THE MADNESS OF TREES

SHOSHANA EDWARDS
THE MADNESS OF
TREES
A HARPER'S LANDING STORY
4 Horsemen
Publications, Inc.

4 Horsemen
Publications, Inc.

4 Horsemen Publications, Inc.
1497 Main St. Suite 169
Dunedin, FL 34698
4horsemenpublications.com
info@4horsemenpublications.com

Cover BY Emily's World of Design
Typesetting by Niki Tantillo
Edited by Gayle Staggemeyer

Library of Congress Control Number: 2023941327

Paperback ISBN-13: 979-8-8232-0264-0
Hardcover ISBN-13: 979-8-8232-0266-4
Audiobook ISBN-13: 979-8-8232-0263-3
Ebook ISBN-13: 979-8-8232-0265-7

DEDICATION

To Rex, who is my rock and my best fan. To Erika and Val and Beau, the best team any writer could ask for. Finally, to David Gerrold, a fantastic teacher and loyal friend, with love to you and your family.

TABLE OF CONTENTS

CHAPTER 1

JIM BURCH HUDDLED ON THE GROVE'S community deck; he was soaking in the warmth of the early morning sun. Despite the chill in the late winter air, Jim was barefoot, relishing the cool, smooth feel of the damp boards. Jim and his wife, Linda, had built their house here, shortly after their marriage two years ago. The scent of jasmine tea announced the awakening of Jen Balanchuk in the house next to his. Jim knew Jen and her husband, Dan, would not come out to join him. Jen's pregnancy was nearing the middle of its ninth month, and she chilled easily.

Two more houses stood side by side on the west side of the deck. Charity Farmington, the Grove's owner, lived and worked in the larger of the two; the other belonged to Bridgette Stevens, Jen's daughter from her first marriage. Bridgette, now eighteen, had been living alone in the small house for two years, spending long hours as Charity's student, studying spells and potions.

The south-side solar panels at the base of the Grove caught Jim's attention as they turned to face the early morning sun. In the winter, the residents switched to power provided by the textile mill, generated by the waterwheel turning in the Martins Way River. But during the spring, summer, and into the fall, most of the Grove's power was solar.

Jim had donned his favorite clothing: a flannel shirt, blue jeans, and a knit hat made for him by Mary Harper. The fabric of the shirt was soft from multiple washings; it clung to his muscular body. The hat provided protection against the chill of the early morning breeze. He wrapped his hands around the hot mug of strong coffee and took a sip, relishing the deep, rich flavor and smell of the freshly ground beans.

He was forty-four and in great shape. But he was also a new father, and the lack of regular sleep showed in his face. Even so, thanks to Will's sleeping through the night for the first time, Jim felt better-rested this morning, ready for anything the day offered.

"Good morning, Jim," said a soft female voice.

Charity Farmington walked slowly across the deck. The tiny woman was barely visible inside her sweater and wool pants. She handed Jim her mug, and he went inside and filled it. When he returned the full mug to her, she wrapped her hands around it with a sigh of contentment, bending her head over it and breathing in the scent.

Jim and Charity often sat together in the early morning. Sometimes they chatted; more often they sat, enjoying the peace and quiet anticipation of the day. They both looked forward to the first birdsong echoing through the orchard. Jim noticed that Charity was looking much older these days. When he came to Harper's Landing, she had seemed little older than late middle age. Now she looked old, with obvious pain in her steps as she crossed the deck from her home. But her voice was still strong, and her eyes were bright and alert.

Charity reached into the bag she'd brought with her and removed two large warm cinnamon rolls. The scent of cinnamon, nutmeg, and warm wheat filled the air. The two sat in companionable silence, enjoying all the sights and sounds the morning had to offer.

The peaceful quiet was broken by Jim's cell phone. He frowned. It was only seven o'clock. Who would call this early?

It was Harve Sanders. Jim heard panic in his voice.

"Jim, sorry to call so early. But you'd better get down here as soon as you can."

"Where is here?" asked Jim.

"Oh, sorry. Jeremy's house, or rather the woods behind it. I don't... I can't... Oh God, Jim. Get down here, please?"

The line went dead. Jim turned to go into his house to retrieve his weapon and his badge. Before he reached the door, Charity spoke with urgency in her voice.

"Jim? Do *not* go alone. Please, trust me on this one. Don't go by yourself."

"What? Why?" Jim was confused.

"I promise to explain everything later," replied Charity. "Don't worry about that right now. It's important, and I will explain, I promise. I don't know what has happened, but when you said it was Harve, I got a sense, call it intuition if you will, that whatever it is, it's related to an incident from long ago. You need to go, but please don't go alone."

Jim understood Charity's distress. Two years earlier, nine people had died by drowning in Sanders Pond in the space of three months. People were still afraid to go near it, despite reassurances from Jim and the Grove's leaders that it was safe. Jeremy and Harve Sanders lived in their family home, up the hill from the pond. For a long time, Jeremy had lived alone in a cottage behind Harve's house. Now the two brothers lived together. Jeremy's former cottage had been converted to a taxidermy studio, complete with display cases, a large workroom, and a walk-in fridge for storing specimens. Jeremy was a world-renowned taxidermist; having such a large workspace had increased his ability to meet ever-expanding demands for his skill.

Charity's agitation, however, was based on something other than remembrance of the horror that had lived in that pond. She knew that danger was long gone. This was something else. It had been a hundred years since a major danger to the Grove and the town below it was last dealt with. Those who had been part of dealing with that long-ago threat had been unable to make it permanent. She feared the threat had risen again. There would be time enough to tell that story. Right now, she needed to protect those under her care.

"Do you know something I should know before I go? Some special protection I and the others might need?" asked Jim.

"Call and tell me what you find after you get there. I'll tell you if you require additional protection. Later, I have to tell you a long and somewhat unbelievable story."

Jim sighed. *More monsters,* he thought. *I hope not.*

"I'm coming with you," said Dan, as he crossed the deck after closing his front door.

Dan Balanchuk was a graduate student, studying for a doctorate in mythology, when he came to Harper's Landing two years ago. Jen had requested his assistance in translating old diaries they had found. His special area of focus was Ukrainian folklore, a logical choice since he had been born and raised in Kiev. He ended up being instrumental in bringing about the demise of the creature which was responsible for the deaths in Sanders Pond and the Martins Way River. He also fell in love with Jen Harper and remained in

Harper's Landing. He and Jen had had a double wedding with Jim and Linda Burch. Dan had recently passed his citizenship test, becoming a United States citizen in a ceremony in St. Louis. He'd also completed his doctoral dissertation at the same time, coming back home with both certificates in hand.

Jim noticed Dan was carrying his weapon in a shoulder holster like his own.

"Charity and Jen will help Linda when the baby wakes up. Don't worry about them," said Dan.

Jen loved helping Linda care for Will; it was also good practice for her, as Jen was pregnant with a girl. Jen and Dan had decided to name her Kateryna Elizabeth, after Jen's great-great aunt and Jim's late wife, Beth. The babies would have no shortage of parents, godparents, aunts, and uncles to fuss over them.

"How did you... oh hell, I should know better than to ask," said Jim. "All right, come along with me. Let's get going."

"We need to pick up Arthur and Finn," said Dan. "We will need them, too. And as of now, I'm back on deputy status, as are they."

Jim stared at him, his confusion and irritation increasing by the moment.

"Harve called me right after he called you, Jim," said Dan. "This is serious business. None of us really believed the hundred-year thing, but now we aren't so sure."

"What the hell is this hundred-year thing?" demanded Jim, as they headed for his car.

"If the stories in the journals are true, and that's a big *if*, then Charity is far older than any of us knew. Plus, apparently another ancient elemental has arisen here, after being asleep for one hundred years. It is a long story, and we will tell it to you and everyone else later, but for now we must get to Harve's."

Dan sat in silence as Jim drove to Havensrest, a bed and breakfast establishment Arthur Willingham had built in the town's original rectory. Originally called The Rectory, Arthur and Finn renamed it shortly after they married. The only car in the parking lot belonged to Finn, Arthur's husband, so there were no guests who would require the men's attention. The season for tourists wouldn't begin for another month or so.

Arthur and Finn were waiting for them; the two were clad in warm jackets, wool pants, and hiking boots. Arthur was the town preacher and a Druid, leader of the pagans in town, as well as the few practicing Christians. Finn McGonigal, his new husband, was also a Druid. Arthur was an Ovate, meaning he followed the path of a shaman, while Finn was a Bard. They could not have been more different in appearance. Arthur was short and a little pudgy, with a snow-white beard and long gray hair he wore tied back in a ponytail. Finn was tall, thin as a rail, with short curly red hair and a closely trimmed beard.

Silent and serious, they climbed into the back seat of the SUV. They both carried thermoses of hot coffee. The four men rode in silence toward Sanders Pond and the home of Jeremy and Harve Sanders. Jim was aching to ask questions and demand answers, but he knew better than to try. They would tell him in due time. It was apparent from their demeanor that he needed to be in cop mode. It was equally apparent that they felt the need to be in Druid mode.

Whoever thought I'd have Druids for deputies? If only my former captain could see me now. Jim sighed. This was going to be a long morning and a hungry one, too. His stomach growled loudly.

"Oh damn, I'm sorry guys," said Finn. "I forgot that Maggie left these with us last night."

He pulled out a bag full of cinnamon rolls and handed them around. Jim told him to hold two of them for him so he could focus on driving. Their scent was intoxicating; by the time they arrived at Harve Sanders' parking lot, Jim was ready to wolf them down whole.

I'm going to have to cut back on the carbs. More eggs; fewer rolls. Damn! Jim thought.

CHAPTER 2

HARVE AND JEREMY SANDERS LIVED SOUTH of Harper's Landing, off Deer Pass Road. The road was not found on any maps, though it did seem to run parallel to State Highway 61 for most of its twenty-mile length. Jim pulled into the long driveway that curved down past the pond and then back up to Harve's house in front, where the two men had marked out a parking lot. Last fall, before the early snows, Harve and his workers had built a greenhouse, in which Jim could see an abundance of plants waiting to be placed throughout Harper's Landing. The City Council had voted to make Harve Sanders the official town landscaper, something he had been doing for some time without a title. The position was more than a title; it guaranteed an income large enough to pay for a work crew of five men in addition to himself. Harve was delighted.

Harve and Jeremy were waiting on the porch. Harve waved at the group to follow and headed for the woods behind Jeremy's house.

"Hold up," hollered Jim. "I want to know what we're getting into before we all go traipsing into the woods."

Harve returned to the porch. Jeremy spoke first.

"I hired a guy who was traveling through. He came to our door, looking for work. Seemed a nice enough guy, backpacking through the Midwest and occasionally working to buy necessities. I needed some new specimens for an order from the Smithsonian. I told him to look for recently dead animals, only kill if necessary, to get the number required to fill the order."

Jeremy and Harve were twins. They had lived together all their lives. Jeremy had been severely burned in the horrific car accident that took both their parents when the boys were in their teens; thanks to the ministrations of Charity and her pupil Becky Sloane, he was beginning to recover from his injuries now that he had come out of hiding and allowed them to help. He still required assistance in gathering his specimens, due to the scarring on his body. Furthermore, his face would forever be twisted and scarred.

"Early this morning we heard screams from down that way," said Harve, pointing southeast. "I got my shotgun and ran down there, but it was too late. You'll see. I'd prefer not to see it ever again. But I'll show you where it is."

Jeremy remained at the house he and Harve shared; he was sitting on the porch, rocking and shaking with anxiety and fear.

"He's been that way since he followed me earlier," said Harve. "Let's just leave him be."

The others set out with caution, following Harve to the scene which had driven him to make his frantic phone call.

"Oh, shit," said Jim Burch.

The body lay in a heap, like a discarded rag doll. Except this doll had no recognizable face and had jagged pieces of bone poking out through the left sleeve and both legs of the tattered jeans.

"Yeah, that about sums it up," said Arthur.

"Jeez, whoever did this had to be incredibly strong. Look up there midway on that tree, Arthur."

Jim pointed to the nearby hemlock, where blood spatter and what might have been brain matter was spread across the middle of the tree, about six feet up.

"Sorry, Jim," said Arthur, as he turned and ran into the bushes—

"Dammit, Jim, I'm supposed to protect this place. Not doing such a good job, am I?" Arthur sighed as he returned to the scene. He took a mouthful of coffee from his thermos, swished, and then spit it out, in an effort to clean his mouth.

Watching with mixed horror and curiosity, Harve and Finn stood back at the edge of the clearing. Dan was walking around it, stopping every few feet to look into the forest and pausing periodically to listen for noises.

Jim pulled out his cell phone and punched the number to Brett Michaels, the town doctor, coroner, and forensic examiner.

"Brett? Jim Burch here. We got us a dead body in the woods, southeast of Harve and Jeremy's. How soon can you get here?"

Brett had moved to Harper's Landing two years ago after spending over twenty years as a state forensic pathologist. He enjoyed the peace and quiet of being a small-town family doctor. It made perfect sense that he would take over the job of coroner from Jim. However, he wasn't quite ready for his vacation from the constant demands of forensic pathology to come to an end. He sighed deeply.

"Give me twenty minutes," he said. "Gotta get my stuff together."

CHAPTER 2

Jim remembered his promise to Charity, that he would call her once he got here. He punched in her number. When she answered he quickly described the situation, leaving out as many of the gory parts as he could. She asked if there were any footprints, strange ones. He was puzzled by her question but told her they had not yet had a chance to search. She again, with as much agitation as earlier, warned him to keep everyone together and be extremely careful.

He hung up, worried but confused by Charity's words. *She's going to tell us another monster story. I just know it. Damn!*

Jim took multiple pictures. He searched around the body, looking for footprints and other evidence. At one point he stopped and placed a marker on the ground next to a strange print. He asked Dan to make a cast of it. Arthur made sketches of the area, including the path they had hiked and any paths leading away.

Finn finally approached, looked at the body, and turned pale. However, he pulled himself together and said, "It's probably too late, but I'm going to sing him on his way anyway."

He sang a hauntingly beautiful chant, and for a moment, Jim could have sworn he saw a cloudy shape rise from the body and hang, floating in the air.

Finn was well-trained in the magic of the Bard. His voice was rich and warm, and the chant filled the little clearing. Jim, Arthur, and Dan stood frozen in place, mouths slightly agape, watching a shimmering path materialize. It began beside the body, rose into the air, and disappeared into the treetops. The hazy shape became more solid, while a young man walked up the path. At one point, he stopped, turned, and gave them all a wave before disappearing, following the shining path into the ether.

Jim realized that, like the others, he was crying. Confused and disoriented, he wiped his eyes with his sleeve. Jim Burch was many things, but primarily he was a cop. A good cop, a dedicated one, with a solid grounding in evidence and truth seeking. He knew what he had seen. It was undeniable. But it was completely foreign to his experience and beliefs.

"Was that his spirit?" he asked no one in particular.

"Yes," replied Finn. "I'm rather surprised you saw it, Jim."

A quiet cough from the side of the clearing got their attention. Brett Michaels stood there, forensic gear in the heavy backpack he carried. He had apparently seen the same thing.

"I've had that happen to me once or twice during an autopsy. I always chalked it up to lack of sleep or inhaling too many lab chemicals. Now, I'm not so sure."

"Let's get busy with the forensics," said Jim. "I don't want the trail growing any colder. Brett, I want a cause of death as soon as possible."

Jim turned to the others.

"Arthur? You and Finn look around in the woods, see if you can find a campsite, anything that indicates where the victim came from. Stay alert. We don't know who killed this guy. They may still be in the area."

The two headed off through the underbrush, their cell phones in camera mode.

"Dan, are you up to helping Brett? I want to get samples from that tree, and I need to do a grid search before we move the body."

"Yeah. I have a strong stomach."

Jim paced around the small clearing, searching for trace evidence. It didn't take him long to figure out where the deceased had entered the clearing. He pulled out his cell.

"Arthur? You guys need to be especially thorough in the area southwest of here. It looks like he came here from that direction."

"Gotcha. Headed there now. So far, we haven't seen anything out of the ordinary."

Jim turned his attention to Brett and Dan. They had finished searching through the victim's pockets and were now examining the body.

"Considering the temp, lack of rigor, and the beginnings of decomp," said Brett, "I'd say he was killed sometime yesterday around midday, early afternoon."

The two men examined the area around the body for any trace evidence. They opened a body bag and carefully rolled the corpse onto the black plastic. Dan zipped it shut. Being careful where he stepped, Brett carried the contents of the victim's pockets over to Jim.

"I think he was Native American," said Brett. "Found this in his front shirt pocket." He handed Jim a necklace of bear teeth. "And I found these in his pants pocket." He gave Jim a Missouri driver's license, a student ID for Washington University in St. Louis, and a money clip with three twenties, two tens, and four singles. He had also found a small plastic bag with two eagle feathers and a small length of braided leather inside.

The driver's license picture was of a young man with a scruffy beard and medium-length brown hair. The name and address on both the license and the student ID were Ethan Burns at Rural Route 22, Box 50, Hannibal, Missouri. Additionally, the student ID had a phone number on the back. The birthdate on the documents showed the young man to be 18 years old, while the student ID pegged him as a freshman.

"We'll have to verify ID with DNA or dental match," said Jim. "But for now, let's assume that these are the remains of Ethan. I'm going to call the parents. I'll have them meet me at Havensrest."

Jim moved to the edge of the clearing and dialed the number on the student ID card. He hated making these calls. A man answered, and Jim identified himself. The man on the phone was the grandfather of Ethan Burns.

"Sir," said Jim, "have you spoken with your grandson in the last few days?"

"Last time was about three days ago. He decided to hike home from St. Louis. Called it his vision quest; he wanted to hike through the forests between the city and home."

"Does he do this often?"

"No, not that far. But he's an experienced hiker. What's this all about, Sheriff?"

"There's no easy way to say this. We've found a body with your grandson's license and student ID in the pockets."

There was a long silence, but Jim could hear the man's heavy breathing as he tried to maintain his composure.

"What was he wearing?"

"Jeans, Nike hiking shoes, and a blue plaid shirt. No cellphone that we found, but we're still looking."

"Does it look like him? You have his picture?"

"Sir, I think you and your family had better come down here as soon as you can."

"It's just me, Sheriff. Me and Ethan. My wife Alice died two years ago, breast cancer. Boy's parents died when he was little, so Alice and I raised him." He sighed. "I'll get my car, come down there. Where can I find you?"

"Come to Harper's Landing; park at Havensrest, next to the church. If you can't find it, ask any of the residents. Everyone knows where it is. I'll meet you there in about two hours. Do you know where Harper's Landing is?"

"Yes. I'll be there in about two hours."

CHAPTER 2

Jim hung up just in time to hear Finn and Arthur call out to him. He hurried down the southwest path toward their voices.

The two men stood in a clearing, staring at the remnants of a campfire strewn about and obvious signs of a struggle in the dirt.

"Jim," said Arthur, "look at how the branches are broken over here. And the brush is trampled."

"And we found scuff marks going up the trunk of this oak here," said Finn, pointing to an old, stately tree with low branches. "Like someone tried to climb it."

"Did you both take pictures of everything?"

"Yeah, I took as many as I could until I ran out of memory," said Finn. "Arthur took over to make sure we got everything."

"How about a sleeping bag? Pillow? Anything?"

"The guy had a full kit," said Arthur. "Over here in the bushes. I didn't touch it."

Jim followed him and saw the backpack. It had been thrown into the brush but was still zipped shut. He took several pictures, then retrieved the pack. It was heavy and tightly packed.

"Looks like there was a heck of a struggle here, Jim." Arthur pointed out.

"I know. Someone put up a good fight, but it looks like our boy took off. He didn't get far. Are those tracks over there?"

Jim walked carefully through the brush, taking pictures as he went. He saw footprints similar to the shoes on the body plus some much larger prints he couldn't identify. They were round with small holes circling each print. They were similar to the strange prints he had seen next to the body. He called Brett.

"Can you spare Dan for a while?" he asked. "I need to make some more print casts."

"Sure. I'll send him now."

"Please. I've got a real mystery here."

Jim sent Finn to stay with Brett. He was not about to leave anyone alone.

Dan arrived, carrying a small bag of casting material, a mixing dish, a stirrer, and a bottle of water. The two men mixed up a batch and took casts of several of the prints.

"Have you ever seen anything like this?" asked Jim.

Dan stood for a while, staring at the prints. "No, but I have a suspicion as to what they are."

"You've been reading those diaries again, haven't you? Are you going to tell me we've got another magical killer?"

"No, not yet. Let's get these casts up to Brett's van, along with that backpack. Brett's been teaching me how to label forensic evidence, so I'll help him. You can go with Arthur and Finn to talk to the grandfather. Can you let me have one of the print casts?"

"Sure. Let's make another."

After that, they were finally ready to leave the area.

"Did we get everything?" asked Jim. "I don't want to leave until we've examined every leaf, bush, and tree."

"We could get Deputy Randle and a couple of boys down here to tape it off, if you want. But we've got the evidence off the tree and casts of prints in the area where the body was found. Plus the casts you and I just made. Frankly, in my opinion, for whatever that counts, the fewer people who know where he was found, the better," replied Dan.

Jim agreed. He was spooked by the area, without knowing why. He was not easily shaken, but something about this whole area, as well as the body, felt *unsettling*. He had no other word for it.

Brett and Dan left with the body and the evidence fastened down in the back of Brett's van. Harve returned to his house and shut the door tightly behind Jeremy and himself, locking it for good measure. Jim, Arthur, and Finn climbed into Jim's car and drove to Havensrest. Once there, they called Morey's Diner to see if someone could bring them some eggs, bacon, and maybe even apple pie. Jim realized he had not had any breakfast, other than the cinnamon rolls, which explained why he was ravenously hungry.

While they waited for the food and for Ethan's grandfather to arrive, Jim called Linda. By now Jen and Charity should be having coffee with her.

"Sorry I've been gone so long. I'll give you the details later. Are Charity and Jen with you?"

"Yes," replied Linda. "They came shortly after you left. Don't worry about us."

"Look, I don't know why, but I feel like it is important that you all stay inside. Humor me. Keep the doors locked. Okay?"

"Charity was saying the exact same thing. It's a bit nippy this morning, so we've got a fire going. Jen and Charity made sure there's enough wood, so we don't have to go out. We'll be fine. Charity is explaining things. I'll fill you in later. Maybe after dinner?"

"I'll be home when I can. I'm going to have a grieving grandfather to deal with first."

Linda sighed. She'd been afraid it would be something like that.

"Be sure you eat," she said.

"Funny you should mention that. Food has arrived. I'll see you at dinner for sure. Love you bunches."

Jim checked his watch. Ethan's grandfather would be arriving soon. The three men ate their late breakfast and opened a second thermos of coffee.

"Okay, Arthur," said Jim. "What the hell did I see out there?"

"A dead boy?"

"Don't play coy with me. You know exactly what I'm talking about. Spill it."

Arthur and Finn looked at each other, wondering who should go first. Finally, Finn spoke up.

"Jim, we Druids who follow the Bardic path have many duties. One of them is to sing the soul on its way to whatever path lies ahead. What you saw was the spirit of that poor boy. His death must have been violent and sudden, enough to confuse him and keep him hanging around. I helped him find his path."

"But," began Jim. "Oh hell, I don't even know what to ask." He paused for a moment, then asked, "Why did I see it?"

"He manifested himself. That happens sometimes. Especially if the soul was a gifted person, if he possessed great power. I'm very curious about who he was."

"Guys," Jim pleaded, with a mock glare, "I'm a worn-out detective from a big, unfriendly city. I've spent my life denying psychics, mediums, seers, charlatans of every stripe. I came here to relax, to live a quieter life."

They all laughed, though there was little mirth to their laughter. The horrors of two years ago, when nine people died in the waters of Harper's Landing, were still fresh.

"Seriously," Jim continued, "I'm aware there was something more than accidental drowning and waterwheels ripping up bodies that caused those deaths two years ago. And yes, I admit to some compulsion that led me here, that caused me to become your sheriff. But this is all a bit much to take in at once."

A light blue Chevy Camaro pulled into the parking lot.

"That's probably Ethan's grandfather," said Finn. "I'll go out to meet him. Bring him in here?"

"Please," said Arthur. "This is the most comfortable room. Jim, let's put this off for a while. I promise, we'll have a long talk. With good bourbon and apple pie. For now, we need to be our best for Mr. Burns."

"You're right. He is going to need us. Do we have a picture that doesn't include the head?"

"In fact, I do. I thought that might be needed. But it wasn't possible to hide the bones. Let's hope we don't have to show them."

Galen Burns filled the doorway to Arthur's study. His hair was braided and tied with a hank of rawhide. Hints of gray showed around the edges, and his face was creased with deep wrinkles. He wore a buckskin jacket over a dark blue work shirt and slightly faded jeans. His high forehead and slightly hooked nose betrayed his ancestry. He confirmed this when he told them, "I am Galen White Eagle Burns, chief of the Osage people who live north of here."

He sat on the one straight-backed chair Arthur kept in his office; he was waiting for the others to speak.

"Mr. Burns," said Jim, "are these your grandson's belongings?"

He handed the man the student ID and driver's license, along with the packet containing the eagle feathers and braid. Everything was bagged in plastic and labeled as evidence. Burns took some deep breaths as he looked at the items. He moaned slightly when he saw the bag with the feathers.

"Please, call me Galen. Yes, those are my grandson's belongings. What has happened?"

"We don't know yet what happened. We found a body in the woods, with these items in the pants pocket. We cannot identify the body as your grandson. Did he have any identifying marks?

"What do you mean? Why can't...?" He stopped. "Oh, dear gods."

Galen reached for a glass of water Arthur was holding and drank most of it. He sat quietly for a few minutes, his eyes closed.

"He had a tattoo, like mine." He stood and turned, lifting the back of his shirt to reveal a tattoo of an eagle in full flight between his shoulders. "Ethan's was a bear. His name is Little Bear. Same as I was Little Eagle until I became chief. When he becomes chief, he will be Standing Bear. He has a scar on his left hand, below the little finger. Crescent shape. Got it from a scythe he was playing with."

Jim motioned to Finn to get Galen a shot of bourbon. Then he stepped out of the room to call Brett.

"Mr. Burns is here. Says his grandson has a bear tattoo on his back, between the shoulder blades, as well as a crescent-shaped scar on his left hand, below the little finger."

He listened for a moment; then his shoulders slumped.

"Thanks, Brett. Let me know the cause of death ASAP in case it is something other than the obvious."

He returned to the room where he found all three men sipping drinks. Arthur and Finn had bourbon; Galen had a glass of strong tea. Jim joined them, pouring a bourbon for himself.

"Galen, forgive my bad manners. I'm Jim Burch, Sheriff of Middlewood County. This is Arthur Willingham, our town preacher who is also an Ovate Druid. This gentleman is Finn McGonigal, Arthur's husband. Finn is also a Druid, a Bard. There's no easy way to say this, so I'm going to give it to you straight. The body we have at our Coroner's Office has the tattoo and the scar you described. We'll still use DNA to confirm, but I feel safe in saying that the body is that of your grandson."

Galen sat silent, eyes closed, fists resting on his knees. Finally, he looked up at Finn.

"Did you sing him on?"

"Yes. We all saw him leave. How did you know?"

"I am not simply the chief of my people; I am also a shaman by training as well as inheritance. Excuse me please, gentlemen. I will return in a moment."

The three men watched through the window as Galen walked out into the springtime sun, lifted his hands, and howled in grief, anguish, and rage. They watched as, once he'd howled all he could, he continued to stand, silent, his arms spread, hands open to the sun. And they watched as he shook his fists in frustration and despair at the same sun. Finally, he sank to his knees and lowered his forehead to the ground, placing his hands flat on the ground. He remained silent and unmoving in that position for approximately ten minutes, while Finn sang through the window Arthur had opened, that same hauntingly powerful dirge he had sung earlier in the forest over the ruined body of Galen's grandson. Finally, Galen stood and returned to the study. Jim handed him a glass of bourbon, which he finished in one large swallow. He declined a second glass, opting for his tea instead.

The sounds of birdsong drifted through the window while the men sat in silence, sipping their drinks. Arthur left the room around noon. Shortly thereafter, Morey arrived with a large pot of beef stew and homemade rolls. They all ate, and still the silence filled the room. Galen continued to sip his tea, also managing to eat a little stew and a roll.

Jim left once to call Linda to explain the situation. He was relieved to hear that Charity and Jen were still with her.

He called Harve to see how he and Jeremy were holding up. Harve was still badly spooked. Jeremy, he reported, had still not spoken and refused to go outside.

"Jim, what the hell? Right in our back yard? I'm beginning to think this place is cursed. First the pond, two years ago. All those dead children. And now this?"

"Let's find out who did it, okay? Arthur and Finn are telling me that Charity thinks something uncanny has entered the picture, again. I'm open to the possibility, but I suspect there's a more mundane answer. Like some really big guy on a murderous rampage for whatever reason. Young Ethan wasn't a big fella. Someone really strong probably could have done all that to him."

"Tell that to Jeremy. He's sure we have somehow brought a curse upon our houses and maybe even Harper's Landing. When you see her, please tell Charity we're going to need her here soon."

"Will do. For now, you got food?"

"Oh yeah; we're always stocked. Jeremy's staying here with me in the house. His taxidermy studio is battened down. I have my shotgun loaded, sitting by the front door, and everything is locked. If there's a killer wandering those woods, he's going to have a hard time getting in here."

Jim returned to the library. The three men were talking about how they would go about finding whoever had murdered Ethan Burns. Galen was visibly switching from overwhelming grief to rage. Jim knew he must interfere, stop the slide before the man felt compelled to act. However, Arthur was way ahead of him.

"Galen? You need to slow down. You are a shaman. Tap into that knowledge. Calm yourself."

The big man took a deep breath, let it out with a sigh, and slumped in his chair.

"First Alice, to cancer. Now Ethan. I'm not exactly alone; my people are my family. But still."

His voice trailed off into silence. Tears rolled down his cheeks. He made no effort to hide them.

"Arthur, Finn?" said Jim. "For some reason I feel a need to have Galen up at the Grove tonight. In fact, I would feel better if both of you were up there, too. I can call Jen and ask if their guest room is still available. Ours is, but we knew a baby was coming before we built. We have a separate nursery. I don't think Jen and Dan do."

"We can stay there for a couple of nights, I'm sure," replied Arthur. "I'm not going to question you about it. Finn and I feel the same need. Why don't you and Galen go on up, and we will make sure Havensrest is locked up tight."

"I'll call and let everyone know they have three extras coming up," said Finn. "You go on, take Galen up there."

"Jim," said Arthur. "I'm probably being a goose about this, but do you think we should issue a town alert?"

"Town alert?"

"Yeah. Morey got everyone's cell number on record two years ago, while you were dealing with all the police work. He thought it would be a good idea to be able to send out a message to everyone if there was a need."

"So that's what he had installed on my computer! He kept promising me he would show me what he had done and how it worked, but with the wedding, building the house, and then the baby, it fell by the wayside."

"I think we need to use it," said Arthur. "I don't want people wandering in the apple orchards or forests until we know what we are dealing with." He stopped and blushed. "Sorry, didn't mean to be taking over your job."

"No, you're right. I'm glad you thought of it. Glad we have the ability. I'll ask Morey to send out a message. Tell people for now to stay out of the woods until we tell them it's okay. I expect a helluva lot of questions."

"Yeah, your phone will probably get a workout. You could ask Morey to tell people there will be a town meeting, say tomorrow? That way we can give them some more solid information and answer their questions."

"Great idea. Now you know why I need you as a deputy. God, what I wouldn't give for a good night's sleep!"

"New babies eventually settle down. You've got about one more month before you will get more rest. If you want, Finn and I can take him for the occasional hour or two so you can catch a nap. Can't have a sleepy sheriff in the middle of an emergency."

Jim slapped his forehead. "Damn, I should be taking Charity up on her offer to sit with him so we can nap. I'm a goofball sometimes."

He turned to Galen Burns.

"Galen, please forgive us. I know you are hurting, and here we are discussing our own petty problems. Do you think you can drive a mile or two up to my home? Follow me?"

"It's good to sit and listen to the mundane. Helps me settle. Yeah, I can drive a bit. Which is yours, the Explorer?"

"Yep," said Jim. "Stick behind me. The road gets a bit dicey as we get closer. We don't fix it on purpose. Keeps people away from the power center of town. Or so the other residents tell me. I like privacy."

CHAPTER 3

SHAKING AS MUCH FROM FEAR AS FROM the early spring chill, he sat in the small cave he had cleared out himself. He was afraid to build a fire as it might be seen by someone curious, or worse, by the law. He wanted nothing to do with the law. Especially now. He had perched high in the trees, and he watched as they searched. The big man the others called Jim was obviously the law. The others were different, in a way he couldn't describe. He trusted none of them.

He was a big man, six-foot-seven inches in his stocking feet. He only weighed about 160 pounds. Due to the lack of regular food, he had suffered the last couple of years. His arms and chest were lean now where once they had been heavily muscled; his calves were those of someone who walked or ran long distances. His beard was thick and greasy, reaching the middle of his chest. His hair was equally tangled and dirty. He could have bathed in the great river, a few feet from his cave opening. The current had hollowed out a small inlet, where he got his water, boiling it before drinking it or making coffee. However, he hadn't bathed all winter. He itched and had sores.

The last time he had seen a body like that was in Fallujah. They had come around the corner, checking rooftops carefully, their dog alert for IEDs, going door-to-door, seeking the enemy. Who the hell knew who the enemy was? It was hell, that war. Absolute hell. Little children armed with bombs. One of those children had come up to them, asking for candy, until he got close enough to... *NO, don't go there*, he thought, but it was too late; he was there, shaking in terror and horror as he stared at the body of his best friend, destroyed beyond recognition.

And now, here in his woods, he had seen a body like that. *Did I do that? No! No! I couldn't. But I don't know. Did I do that?* No, he remembered; the boy was dead when he found him. *I can't go there, not again. I must stay alert, ready to hide or to fight if necessary.*

He sat unmoving, vigilant, listening for the slightest sound that might signal danger. He had been careful to remove traces of his presence at the scene of the murder. The boy had already been long dead when he found him. He knew that even the most careful soldier could make mistakes: a broken branch, a trampled plant missed in his retreat as adrenaline coursed through his veins.

After several hours had passed with no intruders, he dared to light a small fire. He heated a pan of water, added some berries and edible roots he had found, as well as the rabbit he had skinned last night in preparation for today's meal. He needed more food. His body was shrinking. The daily workouts kept his muscles toned, but fishing had become sparse. Today should have been a hunting trip. Now he must wait a few days at least, until he was sure those who sought the boy's killer were gone.

It wasn't me, he thought. *Please, don't let it be me. I don't remember. Why was I there? It wasn't me! It can't be.*

He pondered his situation. He needed food, but he needed not to be found even more. *I could go north along the river.* He had never before thought of traveling along the riverbank, but as he considered it, he realized he might encounter beavers, raccoons, or perhaps even a thirsty deer. Tomorrow he would head north, keeping to the edge of the forest with the great river on his right. He could easily hide from prying eyes. *Perhaps I will have more success at hunting,* he thought. He checked his bow and handmade arrows. He had dropped them when he first saw the body. They were still whole, undamaged.

It was scarcely sundown when he carefully doused his fire, rolled up in his blankets, and fell into a deep sleep. As always, however, his sleep was populated with nightmares, the ghostly remnants of a soldier still lost in the middle of a war he should never have had to fight. He awoke at dawn, barely rested, instantly alert to all the sounds around him. He made coffee over a much smaller fire than last night's, noting that he would soon need to get more ground beans. He felt bad about taking them without asking from the nice people who owned the diner. He always left money if his VA check had hit his bank account, or freshly caught fish if not. He used the town's ATM after dark, making sure to tape over the camera by reaching around from the side before he withdrew money to pay for his coffee.

He always got his coffee on the first of the month. Last month, he had money to leave. He was surprised to find a bag of ground beans waiting outside for him, along with a bag of cinnamon rolls, a small meatloaf, and, wonder of wonders, an apple pie. There was a little note with them.

> *"You've been paying too much for the coffee. Please take this food. If you ever feel comfortable enough to come during the day, come to the back door here. We will sell you whatever you need."*

He was profoundly embarrassed that this kindness left him crying, tears so copious and sobs so overwhelming that he was unable to move for nearly an hour. He wondered if he would find more than coffee this time. It must be close to the first since he was nearly out of coffee. He would risk going into town after he returned from his hunting trip.

He dug out a sliver of soap, undressed, and bathed in the cold river. It felt good. He washed his hair and beard, then scrubbed the sores to make sure they had not become infected. He carefully burned his lice- and flea-infested clothing and dug out the clean ones he had folded at the bottom of his rucksack. He shrugged on his jacket after shaking it thoroughly and checking for any stray vermin. He made sure his knife was on his belt, slung the quiver and bow over his shoulder, and set out along the riverbank, close to the forest edge.

CHAPTER 4

SMALL TENDRILS OF SMOKE ROSE OUT OF the chimney at Jim's house as he and Galen pulled up in front. It was approaching sundown, and the air had turned chilly. Both men were looking forward to a warm house and a hot meal. Arthur and Finn parked behind them.

The Grove had changed dramatically in the last two years. Where once there had been a well and four small stone cottages, there was now a large deck connecting four houses, two of them fairly large, plus two small buildings. In the center was a round building which housed showers, a cedar-lined steam room, and access to the outdoor hot tub. There were separate toilets and dressing areas for men and women. On the southwest side of the deck was a fourteen-by-twenty-foot structure.

The south-facing wall harbored floor to ceiling windows which looked out on the orchards and the forest beyond. The room also had a large fireplace, a television, several comfortable chairs, and a large game table. There were bookshelves on the north and west walls, filled floor to ceiling, with library-style ladders on a track that ran the length of both walls. Everything had been built of logs, polished to a high sheen, held together by mortise and tenon joints. Inside, the walls were finished with oak planks, laid shiplap style with heavy insulation boards between the outer logs and the planks.

Jim suggested that they all go to the social hall. They could have dinner there and enjoy the relaxed atmosphere while they waited for Brett and Dan to arrive. No sooner had they gotten settled, though, dinner in place for everyone, than the two arrived, files in hand.

"You'd better have some of that food for us," said Dan. "Otherwise I'll have to go out and find myself a bear to eat raw."

"Me, too," said Brett. "Miranda will be along shortly. She had to feed the dogs and put them in their crates."

Miranda was Brett's wife. She was also a forensic technician, formerly with the state of Missouri. She and Brett had worked together for years and got married just before they moved from Jefferson City to the quieter life of Harper's Landing. Miranda was also a highly skilled nurse. The previous year she'd finished her midwife training, just in time as it turned out. There seemed to be a baby boom happening in Harper's Landing.

Galen sat quietly watching the friendly efficiency of a group of people who were accustomed to one another. Plates were filled with hot roast beef, potatoes, and other veggies, while plates of rolls were set out on the back counter, along with freshly churned butter and homemade berry jam. Dan, Brett, and Finn sat at the game table; they were playing a furiously competitive game of dominos while they wolfed down their dinner. The others chose comfortable chairs with end tables or simply held their bowls in their laps. Galen was persuaded to take a plate. He was surprised to discover that, despite his pain, rage, and grief, he was ravenous.

Finally, they were done, including Miranda, who'd arrived shortly after everyone else was served. Jen turned on some quiet, soothing music, while Bridgette lit a fire. Linda was nursing Will, who was nearly asleep. She finally tucked him into the baby tote where he snored softly. Jen brought out warm pieces of fragrant apple pie. Even Galen took a piece and gasped when he tasted it. The others looked on with amusement. It was always a joy to see someone eat their first piece of Maggie's apple pie.

As Jim had predicted, his phone rang every couple of minutes. Finally, he recorded a message stating that there would be a town hall meeting to inform people why the warning had been issued. He then turned off his cell, letting all the calls go to voicemail. He turned his attention to the conversation.

"Miss Charity," said Galen. "You're the Guardian, aren't you?"

"Yes."

"And you," he said, looking at Brett, "are the Healer. Though you may not know it yet."

"I've known since I came here. Arthur and Finn helped me and Miranda understand why we felt such a strong need to come here. But I have no special powers beyond being a trained physician, with good people to assist me."

Galen looked around.

"You," indicating Dan, "keep the history. And you, Bridgette, will one day be the Herbalist. And you," he said, looking at Jim. "You must be the one they call 'He Who Does Not See.'"

Everyone laughed, including Jim, who held up his hands in protest.

"Somebody has to keep their feet on the ground around here. And it isn't true that I don't see. I don't let my emotions or beliefs get ahead of good, solid police work."

Galen turned his regard to Linda. "You have something special waiting for you, but I don't know what. We will know in good time."

"How do you know all this?" asked Charity. "We thought we did a pretty good job of keeping under the radar here."

"I am shaman and chief, White Eagle of the Osage, seer in the night and speaker for the dead. I walk these forests, and sometimes the animals come to me in my dreams with information, guidance, and warnings. They have told me about you and the community you have built. It is why my grandson was here in your woods."

He stopped, unable to speak for a bit. He then continued.

"My people remained here in hiding when the other Osage were driven to reservation lands. We are one of the last remaining traditional Osage communities, living in the forest to the north. My grandson was here because we wished to ask you if we could move here."

"You are more than welcome," said Charity, looking about as if daring anyone to say otherwise.

Galen suddenly felt horribly, utterly spent. The weight of the day descended upon him.

"Can we continue this tomorrow?" he asked. "I would like to know how my grandson died, but first I want to sleep. Tomorrow will be soon enough to face the horrors of the day. I also need to contact my people and ask that someone bring something of Little Bear's so that your doctor here can make a positive identification. Yes?"

"Yes," said Brett. "It shouldn't take long. A toothbrush or hairbrush will do."

"Then let me step out and contact them."

CHAPTER 5

SHE STOOD IN THE SHADOWS, AGAINST THE trees. She stared at the buildings, the smoke rising from the chimney, and listened to the laughter and chatter of the inhabitants. She turned in anger and stomped off into the depths of the forest.

"ZANDAR! I KNOW YOU CAN HEAR ME. COME TO ME, HUSBAND. NOW!" She sat on a log, lowered her head to the tree behind, and rested. One hundred years! She had paid her penance, obeyed her god, remaining in the in-between. For what? To awaken to this? This desecration, this mockery? "ZANDAR! WHERE ARE YOU HIDING, YOU DAMNABLE COWARD?"

"No need to scream, Zoya. I am here."

A tall, thin, humanoid figure entered the small clearing. Zandar had antler-like growths on his head. His hair was green and mossy, as was his beard.

"How could you?" she said. "How could you let this happen, this destruction? And orchards? For them? Bad enough that we get brought to this strange land. It was so unjust, what Porewit demanded of me. I have lain quiet for one hundred years, while you cavorted with these humans."

"Calm yourself, Zoya. This is their land. We are the strangers here. They have welcomed me, helped me preserve and protect our children, who are fine, strong trees now. You were the destroyer, or have you forgotten that?"

She rose, rage turning her eyes red, and clenched her fists. "I am the protector, not the destroyer! As should you be also. But you chose them over me! You will regret it. You are no longer my husband. Do not think that you can call Porewit again to deny my right to MY forest!"

She stomped off into the dark, ignoring Zandar's pleas to return, to discuss things. He sank to the log, holding his head in his hands. He was torn. He longed to warn his human friends. But he had obligations to his wife and to Porewit. What was he to do? He remained sitting, silent, undetectable in the trees about him. *She is the same, filled with rage and grief. The long silence did not heal her. I must contact Porewit, however distant he may be. This is beyond my ability to control. She is more dangerous than ever.*

Finally, with a deep sigh, he rose and melted into the forest, following the path his angry wife's stomping feet had left. He needed to find her before she did any more damage.

CHAPTER 6

THE TOWN MEETING WAS HELD IN THE courthouse, the only room large enough to hold all the people. Brett, Miranda, and Melanie, his office assistant, were at the clinic; they were dealing with an emergency, an injury to one of the textile mill workers. Most of them had stayed at work, but their spouses came, many with children in tow.

Morey called the meeting to order, asked Mary Harper to keep notes of the proceedings, and addressed the crowd.

"Yesterday, you all received an emergency text asking you to stay out of the forests and orchards. I apologize for the brevity of the message, but the people who could best inform you why were busy taking care of an unfortunate occurrence in the woods near Harve and Jeremy's home."

The crowd murmured among themselves at this announcement. Harve and Jeremy were already the subjects of wariness among many residents since most of the deaths two years ago had occurred in their pond.

Morey held up his hands, requesting silence.

"Before you go speculating, I want you to hear Jim out. He can fill us in on most of the details."

Jim rose to his feet.

"Yesterday morning I and my deputies were called to the forested area southeast of Sanders Pond, on the opposite side of State Route 22. When we arrived, after a brief search, we found the body of Ethan Burns."

The crowd erupted in exclamations and waving hands, as people vied to get Jim's attention and ask him questions.

"Hold on!" yelled Jim. "I'll get to your questions in a minute."

The crowd reluctantly settled down.

"At this time, we do not know who is responsible for Ethan's death. The cause of death has been determined to be a forceful blow to his head, the result of him being swung hard against a tree. He was probably held by his feet or ankles. Even though Ethan was small in stature, it would have required a person of considerable height and strength to swing him hard enough to cause fatal damage to his skull.

"Ethan was the grandson of Galen Burns, who is here with me today. I would ask that, for the time being, you refrain from asking Galen too many questions. I do have a request from him to you. The proper person to convey that request is Morey. He will tell you shortly.

"First, we are asking you to refrain from going into the woods or the orchards near the Grove. If you are going fishing, please take Route 22 to Big Bass Pool, or a similarly easy access point. Saul Grossman has agreed to allow fishing above and below the waterwheel on the textile mill grounds. Please do not go alone. Not until we find the person or persons responsible for this murder. I'll try to answer any questions you have now, then Morey will take over."

Zak Millbank was the first to raise his hand as he leaped to his feet.

"Jim, what about all the guided fishing tours I've scheduled? They're supposed to begin next week."

"I think you should be okay, as long as you stay in a group. Perhaps you can persuade your clients to stick to Big Bass Pool or up by the textile mill?"

"Yeah, I guess so."

Zak was one of the few townspeople who had some inkling that the deaths two years ago had been something other than accidental drowning, but he was too cautious to bring up such an explosive topic as magical beings populating the forests and waters of Harper's Landing.

Unfortunately, Benny Jackson's mother Lois was not so circumspect. Benny had been one of the victims two years ago, and she was still grieving. Brett had tried to get her to take anti-depressants, but she refused. Now she stood up, pointing her finger at Jim.

"You know, Jim Burch. You know that *something* killed my son. He was a good swimmer; he didn't drown. I don't believe that waterwheel tore him apart. It was a monster; a monster in the waters, probably brought here by Harve's ancestors. Now there's another monster among us. Tell us the truth, Jim."

By now she was screaming, and her thoroughly embarrassed husband pulled her out of the room. Maggie Farmington held her other arm, speaking in low, soothing tones. At a nod from Charity, Jen hurried across the street to the diner, where she secured a small piece of apple pie, muttered a few words over it, and brought it to Lois.

"Here, Lois, have this. And I've brought you a drink of water. We'll come talk to you later, okay?"

Lois reluctantly ate the bite of pie and drank some water. She visibly relaxed, her voice trailing away into a sob. She leaned against her husband Ben, looking back at the crowd.

"Should I go apologize?" she asked.

"No," said Jen. "We understand. Let Ben take you home and tuck you into bed. We'll talk soon."

Back in the courtroom, Barry Sloane had risen to his feet. He was the father of Becky Sloane, the sole survivor of the last of the drownings.

"Jim? I'm not going to go ballistic, but could there be something to what Lois is saying? I mean, you remember my daughter saying she saw a monster. I know kids get confused when they are scared, but Becky's always been pretty level-headed. Could there be some mutant from that nuclear plant upriver?"

"Honestly, I don't know. Right now, I'm operating on the assumption that someone, probably a man, happened upon Ethan and tried to take his stuff away. I'm going up to the area tomorrow, to look for any signs. We searched the immediate area pretty thoroughly after we found the boy, but I want to follow the paths, go through the woods, perhaps down along the Mississippi. I'll take Dan and Finn with me. In the meantime, I don't want anyone out there possibly messing up any evidence or putting themselves in danger."

People muttered among themselves, but then everyone agreed that this was probably for the best.

Finally, Morey stood up.

"Galen Burns here, Ethan's grandfather, is also chief and shaman for a small group of Osage who have been living in the forests north of us, about halfway between us and Hannibal."

Jim sat beside the man, Linda on his other side, an arm draped across Galen's shoulders.

"He has requested that his people be allowed to move down here with us, to establish a small sweat lodge and gathering hall next to the Grove. The families would like to move into some of the empty houses in town."

"How many?" asked Terry Rutledge, the town's sole private attorney.

"Forty-five adults and fifteen children," said Galen. "Our adults are skilled in many things, including farming, carving, weaving, and training hunting birds. We would like to open a small store in town, to help attract the tourist trade in the late spring and summer."

"There are currently twenty-two houses in town that are empty. Most of them need some work, updating, a new roof," said Morey. "Would that be adequate for the number of people? Each house has three bedrooms, some have only one bath, but most have two."

"That would be more than adequate," replied Galen. "Be assured, we have money to pay for them."

"Charity has given her permission," said Morey. "She owns most of the land around here. She has, however, asked that the town also vote on this, since it is the intent of the tribe—may I call it that?"

Galen nodded.

"It is their intent to blend in with us, to share their ways, to learn ours. This is a hard time for Galen. There will be plenty of time later for more questions, but I personally think this will be a good thing for Harper's Landing. And Galen, the matter of money? That's something you and I will discuss later, but it isn't something your people need worry about at all."

Galen raised an eyebrow; a look of puzzlement crossed his face. Linda gave him a reassuring hug.

"Morey will explain later," she whispered to him. "I think you will be surprised."

"Why have you chosen Harper's Landing?" asked Saul Grossman.

"My grandson chose it," replied Galen. "At the time of his death he was on a vision quest of sorts. He was searching for a place for us, hoping that something would reveal itself to him. We currently live near Hannibal, and our children go to school there. They are not welcome. The little ones are teased about their hair and their clothing. The older children try to blend in, but many of them are bullied also, because they do not like having to wear the clothing so popular with urban teenagers."

"He was seeking a place of acceptance?" asked Maggie.

"Yes. The night before he died, he called me. He was so excited. He had first met the Sanders men, and Jeremy had hired him. He had also gone into the town, which he said welcomed him. Not just the people. He said the actual town welcomed him. He told me this was where we needed to be."

Galen's voice choked up a bit, as he related his grandson's excitement over his discovery.

"Despite what happened to him, I share his opinion that this is, indeed, where we want and need to be. Not so far from civilization that my people cannot use cell phones and computers, perhaps even learn to drive stinking, dangerous automobiles, as I do. Still removed enough to allow us to live as close to the Old Ways as we wish. We want to stay. We want to be a part of your community."

"Then let's put it to a vote," said Terry Rutledge. "I hereby make a motion that we allow Galen Burns and his people to settle here."

"I second the motion," said Linda Burch.

"All in favor?" asked Mary Harper, the official county recorder.

The ayes were unanimous. Galen's people had found a new home.

CHAPTER 7

IT HAD BEEN A WEEK SINCE ETHAN BURNS was found. Brett had finished the autopsy and confirmed his identity through DNA comparison with the hair Galen had brought. Galen called him to ask when they could deal with his grandson's body.

"What are your rituals?" asked Brett. "Should I embalm or prepare him in any way?"

"We do not burn our dead, nor do we embalm them," replied Galen. "We bury them, wrapped in a ceremonial blanket, so that they may return to the earth. My people, my small tribe, shunned the conversion to Catholicism that so many of our people accepted. When they left for Kansas, we remained, staying true to the Old Ways. There will be songs, prayers to the old gods, and the burial."

"Do you look upon the body?"

"We do. But you have told me that his face, his head, is ruined."

He choked back a sob.

"Let me see what I can do about that," said Brett. "Can you wait a couple more days, let Arthur and Finn help arrange things? Charity has agreed that you and your people may come here and make this your home. For that reason, the town will mark off a section of the cemetery for the burial of your people. May we arrange that for you? Will you consult with Finn and Arthur while I care for your son's body?"

Galen agreed readily and left to find Arthur and Finn. Brett called Jeremy.

"Do you know how to restore faces?"

"I've done animals, even some large ones. But never a human if that's what you are asking."

"Yes. I have some modeling material that morticians often use when there has been severe damage. Can you give it a try? I have pictures to help you."

"I'll come as soon as Harve is free to drive me."

The funeral for Ethan Burns, known to his people as Little Bear, was held two days later. Jeremy's work had been meticulous and astonishing. The damage to the young man's skull was hidden by the long black hair Jeremy provided and carefully fit around his face, the braid falling to the middle of his back. Jeremy worked the modeling clay, along with his air brush, using the student ID picture as a guide. It was difficult to tell that any damage had been done. Galen dressed his grandson in tribal garb. The grave was deep. Little Bear was placed in it in a sitting position with rocks lining the bottom and sides of the grave in traditional style. The entire community of Harper's Landing attended, as they did for anyone who died among them. Galen's small tribe stood around the grave and silently paid honor to the boy who would have been their next chief. The only departure from the ancient traditions was Galen's request that Finn sing.

The townsfolk left, out of respect for the tribe's privacy and traditions. They returned to Havensrest, where Morey and Maggie had been cooking all day. The men set the tables, and the women helped with preparing the food.

At the graveside, Finn sang of nature, of life, and of spirit. Tears ran down his cheeks as he sang the name of Little Bear and of Ethan Burns, the young man lost to two worlds at the hands of an unknown killer. Other members of the small group sang their own songs. Galen sang last, the song of the shaman, so private, so haunting that even the others standing at the grave turned their gaze upward and plugged their ears.

After they had covered him with the earth to which he would return, after the grave was filled and mounded, Arthur came out of Havensrest; he was carrying a piece of wood affixed to a stake. It was a simple plaque with Ethan's indigenous name, spelled in the language of the Osage, and his American name carved and burned into the wood.

"It would honor me," he said to Galen, "if you were willing to use this to mark his grave."

Galen accepted it gratefully, placing it at the head of his grandson's grave. The others left, going into Havensrest to the warmth and the comfort of food lovingly prepared. Galen remained, squatting at the graveside, staring at the sign. Arthur sat next to him on the ground, his legs crossed and head bowed.

CHAPTER 8

BRETT WAS PREPARING FOR THE OPENING of his clinic day when his phone rang. It was Peter Wilson, husband of Melanie, Brett's office assistant.

"Brett? Have you seen Melanie?"

"What? No, not yet. She isn't due here at work until 10:00."

"I know. It's just that usually she's back by now, showering and getting ready for work."

"What do you mean, 'back'?"

"She goes for a run every morning, down the Old Slope Road to where it joins Highway 22, and then across the field and through the forest up by Harve's. It usually takes her about an hour. She keeps wanting me to go with her, but I prefer to bike, which I do in the evening."

Brett swore quietly under his breath.

"Did you guys ever sign up on Morey's cellphone alert program?"

"No. What's that?"

Brett swore silently again, then replied, “It lets us send notifications to everyone. Remind me to get you signed up today. Anyway, how long ago was she supposed to be back?”

“About an hour. Thing is, Brett, she always takes her cell with her, and she’s not answering.”

“I’ll let you know as soon as she comes in. She probably stopped to admire the early spring blooms. You know how easily distracted she is, Pete.”

“Yeah, but she’s been ravenous lately, when she hasn’t been throwing up.”

“She’s pregnant?”

“We were going to have you test her today. That’s why I’m so worried. This is an important day. I can’t see her missing that.”

“You work up at the textile mill, don’t you?”

“Usually. I took today off so I could come in with Mel, for the test. We’ve been trying for a while.”

“Would it make you feel better if we went out there and looked for her?”

“Who’s we?”

“Jen’s husband, Dan, has been helping me out with something this morning. We could go out and check Old Slope Road if you want.”

“She called me as she was turning off, to go through the forest down to Harve and Jeremy’s. Said she might call again from there to have me pick her up. She was feeling a little nauseous this morning.”

“I know the path,” said Brett. “Dan and I were going down to Harve’s anyway, so we can check the path through the forest. Maybe she turned an ankle or something minor. I’m guessing you called Harve?”

“Yup, right before I called you. He hadn’t seen her but said he’d keep watch.”

"I'll call you as soon as I find her," said Brett.

"I want to come too. I don't have a good feeling about this. Can't tell you why; I just don't." Pete sounded nearly frantic.

"Okay," said Brett. "Meet me at Harve's. And Pete? Please don't go into the woods alone. Wait for us. Trust me on this one."

"What aren't you telling me, Brett?"

"Nothing. I have no idea what has happened to Melanie, but don't worry. We'll find her."

Brett hung up and immediately dialed Jim.

"You and Arthur had better get out to Harve's. Bring Finn, too. And wait for us there."

He hung up before Jim had a chance to ask questions. He and Dan hurried out and climbed into the van, Brett filling Dan in as they sped toward Harve's. Brett felt nothing more than an old lawman's intuition about death and crime, but he knew that Dan and the others who lived at the Grove had a different understanding of the world. He respected their insight, their sense of the world's balance.

"We need Charity," said Dan. "She has to come with us. We will protect her, but go to the Grove first and get her. I'll call and have her ready."

Brett made the turn toward the Grove Trail without question. Dan was talking softly to Charity, but Brett caught most of his side of the conversation.

"Yes, I think it is her. If it is, she is no saner than she was a hundred years ago."

"I won't ask," said Brett. "If I do, it will be later over a liberal amount of good bourbon and a cigar on Jim's porch."

"That would be wise," said Dan. "Charity's going to ride Birget down to Harve's, so we can go there instead of the Grove." Brett turned around.

Birget was the Icelandic pony Charity had purchased a few years back to pull the wagonloads of apples to town for Morey and Maggie Farmington. Brett half-suspected it was the apple pie that was responsible for attracting most of the residents who had not been born and raised in Harper's Landing.

Charity often rode Birget bareback or with a soft blanket to sit on. She was a good rider, and Birget took extra care where she stepped when Charity was on board. When Brett and Dan finally pulled into Harve's driveway, they saw Birget tied up, munching on hay, next to the barn. They also noted Jim's Explorer parked next to Harve's work truck. Brett was not surprised to see Pete's Jeep Wrangler there also, though he wished the man had not come. He was also surprised to see Galen with the party.

Charity insisted on leading the way into the forest once they were all assembled. She rode on Birget, with Jim walking alongside. Dan and Brett came next, with Arthur and Finn bringing up the rear, keeping company with Pete and Galen. The party moved slowly and quietly, at Charity's insistence. Suddenly, Birget snorted and threw her head up. She stopped, refusing to go farther.

"Jim," said Charity, "you need to go into that clearing ahead. Please wait for Dan and Brett to join you. I'll stay here and send Finn and Arthur along. Don't worry; I'll keep Galen and Pete away from the scene, at least for now."

Jim, Dan, and Brett moved slowly into the clearing when Brett suddenly broke into a run. He had spotted a body on the far side of the small meadow.

"It's Melanie. She's still breathing."

He knelt beside her, urging her not to move. A long slender branch, about an inch in diameter, had impaled her chest. He examined her carefully to make certain that the branch had not pierced her lung. She was barely conscious. Brett urged her not to say anything.

"Don't worry. We're here now, and we will take care of you. We'll talk later."

He turned to Dan and Jim.

"We need to get her back to the clinic," he said. "It's a miracle she's alive, but we must find out as soon as possible how much damage has been done. We'll have to take extreme care moving her to the van. Jim, could you and Dan go get the gurney? Finn, do you have any songs in your repertoire that will help keep her calm?"

Finn knelt down next to her and sang softly. Brett noticed that Galen was keeping Pete back at the edge of the clearing, talking to him quietly, a firm hand on his shoulder. Finn marveled at the resilience of the man, to be so compassionate for another after having recently lost his only grandson. He could not see Charity, but he was fairly sure she was also helping to keep Pete calm.

Arthur walked around the clearing, looking for signs of a struggle, other footsteps, and any clues as to what had happened. He thought he saw movement out of the corner of his eye, but when he turned to look closer, he saw only dense forest. *Must have been the leaves in the wind,* he thought. Then he realized there was no wind.

He stood still, peering deeply into the woods. He sensed someone beside him and glanced over briefly to find Galen also staring into the woods. Pete stood next to him; he was shaking but obviously calmer.

"Is this the same clearing where you found my grandson?"

Arthur turned to stare at him and then looked around the entire area. He noted the marks on the tree trunk and realized that they were exactly where Ethan Burns had been beaten to death.

"Yes, it is. I'm sorry, I didn't realize at first."

"I hope he left peacefully. There is a feeling of anger that lingers, but it is not my grandson's anger, nor do I think it is from that young woman. Someone or something else has been here, may still be here watching us."

Arthur scanned the woods. He opened his mind and turned on his Druid sense, seeking any touch of another mind as well as a sight or feeling of something other than trees. *It was probably a deer or even a rabbit,* he thought. But he suddenly froze. He detected a hint of another mind, something quite foreign, filled with malice. No, not malice. Fear and rage. As dangerous as malice, if not more so.

"I sense it, too," Galen murmured. He had resumed his position next to Arthur. "I do not know what or who it is, but we must get Melanie safely out of here, to Brett's clinic."

"Jim, Brett, and Dan are here," said Arthur. "Will they need our help in getting Melanie onto the gurney?"

"We are better used as lookouts, protection," replied Charity, riding up to their side.

"From what?"

"I am not sure yet. But that is no deer out there. Whatever or whoever it is, I think it means us harm."

Brett turned to Pete.

"Pete, this is an awful injury, but I'm sure I can get this branch out, once we get her to the clinic and can do an ultrasound and other tests."

"I want to be with her," said Pete. He was shaking badly.

"I'm happy to have you," said Brett, "but only if you remain calm. Breathe deeply; let us get her on the stretcher and into the van. You can hold her hand on the way to the clinic.

Pete swallowed, took a deep breath, and then said, "I can do that. I'll save my freak-out for later."

Brett and Dan laid a backboard on the ground next to Melanie. Brett gently worked his hand under her body until he felt the branch. He cursed softly. It had pierced through her and into the ground. He opened his bag and withdrew a syringe and a bottle of morphine. Carefully, he drew out a small dose and injected her. After waiting a few minutes, he again put his hand under her body and gently pulled on the branch with his free hand. He was also alert for any bleeding. Dan was carefully monitoring her breathing. Pete simply crouched, holding her hand, his eyes closed. His lips moved in prayer. Finn continued to sing softly, as much for Pete and the others as for the gravely injured woman.

After pulling the branch up only an inch or so, Brett felt the end come out of the ground. There was no excessive bleeding, nor did there appear to be a change in Melanie's breathing or heart rate. He and Dan gently rolled her on her side far enough to slip the rigid backboard under her, using it to help stabilize the branch. They then lifted her onto the gurney and slowly wheeled her up the path to the waiting van. Pete went along, and the three men drove her to Brett's clinic. Jim joined Galen, Charity, Arthur, and Dan at the edge of the woods.

"Are we all going into town?" asked Jim.

"Not today," said Charity. "First, I want you to accompany me back to the Grove, where I would like Arthur and Finn to stay, to arrange protection for your family and the other residents. You need to go see Brett. It could be that when Melanie awakens, she will remember what happened to her."

Jim suspected that Charity was guarding her words carefully, but he decided to wait until later to push her for more information. He was curious as to why she felt that the Grove residents needed protection.

"I believe I will stay at the Grove with Charity, Arthur, and Finn," said Galen, pensively. "I've had more than my share of excitement. If you don't mind, I might ask your wife for some of that tea of Charity's I've been hearing so much about."

"Be my guest," said Jim. "Stay alert. It seems we have a killer on the loose. And I'm certain Charity knows more about it than she's letting on to me."

Charity rode Birget back to the Grove, where Arthur, Finn, and Galen met up with her. The others followed Brett to help with Melanie.

"Galen," said Charity, "when are your people arriving? I love that you have been staying here with us, but it has been three weeks since I gave permission for the rest."

"They are preparing. We need to pack everything, then take down the wickiups for transport. We want to be sure we can go right into the houses in town. I don't want to risk anyone in the woods, even close to the Grove here."

CHAPTER 9

LATER THAT EVENING, AFTER DINNER, everyone sat around the fire in the community area. Charity and Galen were together on a small loveseat that had once graced Jeremy's living room. Finn and Arthur sat together on the large couch, with the newest addition to the Grove draped over their laps. Marvel was an Irish Wolfhound. He had shown up one day at the Grove, hungry and tired, with no collar or chip to indicate who his owner was. He'd taken a long drink, eaten all of the venison steak and sweet potato Charity had put down for him, then collapsed on the floor in front of the fireplace, where he'd slept for several hours. He had been with them ever since.

Once everyone, including Marvel, had pie, and drinks were poured, Charity began her story.

"The Grove was originally established by Stephan, Jane, Kateryna, and Mikhail. They all took the last name of Farmington when they arrived in the late 1800s. My mother was their niece. She and her twin sister, Aleksandra, came here to live with them in 1900. By then, Kateryna and Stephan had moved south of the Grove and built the first home of what would become many in the town of Harper's Landing."

"Why is it called Harper's Landing?" asked Finn.

"For the simplest of reasons," replied Charity. "Harasemchuk was too much for the immigration officer, so he shortened their name to Harper. That happened a lot, I am told. And when they arrived here, they announced they had 'landed.' And so, they called it Harper's Landing."

"Huh," said Finn. "I was hoping for something more romantic."

Everyone laughed. Once they settled down, Charity continued her narrative.

"The twins were fourteen when they arrived in America in 1900. They had spent their entire lives on a small farm in the forests of Ukraine, so even a town as small as Harper's Landing was fascinating to them. They learned the joys of indoor plumbing, indoor lighting, and the telephone. By then, Harper's Landing had grown to forty-two families, all immigrants from various parts of Eastern Europe. There was a school, a small general store, and many houses. Electricity was provided by the giant waterwheel which powered the generators for the town, as well as the textile mill where most of the people worked. Indoor plumbing had been brought to Harper's Landing and installed by the father and son of a family who came upriver from St. Louis, seeking a simpler life. Harper's Landing was quite modern, despite its small size. The twins were dazzled by all they saw."

"Sorry to interrupt," said Brett. "Why did they come here?"

"To escape persecution," replied Charity. "Revolution was brewing in Russia, and if you weren't pure Russian or were different from others in any way, you were a target of the Bolsheviks. Stephan and his siblings foresaw this, long before it began, and came here when land could be had by claiming it. Many Ukrainians settled south in the area known as the Ozarks. Stephan and the others came further north and were later joined by other family members and friends."

"It makes sense," said Dan. "The land is much like Ukraine. They would have felt at home here, if a bit lonely for other Ukrainians."

Charity continued.

"Two years after my mother and aunt settled in, a handsome young man and his family came to live in Harper's Landing. His name was Gerhard Frohm. His family had not been forced to flee their homeland of Germany. They simply felt that America had more to offer a young, intelligent, and gifted child such as Gerhard than Germany did. Additionally, the Frohm family was partly Romani, which meant that Gerhard would never have been accepted into the great universities in Berlin or even Prague.

"The plan was for Gerhard to travel south to attend Washington University in St. Louis, where he could study engineering and architecture, his two greatest joys. The year before he left to attend the university, Gerhard studied along with Sophie, my mother, and Aleksandra, learning English, as well as becoming familiar with his more esoteric gifts and how to use them.

"During Gerhard's first year in Harper's Landing, he and Sophie fell in love. At first, Stephan and Kateryna, as well as Gerhard's parents, passed it off as a teenage infatuation. However, it became apparent that the two young people were deeply and inseparably in love. After much discussion, and an assessment of Sophie's intellectual capabilities, their guardians decided to send both children to St. Louis. Although Allie would miss her sister, she showed no particular desire to attend a university. She was a gifted artist, working with thread and fiber of every kind. She created works from something so simple as a baby's first dress to an intricately hand-pieced quilt meant for display rather than use."

"So, she was the original quilter here?" asked Linda. "Did she train the Harper women?"

"I would guess she did. Although she didn't survive long enough to do any real training. But that is part of my story."

She paused and wiped her eyes, remembering her aunt and her demise. Then she continued.

"Sophie and Gerhard both sailed through their university studies. While Gerhard was absorbed in learning the intricacies of engineering and the skills required for architecture, Sophie found herself drawn to home economics. She was fascinated with the science behind baking and created new recipes that made their way into the Washington University newspaper and even the *St. Louis Post-Dispatch*. They finished their degrees and returned to Harper's Landing, where Gerhard went to work at the textile mill, helping to modernize the looms and other machines, and Sophie opened a baking business in a small shop on Main Street.

"They were married a year later, in 1905."

Charity paused her story to take a drink of water and then a sip of bourbon. She sat quietly, resting and remembering for a few minutes. Then she resumed her story.

"Gerhard was eager to build them a house of their own, plus he had plans for a city hall, county buildings, perhaps even wooden walkways. Most of all, he really wanted to build a sawmill, both to save money in lumber and to exercise his engineering skills."

"When was this?" interrupted Dan. "When did they build the sawmill?"

Charity thought for a moment. "It must have been in 1906, shortly after I was born."

Everyone in the room sat up in surprise, except Linda, who was nursing Will. He had awakened about halfway through Charity's story and informed the world that he was starving to death.

"1906?" exclaimed Jim. "But that would make you over a hundred years old!"

"Yes," replied Charity. "I am one hundred and twelve years old. I should have left at one hundred, but there were obligations to be fulfilled, and my successor was not yet fully trained."

"Obligations?" asked Linda.

"Yes. I needed to protect the Grove, to train apprentices. I was the oathbound Guardian, tasked with protecting the inhabitants of the land from the north where the Martins Way River begins to where it rejoins the Mississippi in the south. But I grew complacent. Things were quiet for so long that I turned all of my attention to the orchard, the Grove, and my herbs. I failed in finding and training someone to take my place when my time was up. So now, even though I have two wonderful apprentices, it is long past my time, yet I still cannot go. Soon, perhaps. First, though, we must deal with Zoya. And Zandar, too."

"But that would mean you were only twelve years old when you became the Guardian. Who does that to a twelve-year-old?" asked Jim.

"Does this mean, Jim, that you now accept that there are things that your scientific method cannot explain?"

"No. I'm simply confused as to why a twelve-year-old girl would feel obligated to take on a burden she could not possibly have understood."

Charity sighed in frustration.

"You know what, Jim," said Brett. "I think we need to give up trying to understand and accept that this is where we are, and things happen that you and I, as believers in fact and science, cannot explain. Otherwise, we'll drive ourselves nuts."

Arthur and Finn both laughed.

"That's one of the first things you learn when you train as a Druid," said Finn. "Questioning and probing at things that cannot be explained by traditional knowledge only leads to confusion. Acceptance will lead to understanding if you are patient."

"So, what happened when they built the sawmill?" asked Jen. She glared at the others, daring them to interrupt again.

Charity resumed her story.

"The sawmill was built during the fall and winter of 1906. My mother would tell me stories of playing with me, while Father and the other men of the village cut the logs, fitting them together to raise the building. Everything was done by hand, including the sawing and planing of the floor planks."

"Sorry to interrupt," said Finn. "Why did they build in the fall and winter? It must have been cold and difficult to work in the rain and snow."

"It was," said Charity. "Mother explained this to me later, after the fire. It did them no good, of course, since once spring arrived, she arose, discovering what she considered a desecration to her forest."

"She?" asked Arthur.

Charity sighed.

"This is where Jim, Brett, and probably Pete get to exercise their willingness to accept the unacceptable."

"Me, too," said a weak voice from the corner. Melanie was slowly waking up, demanding that Pete raise the head of her bed. She had refused to stay at the clinic, so they brought her to the Grove where Charity and Jen could care for her. "I want to hear this. It might explain what I think I saw before I was stabbed."

"My mother and my aunt were collectors," continued Charity. "They loved to gather leaves and press them between the pages of a book or large sheets of paper if no books were available. They gathered leaves from Ukraine before they traveled to America and brought the leaves along. They wanted something to remind them of home."

"I'm guessing it was early fall when they left," said Dan.

"Yes. Among the leaves they gathered were two unusual specimens, leaves unlike anything either of them had ever seen. They stuck them into their collection bags, intending to examine them more closely during their voyage, but they had no access to their bags until they landed.

"When they finally arrived and joined Stephan and Kateryna on the steamboat trip up the Mississippi to St. Louis, their uncle and aunt immediately sensed something uncanny about their luggage. While the girls were otherwise occupied, the two adults went through the steamer trunk holding the girls' belongings and found the leaf bags. When they emptied the bags, they discovered a strange powder that looked like ashes at the bottom of each bag. Stephan believed it to be the remains of Lesheye."

"What the hell is a Lesheye?" asked Jim. "Another damn monster come to wreak havoc?"

"I will explain it all," said Charity somewhat impatiently, "if you will please quit interrupting me."

"Lesheye!" exclaimed Dan, ignoring her impatience. "Surely not. Don't they die every fall?"

"Yes," replied Charity. "But according to what Stephan and Kateryna could discern, the legends about Lesheye turning into leaves and burying themselves under other leaves was true. They had no doubt that the white ash found in each girl's bag was the remnants of Lesheye."

"And they brought them here? Did they rise again in the spring?" asked Dan.

"Yes, we assumed they did, and my aunt and uncle thought they had accepted our forest as theirs. They could not have known how wrong they were."

Charity leaned closer to Galen, sitting on the couch. Jim noticed she was holding Galen's hand. This was getting far more complicated than he had expected. He forced himself to sit back and listen without judgment. Dan explained what the Lesheye were.

"The descriptions we have been given in the diaries of the early residents of Harper's Landing certainly fit with the Old-World descriptions of them. The male is a Leshy, the female a Leshachikha. They are immortal, tutelary deities charged with guarding the forests and the creatures that dwell within. The legends say that they die every fall, then resurrect the following spring."

Charity resumed her narrative. "Since Lesheye die in the early fall, at the equinox, the adults operated the sawmill only in the fall and winter and ceased operations at the spring equinox. No one was anxious to encounter an angry Lesheye. Even the hunters in town respected the seasons and confined their activities to fishing during the spring and summer, though some of them traveled farther south to hunt deer and rabbits."

"Charity, did anyone ever actually see a Lesheye here?" asked Dan.

"Yes. But before I continue, I want some more pie. Then I will tell you the rest of the story. It is sad, it is painful, and Will needs to be changed and tucked into bed. Get me some pie. The rest of you can walk around a bit, while Jim and Linda kiss their son goodnight."

Charity polished off the rest of her bourbon in one swallow then held out the glass to Arthur for a refill. She leaned back, discovering that Galen had put his arm out so that he could hold her gently against his chest and shoulder. Breathing deeply, she sank gratefully into his comforting hug. It had been a long time since she had felt so loved and had enjoyed the scent of a man.

Jim added logs to the fire, as it was getting late. He wondered if it wouldn't be better to take up the story tomorrow. He wanted nothing more than to make love to Linda and drift off to sleep. He needed to clear his head of the horrors of the last few weeks. The image of the ruined Ethan was gradually fading, and hearing Melanie speak had lifted his heart. However, he feared that this was the beginning of another series of tragedies. The horrors of two years ago threatened to rise again. So many had died, and he had been unable to stop it. He needed to prevent that from happening again if he could.

There is a fine line between caution and fear. Those who choose the path of being Guardians must walk both sides of that line. And they must retreat from time to time, restoring their energy, reminding themselves why they have chosen this path.

Jim realized that most of the men in this room had chosen that same path. Each had his own weapon: Jim and Dan, and sometimes Brett, used guns; Arthur relied upon his staff and his spells; and Finn had that incredible voice that seemed capable of both attracting and repelling almost anyone or anything. It remained to be seen what path Pete Wilson would walk, or if he had already chosen one. The women had also chosen to be Guardians, but their duties were foreign to him.

"Charity," said Jim, "would you mind continuing the rest of your story tomorrow? I need a break. I need time with my wife."

"I agree," said Galen. "Your story can wait for the morning. We can hear the rest over coffee. Okay?" He looked down at Charity, who was now snuggled into the crook of his arm. He realized that she was sound asleep. He gently picked her up and headed toward her door. He told the others as he walked away, "I'm going to stay with her. I will lock the door."

Galen gently put Charity on her bed and covered her with one of the quilts that lay at the foot. He then went into the main room to make sure the door was locked and the wood stove was stoked. The room warmed quickly while he sat, looking about at the altar, the woven hangings, the knitted afghans, and the homemade furniture. This was a house built of love, built by a community for a woman they adored and perhaps feared a bit. Her power was undeniable.

Galen was not disturbed by the difference in their ages. He was in love. It had happened instantly, and he was overwhelmed by a desire to protect her and guide her. He also wanted to accompany her on her next journey, which he knew would come soon, if she would let him. He was determined to help her solve this threat to her people because soon they would be his people, too. It was time for him and his small troop to become part of a greater and more diverse community. The Old Ways had served them well, but they needed modern ways to balance them.

He dozed lightly in the rocking chair by the stove; then, he was awakened by a gentle touch on his shoulder. Charity handed him a cup of her famous tea. They sat in companionable silence and watched the fire burn down to coals. When the tea was gone, Galen gently lifted her and carried her into the tiny bedroom. He laid her on the bed after folding back the quilt and the blankets. Slowly he removed her clothing, a piece at a time, waiting for either encouragement or a refusal. In response, she reached out and unbuttoned his shirt. As each piece of clothing fell, revealing more skin, they touched and explored each other, first with hands, then with lips and tongues.

Young sex is passionate, athletic, and often rushed. Age does not dim passion, as some might think. But the passing of time brings patience, often born of necessity. Old muscles are slower and passions are deeper; therefore, lovemaking takes time.

Charity and Galen explored each other, and when they joined it was with eyes wide open, looking deeply into one another's souls. It was lovemaking unlike anything Charity had ever known. When her husband died so many years ago, she had never expected to love again. Yet here she was, her body on fire and filled with desire. Her heart and mind sought to join with this man she had just met yet felt she had known forever. Galen was experiencing much the same emotions and physical response. His wife had died two years ago, and he, too, had thought he would never love again. Yet here he was.

They made love, slowly and passionately, and finally fell asleep; both were spent and relaxed. In the middle of the night, wonder of wonders, they awoke and made love again, this time with joy and exuberance. Then again, in the early morning light, just before dawn, when the world is quiet with anticipation of the coming day, they made love until both of them cried out in passion, love, release.

If the entire Grove heard them (and they did), no mention or hint was made of it over breakfast. There had been a great deal of lovemaking going on that night in the Grove, mostly because two people of great power had let their passions loose, to fly through the night affecting all who came in contact. All, that is, except for Jen and Dan. When they did not appear for breakfast, Arthur went to their house and knocked quietly. He was greatly relieved when Dan came to the door. His relief was short-lived, however, when Dan announced that Jen was in full labor and thought she would deliver soon. Charity immediately went to Jen's bedroom while Jim called Brett and Miranda and told them to hurry when Charity announced that Jen's water had broken.

Kateryna Elizabeth Balanchuk was born with curly red hair and brilliant blue eyes. Her squall awoke Will Burch, sleeping in his mother's arms in the common room. He did not cry but looked around seeking the source of this new and interesting sound. When Jim learned that Kateryna's middle name was in honor of his late wife, he was overcome with happiness, lightly tinged with grief. Charity giggled with joy to learn that the baby had been named for her late aunt.

It had been a night of lovemaking, a morning of birth. The Grove seemed to vibrate with the emotions running through everyone. Pete and Melanie had spent the night in the common room; they were holding hands and trying to sleep, without much success. When Melanie finally slipped into a deep sleep, Pete let himself drift off as well.

The cries of the newborn woke them both. Despite the few hours of sleep they had both managed, he looked better than he had the previous day and was no longer shaking and watching Melanie constantly. Melanie had recovered a bit of her color and was visibly stronger.

At Melanie's request, Brett brought Kat into the common room briefly for her to see. When he returned, she and Pete asked if the pregnancy test they had planned for the day before could be performed. Brett readily agreed.

The test was simple, conducted behind a makeshift screen.

"How many periods have you missed?" asked Brett.

"Two," replied Melanie. "I should have checked sooner, but we've been trying for so long that I was afraid to take the test. Then Pete said that since we were going to ask you and Miranda to be godparents anyway, we might as well go ahead and have you do the testing."

Miranda asked Linda if she had a home pregnancy test. She brought it into the room and handed it to Brett. Brett conducted a quick examination along with the home test. Both were positive. Pete and Melanie were overjoyed. But Melanie quickly grew anxious.

"Was the baby at all affected by my injury?"

"Not that I can tell," said Brett. "It's really too early to clearly hear the heartbeat. I'm going to assume until I discover differently that you are both fine. Now let's go join the others for breakfast. I'm starving. Take it nice and slow, Melanie, and hold onto us."

Breakfast was already being served when they arrived in the southern part of the common room.

"I'm gonna be a dad," blurted Pete, blushing furiously.

Everyone congratulated them, agreeing that this had, indeed, been a momentous night and morning. New life, a life spared, and now another new life on the way. Plus new love, though Charity and Galen knew it was old love, as close to its end as its beginning. Now, however, was not the time to tell that story. Tomorrow would be soon enough.

They were all so caught up in the events of the morning that none of them noticed the large man, standing next to a tree, watching them.

CHAPTER 10

SHE'S OKAY! SHE DIDN'T DIE. THERE'S A NEW baby. I haven't seen a baby for so long.

He sat beside his small fire and counted his arrows. They were all there. He had seen the shaft that pierced her and was about to go to her when the others arrived. It looked like one of his arrows from a distance; his inventory said otherwise.

What could it have been, if not an arrow?

Trying to remember the events of the previous day, he chewed on a piece of squirrel. He went hunting, had the squirrel to show for it and a rabbit, too. He remembered shooting them, cutting their throats swiftly so they would not suffer in case the arrow had not killed them. All of his arrows were here. However, the blackouts were coming more often. He had long periods of time he could not account for. What if he had shot her?

I need help. But with that boy dead, and now this woman injured, will they help me or blame me? Perhaps I am worthy of blame?

Ready to sleep despite the early hour, he had wrapped himself in his tattered, filthy blanket. The sun was setting; night was far away. He wanted to be asleep before the darkness came. There were demons in the darkness, demons he could sometimes avoid by sleeping, but not always. The worst were the ones that came in his dreams. He still had some of the pills the VA doc had given him in St. Louis. He hated them. They made him feel groggy and dull in the morning, but they let him sleep without dreaming. Tonight, he took one, rolled over next to the dying fire, and slept until the morning sun touched his face.

And now, in the clear bright light of morning, he stood hidden behind a tree. Longing tugged at his soul. Fear of rejection, or worse, accusation, kept him from approaching them. He watched them laugh and talk and eat and rejoice over the new baby until he could bear it no more and slipped back into the forest to return to hiding.

CHAPTER 11

THE PLAN WAS TO HAVE CHARITY RESUME her story after breakfast the next morning. She and Galen woke up late, and the others joined them in a late brunch that extended well into the afternoon. The events of the morning, a new baby and another on the way, drove all thoughts of forest monsters and long stories away.

Charity privately rejoiced that no one asked her to continue. The memories were painful, which is why she preferred focusing on the present. Galen was a joy, an unexpected presence in her life. She intended to treasure every moment she had with him.

"We will need to get the sawmill running," she said quietly.

Everyone turned to stare at her.

"But we must cut the wood quickly."

"Of course," said Galen. "We can work fast, but if it would be better, we can wait until fall, when she dies. We should be able to finish before the snow sets in. We will need to assess the condition of the houses in town first to determine how much lumber will be required." Galen looked quite worried. "If necessary, we can have lumber and roofing materials shipped upriver from St. Louis."

"Why do we have to wait?" asked Jim.

"Because we don't want to anger the Leshachikha more than she already is."

Jim sighed. *I know I will get the rest of the story when she is ready. I still need to know more now, though.*

"Why is she angry? I don't need the whole rest of the story now, but it would help to know what has pissed her off."

"She sees the trees as her children," said Charity. "When we cut them down, make lumber out of them, we are, in her eyes, murdering her children."

All of the parents in the room stared at her in horror.

CHAPTER 12

ASHLEY SWANSON WAS FIFTEEN YEARS OLD and fiercely independent. She was the daughter of Norm and Wanda Swanson, who both worked as loom programmers at the mill. She had convinced her parents that she was old enough to spend time on her own for the summer and had promised never to go near the river or Sanders Pond. She had also signed up for a four-hour-a-week shift at the *Harper's Landing Gazette* as a reporter. She had not promised them she would avoid boys and was happy the topic had never come up.

The primary reason for her happiness was sitting next to her, under a large apple tree in the middle of the orchard. Davin Crow was sixteen, captain of the football team, and rumored to be first in line for quarterback next fall. He was intelligent and extremely good-looking. He was also utterly besotted with Ashley, though whether it was because of her quick wits or her physical charms was a matter of debate among several of their mutual friends.

It had been three weeks since Sheriff Jim had told everyone not to go into the woods. They both knew about the dead boy found near the orchard and about the attack on Melanie. But nothing more had happened since then, so they decided with the certainty of mid-adolescence that it was safe to be in the orchard.

They were enjoying a picnic of pulled pork sandwiches, potato salad, pink lemonade, and chocolate chip cookies. The looks they exchanged when they accidentally touched hands suggested they were both contemplating other enjoyments once lunch was done.

"I think we need some fresh fruit," said Davin. "All this meat and potatoes isn't healthy."

He reached up and shook a low-hanging branch. Two ripe spring apples bounced on the ground. He pulled out a pocketknife, picked up one of the apples, and deftly cut it into slices. He handed one to Ashley. She ate it delicately, exclaiming at its sweetness.

"That might be the best fresh apple I've ever eaten," she said, swiftly finishing the remaining slices.

"Let's carve our initials in the tree," said Davin. "They will be there forever."

Davin was about to cut into the tree when Ashley began to cough. She turned red in the face, while her lips began to turn blue as she coughed and choked. He rose in concern and tried pounding on her back. She continued to choke and gag.

He stood her up and clasped his arms around her midsection, applying the Heimlich maneuver he had recently learned. Instead of a piece of apple popping out, Ashley opened her mouth wide, and a gush of vomit poured forth. He recoiled in horror, when not only her entire lunch, but also a considerable quantity of blood came out.

Davin laid her on the ground on her side with his shirt rolled up under her head. He then dialed Sheriff Jim's number. Before the call could go through, his legs were suddenly and violently pulled out from under him. A pair of long branch-like hands wrapped themselves around his feet and ankles. He fought to get free, reaching for his knife to cut and slash at them. He was lifted high into the air and then swung violently against a nearby tree. Once his head had burst like a melon, his attacker tossed his body to the ground.

The being who had brought about the demise of Davin approached the prone body of Ashley. The girl was barely breathing. The creature was a female, with trunks for legs and branches sprouting from her torso and from her head, draped in moss. She bent down and removed the shirt from under Ashley's head. If the girl survived to retch again, she would drown in her own vomit. She dropped the shirt, watched the two bodies for a while, and then, with a grim smile of satisfaction, melted back into the orchard.

CHAPTER 13

BRUNCH WAS CLEARED AWAY, WATER glasses were filled, and babies were sound asleep. Charity was about to resume her story when Jim's cell phone rang. He frowned at the screen. It was a number he didn't recognize. The Caller ID said Davin Crow. Jim vaguely remembered the name as a boy on the high school football team. He answered by the third ring.

"Is this the sheriff?" asked a deep, brusque voice.

"Yes. Who is this? Why are you on Davin's phone?"

"Well, first off, it wasn't me. I know what it was, or at least what it looked like, but it wasn't me, Sheriff. Ya gotta promise me you believe me."

Jim stared at the phone for a moment as if it had grown legs.

"Who is this? What doesn't... Why are you calling?"

"My name doesn't matter much, but it's Master Sergeant Michael Cullen, sir. I'm down here in this apple orchard. I think you need to come right away. Are you at that place they call the Grove?"

Jim felt some alarm. Who was this Cullen fellow and how did he know so much about them?

"Yes, I am."

"Then come due south, through the orchard to the middle. Sheriff?"

"Yes."

"Bring some help, some evidence-gathering people, and a doctor if you have one."

Jim ended the call abruptly and leaped to his feet.

"Brett, get your bag. Dan, grab the forensics stuff. You," he said, pointing at Jen, Charity, Galen and Linda. "Go inside my place and lock the door. Linda, show Galen where I keep my extra weapon. Keep the curtains closed, and your phones at your side. Pete and Melanie went home, right?"

"Yeah," said Brett. "Miranda went with them."

Linda was looking truly alarmed, while Galen was busy herding everyone inside. Charity stood, deep in thought, staring into the orchard. Jim noticed that her lips were moving, but he did not interrupt. Finally, she turned to him.

"Take Finn and Arthur with you. Keep them close."

She turned without further comment and entered his house, firmly locking the door behind her.

Jim, Dan, Finn, Arthur, and Brett set out into the orchard. Jim and Dan led the way, Jim's gun loose in the holster, ready to be drawn if needed. Arthur carried his stout walking stick which Jim suspected was weighted at one end. Finn and Brett walked behind Arthur, constantly scanning the sides of the orchard as the group headed south.

They finally reached the clearing which Charity called Heart's Center. It was precisely in the middle of the orchard, circular, and marked by lush, thick grass and meadow flowers.

Today the normally peaceful and beautiful clearing was the site of grisly mayhem.

It was obvious that Davin was dead, his head a gut-wrenching ruin. Brett ran to Ashley. She was still alive, though barely. He rolled her onto her side, cleared her mouth of vomit, and checked her vital signs. He then called Miranda.

"Get a car down here, now," he said urgently. "Jim, get the portable stretcher out of my bag, please. Dan and I are going to carry her as quickly as we can to meet the car."

Brett did a more thorough examination of Ashley's mouth and throat. She appeared to have stopped bleeding; however, her throat was raw and swollen. He knew he needed to get her to the clinic and on oxygen and fluids as quickly as possible.

While all this was going on, Jim noted a man, dressed in black, tattered clothing, standing beyond the edge of the trees. He moved over to Brett.

Jim and Dan unfolded the stretcher. The two men gently lifted Ashley onto it; then, Brett and Dan hurried off toward the Grove, traveling as swiftly as was safe for the girl and them.

Jim headed slowly toward the man standing among the trees.

"Master Sergeant Cullen?" he asked, holding his empty hands slightly raised.

"Yessir," replied the man.

Although his clothes were tattered almost to rags and his hair was matted as was his beard, Mike Cullen was apparently sober. He was badly in need of a bath and probably medical attention. He did not run but maintained a wary stance, as if ready to bolt if Jim made any aggressive moves.

"Why don't you come on out, sit with me on this log, and tell me what happened?" asked Jim. "I know you asked me to believe you, told me it wasn't you. So, tell me what you know."

"How do I know you won't arrest me on the spot?"

"You don't. You can't expect me to believe you without having something to go on, though, can you?"

"Yeah, you're right."

Cullen stepped into the clearing. He was obviously in poor shape, far too thin for his tall, broad frame. He carried a bow over his left shoulder, ready to be drawn quickly, with a quiver of arrows on his back. A large buck knife was holstered on his belt. Jim could also see he did not have a gun, at least not one that was visible.

Finn walked directly up to Cullen, a bag of cinnamon rolls in his hand, and offered one to him. The big man accepted swiftly, and the roll disappeared in one or two bites. Finn offered a second, and Cullen ate it more slowly than the first. He sat on a stump and licked his fingers.

"Sorry about that. Haven't had much but a couple of squirrels and a coney last week. Plus, I ran out of coffee."

He looked hopefully at the thermos Arthur was carrying on his belt. Arthur quickly poured some hot coffee into the cap and handed it over. Cullen sat for a while, savoring the hot coffee with still another roll that Finn pulled from his seemingly endless supply.

"Was going into town tonight to fetch some coffee beans from the nice lady at the diner. I go near the first of the month. She leaves me food sometimes, sometimes leaves that apple pie, and I leave her rabbits or fish that I catch, and a little money."

Cullen's voice was less ragged now. He had obviously not spoken with anyone for a long time. He sat on the stump, staring at Davin's lifeless body with the mangled head. Tears began pouring down his cheeks.

"I couldn't stop her. She was too big and scary."

"Stop who?" asked Jim.

"The tree-woman. The one who did this."

Jim sat on a log near him, waiting for him to continue. Cullen sat in silence. Finally, Arthur spoke up.

"Can you describe her? Do you mean she lives in a tree?"

"No. She is a tree. She doesn't have feet like you and me. More like stumps, with roots. Her fingers are long and pointed. She has plants and moss growing out of her head."

He glared at them, daring them to question his story. He was used to being treated like a dimwit or drunk, though he was neither. He was embarrassed at having cried in front of them and now was certain they would think he was crazy.

Instead, Arthur said, "So the stories are true."

"What stories?" asked Jim.

"In the diaries, the ones Charity found in the cottages. They speak of Lesheye living here in the forest. I thought they were long gone if they ever existed. We really need to have Charity finish her story soon."

"You believe me?" asked Cullen.

"Maybe they do," said Jim. "I'm not convinced yet. I do want to hear more, though. If you saw her, why didn't you try to stop her? You're a big man."

"I know. I'm a coward for not trying. Sheriff, she's almost eight foot tall, and her arms are long and powerful. You see what she did to the boy."

Finn spoke up.

"Jim, I know you have a hard time with this stuff. It goes against your training. If the attacker was a Leshachikha, then Mike here would be dead too, if he had tried to stop her. Lesheye are tutelary deities, more than humans but less than gods."

"You know I'm open to persuasion, as long as it's backed up with hard facts; until that's proven, though, Master Sergeant

Cullen, I'm afraid I'm going to have to ask you to come into town with us."

Cullen looked shaken, his posture indicating he might be resistant. However, Jim put him at ease immediately.

"I'm not going to lock you up. I am going to ask you to stay at Havensrest with Arthur and Finn. They will see to it that you get some real rest, good food, and will hear your story when you are ready to tell it."

Cullen visibly relaxed. To his great embarrassment, he had to wipe away more tears.

"Do you have any belongings somewhere we can help you retrieve?" asked Finn. "Arthur and I can help you get them after the others come back for this poor boy's body."

Cullen answered in the affirmative as Jim called Dan, while looking down at Davin's ruined body.

"Will you be able to come back and help me retrieve the body?"

"Yeah. We got Ashley to the clinic. Miranda and Melanie are helping Brett get her settled into the little hospital setup they've been preparing. Her parents are on the way, as are Davin's. What do I tell them?"

Jim swore under his breath. Still another family about to be ripped apart. As he recalled, the Crow family were old time Harper's Landing folks. There would be many relatives and friends needing consolation. He hoped Charity and Arthur had enough energy for them after the horror of Ethan's death. *Of course, they do,* he thought. *They are the backbone of this community. Plus, there is Finn, too. Now Galen, as well. He is made of stern stuff.* He realized that Dan was waiting for an answer.

"Tell them the truth, Dan. It appears their son has been murdered, and his body is being brought to the clinic for examination. By all that is holy, please have Brett try to keep them from seeing him. Especially the mother. Explain to them that we will have to use DNA testing to confirm that it is their boy. Once they arrive, get their house key and permission to go get the boy's hairbrush or toothbrush and take it back to Brett. Then get back here as soon as you can. I don't want them to wait. I'm done with the forensics for now. Ask Brett if it's okay to move the body. It needs to be official, and recorded, in case our newest resident is not as upright as he appears."

"I have a feeling about our Master Sergeant Cullen," replied Dan. "Have you interviewed him?"

"Yes. We'll talk later. I still can't hang my hat on the idea that this town summons people," said Jim. "But there isn't a better explanation for someone always being there at the right moment."

"Don't worry, Jim. You'll grow into it. You're being stubborn, even if you do claim to be open to new ideas."

Dan laughed as he ended the call. *Like I was ready to believe in magic when I first arrived.*

Meanwhile Jim stood watch by the body. He didn't like waiting here, even though he was armed, he had people with him, and there was no immediate indication of danger. He had an itch, a cop's itch, that things weren't right. He was on full alert.

Dan arrived shortly, so Arthur, Finn, and Mike left to pick up Mike's stuff. They were to go directly to Havensrest afterwards. Jim and Dan attended to the sad and grisly tasks of placing Davin's ruined body into a body bag and carrying it back to Brett's van, which doubled as a makeshift ambulance and the coroner's van. Jim carefully placed all the bagged evidence in an evidence locker in the back of the van. He forwarded the pictures on his cell phone to Brett and Dan and called Finn to remind him and Arthur to do the same.

Dan and Jim drove to Brett's clinic. Neither man was in a hurry to meet the parents of the dead boy in the back of their vehicle. Notification of the next of kin was one of the worst jobs in a policeman's life, in Jim's opinion. He wished he could leave the task to someone else, but he always did it.

When Arthur, Finn, and Mike reached Mike's camp, it was clear that Mike had few belongings. The three of them managed to carry it all with no struggle. There were a few books, a camp stove, a cooler, and a small box that held matches, a candle, and a sliver of soap. Cullen had a canvas bag over his shoulder that held his sleeping bag and the few staple goods he had—flour, sugar, and a can for coffee beans that was now empty. He also had a small frying pan, a mortar and pestle, and a coffee pot that had seen better days. Over his other shoulder he had slung his bow and a quiver of arrows. His knife was still secured to his belt. Jim had already indicated he had no intention of asking him to surrender the bow or the knife, but he had made a point of instructing Arthur to secure any other weapons in Havensrest. On that point, he and Arthur were in full agreement.

CHAPTER 14

IT HAD BEEN AS AWFUL AS HE HAD SUSPECTED it would be. Jim sat in Arthur's study, sipping at his second shot of bourbon, staring out the window.

"She kept demanding to see him, Arthur. I tried my darnedest to explain without sending them both into a tail-spin of horror why that was a bad idea. In the end, Brett relented, letting them in. I never, ever want to hear a sound like that again."

He drained the glass, setting it on the table.

"I suppose I should get home to Linda and Will," he said.

Arthur stood up with him, suddenly giving Jim a long enveloping hug.

Jim walked out to his car. The moon was rising over the distant forest. Breathing in the scents of early spring, he stood in the garden. He remembered the stink of the city and rejoiced in his choice to leave. Then trouble had come to paradise, not once, not twice, but multiple times, in ways he could not fully comprehend. Of one thing, however, he was certain. His was the solid foundation this community needed, his insistence upon fact, on what was provable. If their magic could fit within that construct, he would grant the reality of it. First and foremost, though, he was and always would be a man of science, with his feet on the ground. He headed home to Linda, to Will, and to the promise of dinner and companionship and warmth.

Shortly after Jim's departure, Arthur and Finn made sure Mike had settled in. What he had wanted more than anything was a long shower with shampoo for his hair and beard, plus a brush, things Arthur could happily provide.

Finn remained with Mike at Havensrest while Arthur headed for the new hospital wing behind Brett's clinic. He would visit with both sets of parents, comforting them as best he could, as well as seeing how Ashley was doing. When they all went home, they would be as comforted as they could be under the circumstances.

Arthur was a shaman, offering healing to both Ashley and her parents. The girl might survive physically, but healing the inner damage would be the work of many hours of walking and talking with Arthur and perhaps some time with Finn and his music.

Back at Havensrest, Finn sang for the parents of the dead boy. He sang a path to the stars for Davin. He sang for Davin's mother because a mother's pain rends the soul with great and tiny tears, wounds that scar and twist and never go away. Finn's song was to heal, not to offer forgetfulness. The scars would remain, but the wounds would heal with time.

When Arthur returned, he and Finn found Mike Cullen in the library; he was engrossed in a nineteenth-century book on arboriculture. Silently, Mike got up and poured each of the men a small shot of Arthur's excellent bourbon. They sat in the moonlight streaming through the window, the only other light being the flicker of dying flames in the fireplace. Arthur noticed that Mike did not share the bourbon, instead pouring himself a glass of sweet tea.

The two-story-high shelves of books seemed to whisper in the shadows, while a great and overwhelming sorrow swept over the three men. They sipped their drinks in silence, tears coursing down their cheeks. They retired together, Mike to the first bedroom he had known in many years, where he had a dreamless sleep; Arthur and Finn to the comfort of their large, well-appointed bedroom, where they lay in each other's arms.

Silence fell upon Harper's Landing, as the lights went out in town and at the Grove. In that silence, a tall ungainly figure walked through town. He strode down Main Street to stand in front of Morey's Diner for a while, then to Havensrest to stare into the library window, and then to the Grove to listen to the sound of snoring parents, his keen ears detecting the soft whisper of babies' breaths. He walked on, his legs like trunks, his arms long and gnarled, hanging almost to his knees. His head had two large antlers not unlike tree branches, covered with moss. Zandar was a Leshy, brought to this land from Ukraine long ago. Soon he would have to reveal himself to Jim Burch and the other inhabitants of the Grove, to help Charity tell her story. Zoya, the Leshachikha, must be stopped, even if she was his wife. For now, however, all seemed quiet and safe, so he went back into the forest to stand watch, as he had done for well over a hundred years.

CHAPTER 15

EVERYONE AT THE GROVE SET ASIDE THEIR desire to hear the rest of Charity's story. While Jen and Dan remained in their house with their new daughter, letting Jen rest and heal from what had been a long and difficult labor, the others began the painful process of planning yet another funeral.

Ashley Swanson was slowly recovering, although the reason for her condition had Brett completely mystified. Jim and his team gathered samples of her blood and vomit from the crime scene; Brett had drawn blood as well. There was no evidence of any poison, toxin, or bacteria in any of the samples that could account for the severity of the injury to her throat and esophagus. It would be at least a week before she would be able to tolerate anything other than soothing, cool liquids.

At Brett's suggestion, her parents had agreed to the insertion of a temporary feeding tube. Everyone agreed she should remain in the small hospital wing of the clinic until it was removed, and she could eat soft food. She begged to be allowed to attend Davin's funeral, but in the end relented and watched it on Facetime with her parents.

Sandy and Carolyn Harper Crow were descendants of some of the original founders of Harper's Landing. Their great-grandparents had arrived in 1902, part of a third wave of immigration from an increasingly dangerous Ukraine. Their families were close to Stephan's family, so they resisted the urge to stay in the Ozarks with the other passengers they made the crossing with. Instead, they purchased a wagon, a pair of stout horses, and some seeds; and they made their way north to Middlewood County, where they found Stephan and his family in the small settlement at Harper's Landing.

Sandy and Carolyn had known each other all their lives, but love came to them late. It was difficult to feel romantic toward the girl who had once thrown horse pies at you because you had dipped one of her pigtails in a small jar of purple paint. But as they grew older and their friendship matured, so did their attraction for one another. They married in their early twenties, planning for a large family. Then Carolyn suffered several miscarriages. When Davin was born, she nearly died of a hemorrhage that required a hysterectomy. They made up for the lack of their own children by encouraging Davin to bring friends home. The Crow house was known for its constant supply of *pampushky*, Ukrainian donuts that were usually stuffed with chocolate or apple pie filling. Any celebration in Harper's Landing could count on having one of Carolyn Harper Crow's magnificent Kyiv cakes gracing the dessert table.

Now Sandy and Carolyn sat rigid in the front row of the small church. They, like most of the older families, were pagan. The church had been the venue for all manner of services, from a full-blown Russian Orthodox funeral mass to an Indigenous Peoples' burial. Today's service would be one familiar to most of the townsfolk.

As was the custom, the entire population of Harper's Landing attended. Even Galen White Eagle's people, though they had not fully moved into their new homes, were seated in the back. Bridgette and Finn provided the music, both instrumental and *a cappella*. The school choir sang *"Vichnaja Pamjat,"* which roughly translated to "Memory Everlasting."

The casket was filled with wrapped coins, pieces of bread, and flowers, left there during the three days of mourning when those who so desired could visit the dead. It was believed by many who still practiced the Old Ways that the soul remained for those three days. Finn and the others who had found Davin's body knew his soul had already been sung on its journey, but the ancient Ukrainian practice brought comfort to the family and friends, so they said nothing.

Jeremy had worked the same magic on Davin he had employed in reconstructing Ethan Burns' ruined face a few weeks ago. Privately, he hoped it was a skill he would never have to employ again. While he was pleased with his work and grateful to have brought some small measure of peace to the families, he did not wish to continue working with dead humans. It was, in his opinion, a desecration of the art of taxidermy, and, if not checked, could lead to unseemly practices. It was for this same reason he steadfastly refused to practice his skill on departed pets. *Let the dead return whence they came* was the motto he lived by when it came to pets and people.

After the service, Davin's casket was placed in the ground in the town cemetery. When the first shovel of dirt was thrown into the grave, his mother collapsed. She was helped into a car and driven to Havensrest, where food, comfort, companionship, and calm abounded. It was a warm early spring day, and someone brought a chair into the garden for her. Several other women sat on benches or on the ground; they enjoyed the scent of newly blossomed irises, Lenten roses, and violets. The food would come later, though someone did bring Carolyn a cup of tea.

Sandy was inside with the men, where he gratefully accepted a small crystal glass with a finger of bourbon. He sipped at it, finally letting the tears he had been holding on to course down his cheeks. He sat silently at the window, looking out at his wife sitting in the garden. *She is with the women. She is okay. There will be time for us later.*

"Arthur?" asked Sandy. "We are going to need help getting through this."

"Of course. Finn and I will help you. Music and conversation, the great healers. Whenever you both are ready."

Everyone migrated toward the large dining room at the center of Havensrest. Maggie and Morey had provided an amazing array of comfort food, and on a separate table was a significant quantity of apple pie: large pies, hand pies, and even a few dishes of apple pie filling for the few new residents who had indicated they could not consume wheat. Plates were filled, and glasses were lifted in a toast to the memory of Davin. There was even a toast to Ethan, which moved Galen to tears.

Gradually, the conversation turned to dealing with whoever or whatever had killed these two young people. No one suspected Mike Cullen. If Arthur and Finn accepted him, that was enough for everyone. Everyone, that is, except Jim Burch. As sheriff, he had a duty to remain vigilant to every possible suspect. And right now, all he had was a large, expertly trained vagrant who was at or near the scene of all three attacks and the assertion by that same vagrant, and most of the pagans in his community, that there was a powerfully dangerous creature of mythology stalking people through the forests and orchards of his town.

While his instinct was to focus attention on Cullen, Jim had learned to trust the people he now lived with, especially after the events of two years ago. It was for this reason that he pulled Dan Balanchuk aside and asked him if there were any English books in the Havensrest library that were about Lesheye. Dan led him into the room and pulled out two volumes, one large and heavily illustrated.

"This one is the best. The illustrator is a well-known Ukrainian biologist who tracked Lesheye all the way to the Eastern Siberian Taiga. His descriptions of their capabilities, duties, and beliefs are considered the most detailed and accurate. The other volume purports to provide background information, but the shaman of the Taiga dispute the author's findings."

"I think I will stick with the big book. I like books with pictures anyway." Jim grinned wolfishly. "Can't let people be thinking I'm an intellectual, can we?"

Dan laughed.

"You do the hick sheriff routine well, when needed. But you don't fool any of us, Jim Burch."

With that, he headed back to the dining room to be with his wife and new baby, leaving Jim in the peace and quiet of the library. Jim poured himself a small tumbler of Arthur's private reserve and settled in for a long afternoon of reading.

CHAPTER 16

MAY ARRIVED, BRINGING WARM DAYS, bright blooms, and the promise of a long, lazy summer. The snow had melted in early spring, swelling the rivers and ponds throughout the area. Flowers were blooming, some of them early, and birds were returning.

Galen's small tribe had moved into town, the families gratefully accepting the few remaining empty houses. A couple of the larger houses became homes to two families each.

Galen remained at the Grove, sharing Charity's small cottage. His grief over the loss of his grandson was palpable. There was also the necessary task of finding another member of the tribe to take his place when he grew too old. Ethan had been meant to fill that role. It was up to Galen to find another, someone with power. He hadn't even bothered to hunt for power among the others since Ethan's gift had been so strong.

The Osage people who had remained behind with Galen and his father, when the others decided to move to the cities, were strong, determined people. They honored the ancient gods and the ancient traditions. They were a small tribe, consisting of forty-five adults and several small children. Galen was sixty-five, likely their leader for many years to come. Ethan had been his only heir. Although Galen's son and his wife had tried, they were never able to conceive another child.

The tribal council had accepted Galen's request to train his grandson to be the next shaman and chief after the tragic death of the boy's parents in a boating accident. Ethan's training had begun when he reached his tenth birthday. Now Galen would have to start the process again. He would seek the counsel of Charity, as well as Arthur and Finn, in selecting a new candidate. Whoever took his place would need to be able to form a bridge between the Osage ways and the ways of the Druids and pagans who protected the Grove.

For now, though, he needed to focus on getting his people settled quickly and teaching them the ways of their new neighbors. It would be a learning experience for everyone. Some of the adjustments would not be easy, so he anticipated much arguing at their next tribal council.

"We would like to build a sweat lodge next to the Grove," said Galen one morning, while Charity, Jim, and he shared coffee and rolls on the deck. "Also, a meeting house for private council meetings."

"Of course," said Charity. "But will you need to cut wood?"

"No, we will use fallen branches and the tanned hides we brought with us."

"Build away," she said. "But be careful."

"Of course."

None of the men building the sweat lodge and meeting house were aware of the watcher, lurking in the trees to the north of the building site. She was angered at first, but when she saw that their housing was made of fallen branches, animal furs, and sod, she nodded in approval. She turned, disappearing into the growing darkness, knowing she would have to keep an eye on them and stop them if they tried to hurt the forests she was tasked with protecting. She now turned her eyes toward the Grove. The collection of houses and other wood structures was a menace that required her attention. Silently, she moved through the trees toward her intended target.

CHAPTER 17

N*O ONE IS HERE,* **SHE THOUGHT.** *GOOD. NOW how to destroy this? This abomination to MY forest, MY children?*

She stalked around the perimeter of the Grove, examining the steps up to the deck on the south side, facing the orchard. She went to the northern side, where the deck was built flush with the gentle slope of the hill that led to the worst abomination of all: the sawmill. She stomped up the hill. Rage filled her when she discovered that the sawmill had been restored and was now obviously in use.

One hundred years! I lay trapped for one hundred years, and this is what I find upon awakening. Damn these humans and their wanton destruction of my children, my forest!

There was no handy fire for her to use this time. She was determined to destroy it, as many times as it took. She entered the structure through the open back door and looked around. Nothing was familiar. The lamps were gone, replaced by strange small balls attached to the walls. Large white panels traveled the length of the roof. The floor was swept clean. Huge round blades replaced the small saws of a hundred years ago, and there were no foot pedals to turn them. She was puzzled as well as enraged.

The source of her rage was the huge stack of lumber, freshly cut, smoothed by some means as yet unknown to her. It was unnatural, this cutting. That, at least, was unchanged, even if the method of creating them was different. She could have tolerated a small amount of building with logs, fallen from ancient trees or limbs torn off by storms. But this wanton murder of her forest, her trees, simply to provide comfort for humans, could not be tolerated.

She saw a large, strange handle of sorts on the wall near the front door. She examined it thoroughly, cautiously lifting it. When she pushed it all the way up, she sprang back as the building seemed to come to life. Light flooded the spacious area around the various machines, while some of them hummed. She approached one of the larger machines, and upon examination, she found a small protrusion that she could move up and down. Gingerly, she pushed at it, flipping it downward. The blade on the machine sprang into action, moving rapidly up and down.

Carefully, she picked up a small piece of wood, holding it under the blade. The teeth of the blade grabbed the wood, nearly wrenching it from her powerful hands. She was enthralled as the blade moved swiftly through the wood.

That is how I will do it. I will destroy their work. Let them try to remake what I destroy. I will stop them before they can hurt any more of my children. I will force them to try, and I will destroy them. But first, I must destroy this abomination.

She picked up several large pieces of finished lumber and began systematically destroying them with the saw. She laughed wildly as she cut through the planks. Once she had destroyed all the carefully stacked boards, she turned her attention to the various tools that hung from the walls, all of them unrecognizable to her. She was a daughter of the forests, a stranger to the ways of humankind. She pulled over the tables, ripped cords from the walls, and broke the long pieces of metal with teeth on one side, tearing them from their wooden handles.

She picked up a strange item. It was made of metal with a long rope extending from it and another piece of metal sticking out from the end of the rope. The rope was made of a strange material, something she did not recognize. At the end of this strange rope, there was a circle of metal with teeth in it, like the long metal pieces she had broken. She poked at it and discovered that the circle turned. She looked around and saw similar ropes, attached to other strange items. These ropes were attached to strange-looking holes in the walls.

She carried the tool she had picked up, along with its rope, over to the wall. After some experimenting, she discovered that she could stick its end into a hole in the wall, like the other ropes. She held the strange tool up, examining it carefully. On one side, she found a handle, and when she grasped it, her finger touched a movable part on its underside, causing the tool to roar to life, the blade spinning wildly. She barely avoided cutting into herself and dropped the thing to the ground. When she let go of it, the demon-possessed metal went silent.

Perhaps not a demon, she thought.

She picked it up again, this time holding it away from her, and grasped the handle, pressing the moveable part underneath. Again, it sprang to life, and she gingerly pushed it into the floor. The wood made a tearing noise as the great spinning blade cut into it.

Better and better, she thought.

She set to work, ripping great holes in the floor. She turned her attention to the walls and the framework that held them. The great spinning blade cut through them easily, so she began to destroy the entire sawmill.

It was inevitable that eventually she cut through the electrical wiring in the walls of the sawmill. The results were catastrophic. The fresh sawdust exploded when the sparks hit it, blowing out all the windows and causing damage to most of the remaining walls. The circular saw blade warped and began to melt, while the rest of the saw exploded, throwing pieces of metal in all directions. The piles of sawdust and cut wood on the floor caught fire when the sparking wires hit them.

The Leshachikha's limbs began to smoke, and small flames broke out here and there on the moss hanging from her head. She swiftly shape-shifted into an extremely large bat, but not before sustaining some burns that caused her to cry out as she flew through the destroyed window closest to her. If anyone had been watching at that moment, they would have seen a large flying creature heading for the river at high speed, trailing smoke and sparks behind.

Zandar, who had been searching for her, heard her cries and looked up, recognizing immediately his shape-shifted mate. He stood debating. Go after her? Help the humans? Retreat into the forest and deal with her later? He chose the latter. He needed to spend some time pondering how he would approach her.

The entire sawmill was engulfed in flames. The first to realize it were members of Galen's tribe, who had returned to work on their sweat lodge and meeting house. They rushed to the sawmill to make sure that the fire didn't reach the trees next to it, while one of them phoned Galen at Havensrest. Galen relayed the news to Jim, who immediately activated the volunteer fire department alarm while running to his Explorer. He sped to the courthouse, which housed the single fire engine in the garage behind the building. As he fired up the engine, other cars careened into the lot. The volunteer firefighters leaped on board the truck. They grabbed the coats and hats stored on the truck, donning them as Jim sped toward the Grove.

As they sped up the road toward the Grove, they could see the smoke and flames leaping upward. Jim heaved a sigh of relief. It wasn't the Grove; it was the sawmill. His relief was short-lived, however, when he remembered how close the forest was to the north side of the sawmill, plus how much dry brush there was between the sawmill and the Grove residences to the south.

When they finally pulled up between the sawmill and the Grove, Jim saw Galen's people hastily removing the brush which had worried him so much. Most of the volunteer firemen set to work attaching hoses to the tank on the fire engine. Jim and one of the men unrolled another hose, hooking it up to the well pump at the perimeter of the Grove. They attached the other end to the fire engine tank and activated the pump, keeping the tank full and thus providing a steady supply of water to those fighting the fire.

It took four hours for all Galen's people and half the population of Harper's Landing to completely extinguish the fire. Fortunately, there was no wind. Nevertheless, Galen, Mike, and two of the Osage men fanned out through the forest on the three sides of the sawmill to check for any small fires. The remainder of the fighters made certain that all the hot spots in the sawmill were completely extinguished.

Jim and Dan disconnected power to the sawmill, then made certain there were no hot wires anywhere. The damage was extensive. The structure was a total loss, as were all the tools inside. They had managed to save most of the equipment outside: the pump, several benches used for sanding or fine work, and the large shed that housed the tree cutting tools and equipment.

"Dear gods, she's done it again," said a soft female voice next to Jim.

He turned and saw Charity staring at the devastation, most of the color drained from her face. She looked old and feeble. He saw none of the usual joy that radiated from her. Instead, tears coursed down her cheeks as she stared in despair at the ruined sawmill.

"Thank the gods no one died this time."

"Who died in the first fire?" asked Jim.

"My aunt and my father."

Charity stared a while longer, then sank onto a nearby log.

"I can't go through this again, Jim. She's back, and I can't deal with her. I was too young the first time, and now I'm too old."

Galen appeared out of the nearby stand of trees.

"No fires that we could find, nor any evidence of who or what did this."

"You know who did it, Galen," said Charity, a hint of bitterness tinging her voice. "You know she's back. Zandar told you, didn't he? He hoped she would have learned her lesson."

Jim remained silent. He would have to hear the rest of the story, learn more about this Zandar person, later. For now, he was concerned about Charity.

"Charity, do you want Galen to take you home, or me?"

"Galen can do it. You need to check out the sawmill, do your sheriff stuff. Jim? Mike Cullen is not the cause of either this or the murders. If you treat him right, he will be your good right hand."

Galen lifted her effortlessly. She put her arms around his neck, burying her face in his shoulder. He carried her swiftly and silently back to her home in the Grove.

Jim turned back toward the sawmill and saw Mike standing at the edge of the ruined building. He was examining the ground around what used to be the back entrance.

"Sheriff? Come look at this."

"Call me Jim, please. What are we looking at?"

"Prints. These are exactly the same weird tracks we saw at the murder scenes." He paused a moment. "I watched you from the trees, saw you make casts of the prints."

Jim called Dan over and asked him to fetch casting plaster from the back of his Explorer. The three men mixed the material, then Jim made several casts of the prints.

"Those came from the forest," said Cullen. "See how they are deeper on the side toward the sawmill? Whatever made that track was leaning forward, moving this way."

Jim gave Mike a hard stare.

The man was looking much better than the first time Jim saw him. He was far less thin and worn looking, thanks to good food and good sleep. His recently cut hair was combed, his beard was shaved, and his clothes were clean and unwrinkled. He was standing at the edge of the burned building, next to the prints.

"You were Special Forces."

It was a statement, not a question.

"Yup. Army Ranger. Afghanistan, Iraq, Syria. A walk into hell. Glad to be out."

"Glad to have you beside me."

Jim was silent for a while, staring at the sawmill.

"This is the second time this sawmill has burned down," he finally said. "Charity seems to think the same being did it both times."

"Jim," said Mike. "I learned a long time ago, hanging out in an abandoned building praying that the guys hunting me wouldn't come in: don't rely solely on what you already know. I'll tell you the story some day of how I escaped discovery. It's pretty much unbelievable."

"I'll hold you to that."

The two men walked back to the Grove, while Dan stored the casts in Jim's Explorer.

"Can I borrow your keys, drive these down to Brett's lab?" asked Dan. "I'll be right back. I want to get a hot shower, maybe a bit of a soak, and some of your top-shelf bourbon."

Dan stood, waiting beside the driver's door. Jim tossed him the keys while he motioned Mike to follow him up the front steps to the deck. Linda and Jen were sitting in the warm afternoon sun; they were nursing their babies. Jim could tell from the tension in her neck and shoulders that Linda was trying to hide something, probably fear. He suspected Jen felt the same way. Charity was probably napping with Galen at her side. She had taken to doing that every afternoon lately. Arthur and Finn were standing on either side of the deck, both of them staring into the forest beyond.

Trying to avoid looking at the nursing women, Mike sat in one of the Adirondack chairs Arthur had made the previous winter. He loved the casual closeness of this group, along with their obvious affection for one another. He wondered if he could ever get used to it. He realized how much he had missed human companionship. He had been alone for an exceedingly long time. Perhaps he would never really feel comfortable among groups like this. The night horrors sometimes threatened to appear in the full light of day, and there had been times when he could not remember what had happened when they took over. He wanted to belong, with a longing close to desperation. He had lost so much. He would redouble his efforts with Arthur and Finn to heal the deep wounds in his soul. Additionally, though he did not know why, he was certain that the good people of Harper's Landing would help him too.

Jim leaned over and kissed Linda and Will. He headed for the shower house, in time to meet Galen, headed the same way.

While the men were showering, Charity emerged and took a chair next to Jen and Linda.

"I suppose we need to tell them," said Jen.

"Tell them what?" asked Linda. "Which 'them'?"

"Galen knows about Zandar. Though come to think of it, Linda, you haven't met him, have you?" asked Charity.

"No. I don't even know the story, except for what you have told us so far."

"Galen thinks I should assemble everyone and invite Zandar for all of you to meet. What do you think, Jen?"

"Bridgette is simply dying to meet him. Further, it certainly would be easier to persuade Jim and Mike. Those two are of a kind: hard-headed, stubborn, and wed to reality as they know it."

"I think there's more to Mike Cullen than any of you know," responded Charity. "But yes, Jim has really earned his nickname."

"Nickname?" asked Linda.

"He Who Does Not See," answered Jen with a short laugh.

"Oh, that. Jim sees well enough. It should probably be 'He Who Does Not Wish to See.' He knows there are things his science cannot explain, things that all the forensics in the world will never explain. But that doesn't mean he'll give up trying." Linda laughed. "God help us if Will has inherited some ability yet to be revealed. I don't know how Jim would deal with that."

CHAPTER 18

LINDA BEGAN MAKING PHONE CALLS WHILE still nursing Will. Jen tucked Kat into her bassinet, then went in to prepare dinner, which included a roasted wild turkey and two loaves of fresh bread. Bridgette arrived to help, having completed her reading assignments in Havensrest's library. Charity closed her eyes, looking to be deep in thought. Her lips moved briefly now and then. Linda wisely ignored her. She managed to contact everyone she called: Brett and Miranda, Pete and Melanie Wilson, and Jeremy and Harve Sanders. They all agreed to come.

Charity finally opened her eyes, holding out her arms for Will. Linda went in to help Jen and Bridgette with dinner, which they decided to set up out on the deck.

"It's warm enough, and Zandar will appreciate it," said Jen.

People began arriving just as Jim, Mike, and Dan finished their showers. Dinner was a leisurely affair, at least until Bridgette glanced out toward the orchards, let out a shriek, and dropped her glass, sending liquid and shards everywhere.

Jen hurried inside to grab a broom while everyone else turned toward the source of Bridgette's unsettling.

A tall figure had emerged from the orchard. He stopped at the bottom of the steps, waiting to be invited to come up. Charity gestured to him to come join them. The being in question, a male, was approximately seven feet tall. He had a human face, but antlers sprouted from either side of his head. His hair and beard were bushy, the color of springtime moss, while his eyes were brilliant blue. His body was powerfully muscled. He wore a long robe of muslin and carried a walking staff taller than himself. His expression was kind, but everyone on the deck was instinctively aware that could change in a moment. This was an incredibly old being of great power. No one was deceived by the benevolent attitude he was currently projecting.

He walked across the deck to Charity, then bowed deeply.

"Hail, Guardian. Why have you summoned me here?"

"We need your help," Charity replied. "It is time you introduced yourself to the other residents of the Grove."

He drew himself up to his full height. His power was palpable. They were in the presence of a deity; everyone, including Jim and Mike, the least impressionable of the lot, realized this.

"What are you?" asked Jim. "Charity has said you are a Leshy, but what does that mean?"

"I am Zandar, protector of the forests and the creatures who dwell therein. This is my duty, even in this strange land that is not my home. I have dwelt here for over a century, guarding these trees from harm. Because you live here, I have tried to guard the humans also. In this, I fear, I have failed."

"If you are referring to the deaths that happened two years ago, that was not your failure," said Jim. "The people who died were the victims of accidental drownings. That was not something anyone could have predicted."

"Ah, Jim Burch, yes?"

Jim nodded.

"He Who Does Not See."

"Dammit, I wish all of you would stop. I see fine. I require proof is all, facts, not fairy tales and wishes."

"You see with your eyes, Jim Burch. However, you have turned off your soul. You deny the reality of what you cannot see or do not understand. That will change with time. Do not attempt to deceive me. I know full well how those people came to die, at the hands of a *bolotnik*."

He's right there in front of me. Like that thing in the water was right there. I could feel it in my head. I can see this one. I'm a scientist. He wants me to be patient. Okay, I'll be patient. Jim felt the beginnings of a major headache. He decided to stop questioning and listen.

Zandar sat on one of the benches next to the deck railing and contemplated the people gathered before him. He looked weary, sad, and worn down by time and some great sorrow.

"I fear, Guardian, that the century of silence has done nothing to temper my wife's madness."

"So, she again haunts our forests and homes?" asked Charity. "Is she as murderous as ever?"

"Murderous? Yes, I suppose you would see it that way. She believes she is protecting her children. When you cut a tree, you cut her child. When the Sanders boy kills a rabbit or a fox, he kills her children. When you shoot a deer for food, you kill her child. Can you possibly understand this?"

"She killed my father, my aunt!" snapped Charity. "She left me and my mother alone, bereft of the family we loved, dependent on the community. If it were not for Stephan,

Kateryna, Mishka, and Jane, we would have died of hunger or worse. She killed my father!"

Charity turned, burying her face in Galen's shoulder, and sobbed quietly.

Suddenly she stood, her body rigid with anger.

"You!" She glared at Zandar. "You and Porewit decided all on your own that I, who was merely a child, should be chosen to be Guardian! To assist you in doing her work, while she rested in the beloved ground, waiting to come again! I will not forgive her, Zandar! I have done my job, the gods know, and done it well. Yet you and I are not enough to quell her madness, her rage. Do not dare call it a mother's love. It is the rage and fury at being robbed of power, not of love. Do not defile our love of this place by calling her a defender. She is the despoiler, the defiler!"

Zandar bowed his head before her. *She is right,* he thought. *Zoya is the destroyer, and now I must ask them to help me destroy her.*

Jim broke the silence.

"How do we stop her? If I remember correctly from my reading, you are a tutelary deity. Does that mean you are some minor gods, perhaps immortal?"

"We are tasked with guarding the forests and the creatures therein. We die every fall, resurrect every spring. I do not know if we can be killed in the sense that you humans mean: die permanently. It is not something we dwell on. Porewit would know, but I do not wish to call him yet."

"Who is Porewit?"

"He is our god. There are many gods, Jim Burch. Each of them has its own job."

"So, if I understand you, managing your wife, determining her punishment, is something you would prefer to handle without your god. You need to understand, Zandar. This is my town. These are my people; I am charged with caring for them, much the same way you are charged with caring for the forest. I would not want to clash with you, but your wife must face our justice, not yours. You live in our world now."

"Zoya will never allow herself to be taken captive by humans," Zandar replied. "Nor would I willingly hand her over to you. The point is moot anyway. If you were to execute her for her crimes, she would merely resurrect the following spring."

"Let's don't talk capital punishment. Don't like it anyway. Makes murderers of us all. Can she be restrained?"

"With sufficient rope, or a strong enough cage, yes. But again, she would die in fall, resurrect anywhere the following spring. Zoya would simply resurrect where it suited her, continuing the havoc. As long as Zoya is here, the humans of Harper's Landing are not safe and never will be."

"What will you do?" asked Arthur. "At what point do you give in and call upon Porewit?"

"If I call him, he will come if it is his will. In the meantime, I will find her. I will try again to reason with her, perhaps take her far north, beyond the end of the great river. I have heard the forests are thick there, with few people. Perhaps that will be enough."

Zandar rose to leave, carefully climbing down the stairs. Without a word, he melted into the forest, leaving them staring, each lost in their own thoughts. Jim finally broke the silence.

"Well now, that can't be unseen."

Everyone laughed, the tension broken.

"I am obligated, as shaman of my tribe, and as a follower of the Old Ways, to seek the guidance, tutelage, and instructions of the elders of my tribe," said Galen. "There is a great deal I cannot tell you, but what I can reveal is that we—all of my people, as well as the creatures who come to me in my dreams—have never encountered a being like this before. We were not even aware of his existence. While I do not sense any hostility from this one who calls himself Zandar, I feel we must take seriously his warnings regarding his mate."

The sun had set about an hour earlier. No one had noticed that Jen and Bridgette had lit the citrine candles while Zandar and the others were talking. It was growing dark, the babies nursing before being put down for what their parents hoped would be a full night's sleep. For Jen and Dan that was wishful thinking, but Will had been sleeping through the night for a few days now, much to Jim and Linda's relief.

Jim and Finn lit the firepit, while Arthur and the others gathered up the dinner dishes and took them into the communal kitchen. They laughed and exchanged gossip while cleaning up. Mike sat back, watching them. It had been so long since he had been part of a community, and the last time he was, it was a community committed to violence and the protection of one another. He wondered how long it would take for him to relax, to feel a part of this group. If he ever could.

Finn fetched his guitar and started to play a tune, a gentle lullaby. Mike listened to the music for a while, then added a deep, rich baritone to Finn's music.

Midsummer night, sleep little baby.
Midsummer night, sleep little child.
Momma is here, and Daddy is too.
Sleep little child, while the night is still new.

Birds in their nests, rabbits in burrows.
Trees hide the owl and the new little squirrels.
The world falls asleep 'neath a star-studded cover.
Sleep little child, innocent lover.

When the song was over, the others on the deck stared at Mike in awe.

"That is some voice you have," said Finn. "You must have had some training when you were younger."

"From my mom," said Mike. "She was a favorite at jazz clubs in New Orleans. After my voice dropped, she taught me to sing. We used to go to the clubs together, until she died when I was sixteen. I went off to war when I turned eighteen, mostly 'cause of how she died. She used to sing that to me when I was little. It seemed to fit that tune you was playing."

He trailed off into silence. Finally, Jim spoke up.

"What happened to her, Mike?"

"She went to New York, to visit some music mogul who had heard her when he was visiting. He offered her a contract; she was there to sign the papers and make a recording."

"Oh, no," someone muttered. "Oh, no."

"Which Tower?" asked Arthur.

"The first one."

They all fell silent, but everyone noticed Bridgette get up from her chair and walk over to sit next to Mike on the wooden bench he had chosen next to the deck railing. She leaned against him tentatively, slipping an arm around his waist. When he began to sob, everyone quietly left to go to their homes, except Arthur and Finn. They were Mike's ride home, so they waited. Bridgette had recently turned eighteen, showing all the promise of being a magnificent woman, vested with all of Charity's abilities in addition to her mother's own considerable strength. At the moment, as she was holding Mike close, both men could detect the waves of calming energy she was pouring over him.

"I don't think Mike is going to be alone much longer," whispered Finn.

"I suspect you are right. But there's a powerful lot of healing needed to be done before he can commit to a community or a relationship," Arthur whispered back.

"Love heals" was all Finn responded.

It was fully dark when Bridgette and Mike finally untwined, sitting back on the padded bench. Mike appeared exhausted but calm. The tension he had carried so long was released, at least for a while. He wanted to walk from the Grove back to Havensrest, but Bridgette, Arthur, and Finn adamantly refused to let him.

"Where Zandar has been, Zoya cannot be far behind," said Arthur. "You're a damn fool if you think she doesn't know that you saw her."

"I'm no fool about things like that. You're right. I'll take the ride."

He headed toward the steps to the parking lot, stopped, and turned.

"Bridgette?" he asked tentatively.

"Yes?"

"Would you join me tomorrow afternoon at Morey's for some of that pie? I'd like to meet them for real and could use the support. I'm not all that comfortable yet around folks."

"I would love to," she replied, skipping off to her tiny house behind her mother's cottage at the back of the deck.

CHAPTER 19

JIM BURCH SAT AT HIS DESK IN HIS OFFICE. From his vantage point on the first floor of the courthouse, he could see the office of the *Harper's Landing Gazette,* currently occupied by his wife and six-month-old son. He also had a view of the front of Morey's Diner, which was currently full of tourists, brought there by a bus touring the quilt shops of rural Missouri. The travelers would spend the rest of the day at the Harper's Landing Textile Museum and Mill and stay the night as guests of Arthur and Finn at Havensrest.

A large pickup truck rolled by, closely followed by a van filled with six men, outfitted in various colored jackets. It was Zak, headed out with his first fishing expedition of the year. The gear would be carefully packed, tied down in the back of the pickup truck, along with coolers full of lunch delights prepared by Maggie and Morey. Zak's fishing guide business had taken off last year, when one of his customers landed a trophy bass that turned out to be the biggest recorded catch in Missouri. It was caught at Big Bass Pool, so most of the groups wanted to go there. The more experienced fishermen opted for bank trips along the Martins Way River.

It had been a few months since the murders in the forests near Harper's Landing. Jim was no closer to identifying the killer. The town had lost Ethan Burns, Davin Crow, and sadly, Ashley Swanson. The girl had been recovering nicely, but then she inexplicably took a turn for the worse. Brett had no cause of death for her. All her tox screens came back negative; there was no explanation for the new onset of massive bleeding, nor for the subsequent inflammation of her mouth and throat. Brett also could not explain why she had suddenly collapsed and died at a school picnic after apparently having recovered from her earlier ailments. Classmates said she ate a single mouthful of pie with ice cream and then, suddenly, fell over dead.

Jim despised unsolved cases. Even though he had seen Zandar, even spoken with him, he was not yet ready to attribute these murders to an insane female demi-deity, randomly killing people she saw as ravaging her forests. He snorted as he thought what his former bosses would have thought of such a report.

Desk duty at the least; and, more likely, a psych eval and medical leave.

He called Dan, Brett, Mike, and Galen.

"I want to have a meeting," he told each of them. "Can you be at my office at lunch time? Food's on me."

They all agreed to be there at noon.

Jim called Morey.

"Morey? It's Jim Burch. Have you had any problems getting apples?" he asked.

"No. In fact, since Mike began working for Harve Sanders, pruning the trees, we get as much as we can use, sometimes more."

"Mike's pruning the trees?"

"Yeah. It turns out that before he went off to war, he was working for a landscaping company, and they taught him how. The trees are looking great, according to Charity."

"I'm not sure I'm happy about him being out there alone."

"I know what you mean, but Mike's a cautious man. Bridgette goes along most of the time. She does a good job of being a watcher."

Jim mused about that for a moment. *I suspect another romance is blooming.*

"Okay. No one's gotten sick on the pie or anything?"

"Not that we've heard, and we all eat it. Did you ever find out what happened to Ashley? We all thought she was out of the woods, although I heard that someone said it was our pie that did it. It just couldn't be, though, because all the other people who came to the diner that day ate the same pie."

"I don't know, Morey. I'm not going to tell you to stop making it. However, if anyone else gets sick we are going to have to let Brett and his team examine the diner thoroughly."

"Wouldn't have it any other way."

"Can you have the new waitress bring over lunch for five, around noon?"

"Sure. By the way, the new gal is Becky Sloan. She's all grown up now, graduated early from high school. She's learning from Maggie, because some day Maggie's not going to be able to make more pie, not to mention the other stuff she does."

"What about you?" asked Jim. "You're no spring chicken, either."

Morey chuckled.

"You know the veterinarian, Gene Harcourt?"

"Of course."

"Well, it turns out he has a son down in St. Louis, about to graduate from high school this year. After graduating, he wants to do two things: come live with his dad and train to be a chef. I reckon I can teach him a thing or two. Who knows, the kids might like each other, too. This town does bring us what we need."

He hung up the phone. Jim leaned back in his chair.

Yes, this town does bring us what we need. Though damned if I know how it happens.

Jim sat staring at the buildings across from his office. The once empty space next to the *Gazette* was now a craft store, filled with spaces where artisans of Harper's Landing displayed their works for sale, mostly for the tourist season. He realized that tourist season was nearly upon them. Zak's fishing group today was the first. There would soon be many more, including the annual summer quilt retreats that Mary Harper regularly held at Havensrest.

All the more reason to solve this crime as quickly as possible. I've been away from my office for far too long. I've grown complacent. I have a town to protect.

Dan was the first to arrive, parking his battered-but-serviceable old pickup out front. Galen and Brett came next, riding together in Brett's van. The lettering "Coroner, Middlewood County" brought Jim abruptly into the reality of a need for urgency. Privately, he cursed himself for having let this go on for so long, unsolved. He didn't allow himself to wonder why Galen and Brett were together. He'd ask later.

Mike Cullen was the last to arrive, riding Charity's pony. Although the animal was sturdy and strong, the big man looked comical on the little Icelandic pony, causing the rest of them to laugh softly among themselves as he stepped off easily. He then tied Birget to the nearest of the hitching posts the town had installed downtown shortly after Charity had bought Birget. He poured some water into a collapsible bucket he had brought with him, giving her a drink before coming inside.

"We need to solve these murders," Jim said, without preamble. "Tourist season is already upon us. Unless or until we catch the perpetrator, we may have to keep folks away. Which would cause Mary Harper to go medieval on all of us if we try."

"We know who the culprit is," replied Dan. "We have to find her and find a way to subdue her."

"I'm willing to entertain what Zandar told us," responded Jim.

"That's a welcome change," muttered Galen under his breath.

Jim glared at him.

Jim pointedly continued, "I would be derelict in my duty to this town and my personal oath if I did not explore all possible options. So, I want us to go over in detail what we actually know. Not what we think, not what we have heard. Only what we have actually seen, what evidence we have gathered. The facts, the evidence, that is what will solve this crime, even if it is a Lesheye or something or someone else doing the killing."

He pulled the large blackboard he kept against the back wall out into the room.

"I'll write the stuff down," said Brett. "I know your chicken scratches, even on a blackboard. I may be a doctor, but I learned to write so people could read it."

Jim laughed and handed him the chalk.

"Let's begin with what we've seen. Mike? You saw the attack on Ashley and Davin. Let's have the details."

"Let me write it down, please."

Brett handed him the chalk. Mike began a list:

- A LIVING BEING THAT LOOKED LIKE A CROSS BETWEEN A WOMAN AND A TREE. LIKE A FEMALE VERSION OF ZANDAR.

- TALL, STRONG, FAST. PICKED UP DAVIN LIKE HE WEIGHED NOTHING AND SMASHED HIS HEAD AGAINST THE TREE WITH FORCE ENOUGH TO SHATTER HIS SKULL.

- DID NOT ATTACK ASHLEY; TURNED HER ONTO HER BACK.

- NO APPARENT WEAPONS.

"Brett, would you and Dan make a list of the physical evidence we have next?"

"Sure thing."

He made his list on the right side of the board:

- "FOOTPRINT" CASTS FROM BOTH MURDER SITES.

- BLOOD AND BRAIN SPLATTER SAMPLES FROM DAVIN'S MURDER SITE. NO EVIDENCE OF DRUGS OR POISON.

- BLOOD AND SALIVA SAMPLES, THROAT SWABS FROM ASHLEY. NO EVIDENCE OF DRUGS OR POISON.

- AUTOPSIES ON ALL THREE VICTIMS. NO DRUGS, NO POISONS. CAUSE OF DEATH FOR ETHAN: PUNCTURE AND SLASH WOUNDS TO THE CHEST AND ABDOMEN; MAJOR HEAD TRAUMA; LOSS OF BLOOD. CAUSE OF DEATH FOR DAVIN: BLUNT FORCE TRAUMA TO THE HEAD. CAUSE OF DEATH FOR ASHLEY: STILL UNKNOWN.

LOSS OF BLOOD FROM MOUTH AND THROAT WOUNDS INSUFFICIENT TO CAUSE DEATH.

- ATTACK ON MELANIE WILSON. NO DAMAGE OTHER THAN PENETRATING WOUND FROM BRANCH. FOOTPRINTS AROUND BODY SIMILAR TO FOOTPRINTS FOUND AT OTHER SCENES.

Jim sat and stared at the board. He did not like where the evidence was taking him, not one bit. It led down a road he was still reluctant to travel, despite the meeting with Zandar.

"No weapons, no human footprints, no DNA other than the victims'?" he asked.

"Nope," replied Dan. "Jim, at your request we have gone over the sites twice since the initial examination. We have been careful and thorough. What we don't have on that board is that the 'footprints' leading past the Grove and up to the sawmill were identical to the footprints at both murder scenes."

"I think you're going to have to accept Zandar's story, that these murders are being committed by a Leshachikha," said Mike. "I've read the books in Arthur's library, the same ones you did. I don't want to believe it, either. I'm as hard-boiled wedded to facts as you are, but I know what I saw, and it wasn't human."

Jim sighed. They were right. He knew it.

"So, what the hell do we do? Tourist season is about to commence. I can't cancel it. Mary and the others would suffer a real economic hardship, one that we don't have reserves to cover. Hell, even Morey's depends on the tourist season."

"We could create reasons for the tourists to stay in town, not go into the woods," said Dan. "Perhaps spread rumors about an infestation of poison ivy that is being dealt with."

“What did you have in mind as a diversion?” asked Jim.

“How about a real honest-to-God Osage village right on the edge of town?” asked Galen in return. “With crafts, storytelling, dance demonstrations, food, all of that.”

“That would be great!”

Jim was enthused.

“Dan, do you think we could do some Ukrainian culture thing, similar to what Galen is suggesting from his people?”

“Sure. We could have singing, costumed dance, and food also.”

“Zak will raise hell,” said Jim, “but I think we should close off the road through the woods to Big Bass Pool. Leave the main road open from the Interstate into town, and close down all the smaller roads that go through the forests.”

“That is a no-brainer,” replied Mike. “By way of diversion, I could set up an obstacle course and a rock-climbing wall for the teenagers. Heck, let the adults try, too. Never met a man who didn’t want to try to prove how strong he was.”

They all laughed, agreeing it would be a great idea.

“I’ll get some of the high school kids to help me build it.”

“Let’s do an outdoor art show at Havensrest, in the garden,” Dan suggested. “Mary Harper would love to organize something like that. As long as we keep it away from the planter beds, the gardens will be fine.”

“Let’s get these ideas in motion,” said Jim. “I want all of us to meet tonight at Havensrest with Arthur and Finn. I’ll bring Charity and Linda. Dan, you bring Jen and Bridgette. I want all of you there. I want to learn everything we can about how to deal with these Lesheye things.”

As they were leaving, Jim called out.

“I’m going to go talk to Ben Jenkins,” he said. “About using his parking lot for these events. It’s huge. We could probably put everything in one place. I’ll let you know what he says.”

Ben was one of Harper's Landing's longtime residents. He and his brother Will had grown up on a farm outside of town, next to the new road that led to the restored textile mill. The farm had been abandoned, and the land had been sold to Saul Grossman, the new textile mill owner, after Will died of cancer.

The horrible loss of his beloved dog two years ago, after he had lost his brother to cancer, had led Ben down a long and painful road of booze and isolation. Thanks to the kindness of Jim and the tutelage of Arthur, Ben was now sober and thriving. He worked for Harve Sanders in his landscaping business. He used the proceeds of the sale of his family farm to purchase the campground Saul Grossman had built next to the high school. The couple who had first run the campground had decided to retire, so Ben was busy working for Harve part-time and running the RV park the rest of the time. Jim was fairly sure he could persuade Ben to donate the use of the large grassy area in the center of the park for the planned activities.

The campground was a huge success, thanks to the diligent maintenance schedule Ben kept, plus the gorgeous landscaping put in by Harve but maintained by Ben. Although there were only twenty camping spaces, the grounds paid for themselves, providing Ben with a steady, reliable income. There were a few hardy souls from Hannibal up north and St. Louis in the south who even came up in their RVs in the winter. They braved the snows and icy roads so they could enjoy winter fishing on the Martins Way, shopping for woolen fabrics available at Mary Harper's store, and shopping at Crafters' Square without enduring the summer crowds.

Crafters' Square was a large, previously vacant building that the townspeople had renovated to offer selling space to the many talented craftspeople of Harper's Landing.

Enclosed and air-conditioned, it gave both locals and tourists a nice place to shop.

Ben wondered, however, if it was safe to even open the campground for the summer.

"There's something out there, Jim," he said, looking toward the forests to the north and east. "It's killing people. I, for one, am not convinced that whatever it is will stay in the forest. I know it would be a huge hardship for a lot of folks if we don't have the summer trade, but..."

He trailed off, looking worried.

"I have to weigh the danger against the cost to the community," said Jim. "We, meaning me, Morey, Arthur, Charity, and Mary, all agree that if we can provide enough entertainment in the form of activities, classes, and the like, the people who decide to come will be safe. It appears there is safety in numbers."

"Well, as long as I can get Mark Whitaker, the District Attorney, to help me with a waiver, an ironclad one, I guess it will be okay. It will be a great draw for folks who come up for Mary's quilt camps but also want to camp or park RVs," he said. "We should ask Mary to include a list of other available activities in the notices she sends out to former quilt-camp students."

Jim told him about the idea of spreading a rumor that the woods were full of poison ivy.

"I'll make signs," said Ben. "I'm sure you have a good reason for wanting to keep folks out of the woods. I'll include it in the email I send out tomorrow, to people who have requested camping spots."

Jim nodded.

"You ever figure out who or what caused the sawmill fire?" asked Ben.

"Nope. Still working on it. There's not much in the way of clues, but I'll solve it sooner or later."

"Don't close your mind to all possibilities," said Ben, with a slight chuckle.

Jim glared. "Don't tell me you use that stupid nickname, too."

"Oh, you mean 'He Who Does Not See?' No, you see alright. You have a bit of a stubborn streak about you. That's a good thing. I don't much care for people who grab at the easy solution. But, Jim? I've lived here long enough to know that the Farmingtons and the Harpers and the folks related to them have something special about them. This isn't an ordinary town, and you know it."

Jim had never heard Ben talk so much. He was happy to see the man flourishing, even if he didn't much care for this line of conversation. Deep down, though, he knew Ben was right.

"The planners will get in touch with you, about how much space they will need for the various activities. We will stagger events to spread out over the whole summer. I'll let you guys work that out. Ben? Tomorrow night, could you please join us in Arthur's study at Havensrest? There are some things you should know."

Jim walked back to his office. He knew the others would get things done. He decided to order some pie and ice cream and spend some time alone. He needed solitude. His mind had other ideas, though. He was restless, almost agitated, filled with a need to solve this thing.

At last, he gave up his plans for a quiet, solitary afternoon and drove slowly up to the Grove. Entering his front room, he was pleased to find Linda reading a book and Will asleep in his crib. He watched Linda for a while, then finally gave in to his desires. She recognized that look immediately, so they tiptoed carefully into the bedroom so as not to wake their sleeping son.

CHAPTER 20

THE FIRST WEEKEND IN MAY MARKED THE beginning of the tourist season for Harper's Landing. Many of the small businesses, like Mary Harper's quilt shop inside Crafters' Square on Main Street, relied on the tourist trade to survive. The Happy Time Tavern sat on Main Street, next to Crafters' Square. On the other side was the Piggly Wiggly, a small, but adequate, grocery store.

Main Street of Harper's Landing ran from east to west, for five blocks. On the west, it became Old River Road after the fourth block, continued west to the Martins Way River, where it turned south until it crossed a small bridge, then merged onto Interstate 35. On the Interstate north and south of the merger, there were small signs, announcing Harper's Landing. Most people missed it unless they knew where they were going.

To the west, Main Street wound up the hill, where the library, the playground, the community center, and the homes of some of the wealthy retirees who had moved in nestled among the homes of the mid-level management people who worked at the restored textile mill. A two-lane, gravel-and-oil-paved road continued west at the turn and connected with Old River Road. The only people who ever used that road were fishermen headed for Big Bass Pool or Harve Sanders and his employees, headed for Sanders Pond and his home and landscaping business.

If one continued east, the road made a two-lane path through the forests until it came to State Highway 2, which ran parallel to the Mississippi, about five miles east of town. An unmarked turn south led to the road to Harwood, where the Walmart and a rural hospital could be found, along with a small restaurant and a Holiday Inn that had seen better days.

First Street ran north and south, intersecting Main at the bank. Morey's Diner faced Main on the southwest corner; it had grown to take up half of the block. The courthouse, which included the sheriff's office where Jim currently sat sipping his morning coffee, was on the northeast corner, also facing Main. Across the street was the office of the *Harper's Landing Gazette*. Linda Collier Burch was publisher and editor of the weekly paper. She had also expanded her operations to include printing announcements for public and private events. Jim could see Linda's interns busy at work, probably preparing flyers for the summer events.

Second Street crossed Main next to the Happy Time and continued south past the medical clinic and the veterinarian's office, into the residential area. Most of the residents of Harper's Landing lived in original houses, meticulously maintained for over a hundred years. There were a few new houses, mostly next to the combined elementary and high school farther south on Second Street. The street, in fact, ended at the high school, intersecting with Harper's Lane, which led into the residential district.

Second Street North led directly to Jenkins Campground, which occupied the equivalent of eight square blocks. Ben Jenkins and Zak Millbank had formed a partnership of sorts, with Zak attracting large numbers of avid fishermen throughout the season. His skill as a guide was renowned.

The museum at the restored textile mill was a popular attraction for much of the summer crowd. Saul Grossman enjoyed hiring young people to demonstrate the use of the original equipment, as well as conduct tours of the functioning portion of the textile mill. Saul provided most of the fabric sold at Mary's quilt store. Additionally, the two of them had developed their own line of high-quality cotton, with unique and historic patterns and designs.

Havensrest, formerly the residence for the pastor of the church, now boasted twenty rooms, fifteen of which had their own bathroom. A large library, a commercial kitchen, a cozy dining room, and gorgeous gardens completed the charm of the place. Arthur and Finn were the owners. During the tourist season they hired local high school students to help with cleaning and maintenance work.

The Events Committee for the summer, which formed after the ad hoc meeting in Jim's office, quickly set up a series of events for what they called "Art & Culture in Harper's Landing." Linda was tasked with creating and printing flyers. Her interns sent off publicity to travel agencies, newspapers, and cultural organizations throughout the state.

Ben Jenkins reported that the campground was fully reserved for all of June and July, plus most of August. This was in spite of the warnings he had sent to everyone wishing a reservation. He had consulted with Mark Whitaker, and the two of them had drawn up a waiver that everyone wanting a space had to sign. It released Ben and the town of Harper's Landing from any liability should a vacationer wander into the woods and suffer illness or injury of any kind as a result. Throughout the campground, he had also posted signs warning people of an unusually lush poison ivy crop that had infested all of the woods, including the hiking and biking paths.

Zak asked for and received permission to take small groups fishing at Big Bass Pool. He had to agree to take Mike with him on these trips. Zak was called up to Havensrest, along with Ben Jenkins, where Arthur and Finn filled them in on the happenings in the woods and their suspicions as to the origins of the fire at the sawmill. After that, Zak was more than happy to have Mike along, and he made sure Jim understood that both men would be armed. Ben was equally ready to enforce the "no going into the woods" order, to the point of evicting campers if necessary.

Saul Grossman was filled in on the attacks, after which he immediately sprang into action. Within days of his meeting with Jim, Dan, and Mike, a truck pulled into the parking lot at Jenkins Campground. A van carrying four men followed the truck. Soon six men were unloading and setting up an enormous playground. There was a castle to climb on, both open and tube slides, swings, rope climbs, and ladders. Saul informed Ben that it was a gift and would be left there permanently. His only request was that Ben not restrict access only to his guests. Any child who wanted to play would be allowed. Ben hired four high school kids to watch over the playground, to help any little ones who were too timid to try things out alone or too small to be left unattended. Ben was happy to learn, when no one was looking, that the structure was sturdy enough to provide amusement for a fully grown and somewhat-hefty adult. He was especially fond of the slide that came out of the castle tower.

The community center and library up on Jackson Hill opened their doors to visitors. People wandered through the rooms and commented on displays showing the town history, including a large number of old framed prints of the town founders, pictures of horse-drawn carriages, and the textile mill in its original state. There had been a rather-heated discussion about whether or not to include the fact that once the textile mill had been home to slaves. In fact, some of the current families were descendants of those slaves who chose to remain after emancipation. Many of those families lived in the original houses the town built for the newly freed people. When they were consulted, they unanimously agreed that the history of slavery should be included.

"My ancestors, Stephan and his siblings, and the Harasemchuks who arrived later, were aware of the slavery," said Charity, who was a member of the Historical Society Board. "I doubt they liked it, but from some of the entries we have found in their diaries, the town and the Grove had little contact with the textile mill. In fact, it appears at one point the textile mill owners may have attempted to drive away the immigrants who formed the core of Harper's Landing."

The displays were open to everyone. They were such a hit that teachers made a point of requesting that they be set up for the children at the beginning of the next school year.

Tourists began arriving midweek, early birds hoping for a prime spot at the campground. Ben had pre-assigned spaces, much to their dismay. However, the promise of free entertainment, lots of interesting food, and fishing trips was reward enough for most of them. By week's end, the first wave had filled the campground to capacity. The shrieks of happy children swarming over the new playground could be heard all the way to Morey's Diner.

CHAPTER 20

Morey and Maggie quickly realized an opportunity. Since there was plenty of room at the far edge of the parking lot, next to the dense forest on the north, Ben roped off the area and helped Morey and the hired kids put up pop-up tents and install propane stoves. Morey found a propane-powered freezer stored in the back of the Piggly Wiggly and persuaded the manager to let him rent it for the summer. It was moved into one of the tents and powered up. Soon, most of the vanilla ice cream from the grocery store was in the pop-up kitchen, as there was no way to keep up with the demand by relying on their normal homemade ice cream alone. The popularity of the mobile kitchen led to the store manager providing Morey with a fridge too, for storing hot dogs, premade hamburger patties, and corn dogs. The manager also promised to keep up the propane supply.

On Saturday morning, the town awoke to the sights and sounds of a small Osage village in the large grassy area of the campground, complete with sweat lodge, center fire pit, and a wickiup. Tribe members were dressed in ceremonial gear. Galen Burns introduced himself to the visitors as White Eagle, chief and shaman of the small tribe. His hair was pulled back in a thick braid, four eagle feathers held in place at the top of the braid by a band of beads. His face was painted in designs sacred to the Osage, and his pants, boots, and vest were made of soft deerskin.

The women of the tribe were busy cooking, some making fry bread, others tending to the roasting deer being turned on a spit over the open fire pit in the middle of the small village. Their children showed the visitors how to use the various toys native to their people. Samples of fry bread, venison, and a drink made of local berries were handed out. A couple of the tribe members were weaving on a large standing loom, there were drums available for visitors to try, and the small tribe's collection of antique clay pots were on display under the watchful eyes of the eldest women.

Morey and Maggie did a brisk business, with many of the tourists wandering over to Main Street where they filled Mary Harper's quilt shop and the local tavern. There was only a bit of grumbling about the restrictions regarding prowling the forests and their numerous hiking and biking trails.

Jim and Brett decided to forgo the entertainment at the campground. Instead, they sat in Jim's office and pored over the evidence they had gathered, examining and re-examining the notes on the blackboard regarding what they knew and what they suspected.

"Oh hell, Jim," said Brett. "Let's face it. We saw him. Talked to him. Both of us. After two years ago, with what we saw, I think it is time we admit that Harper's Landing is 'different' in ways that the rest of the world isn't ready to accept."

"I know," replied Jim. "But if we accept the reality of Zandar, and the Leshachikha, his wife, we have to go hunt her down. I don't care what Zandar said about needing to do it himself. He admits she's killed, three times that we know of for sure, and possibly more."

Running a hand through his graying hair, Jim leaned back in his chair. "It's a miracle Melanie wasn't killed. It's as if she was protected for some purpose." He shook his head. "Now I'm talking like one of them," he said.

Brett laughed.

"You have to. You know as well as I do that you and I were summoned here. I never had any intention of becoming a rural doctor and coroner of a small, isolated town. Whatever it was you were seeking when you left the city, I don't think being sheriff of a small rural county was first in your mind."

"This town does call the people it needs, doesn't it?" asked Jim.

He abruptly stood up.

"Let's gather everyone who was at the Grove earlier—Arthur, Finn, Pete, Miranda—all of them, tonight, at the Grove again. We'll have dinner and hear the rest of Charity's story. She never finished it. I think we need to hear it now. You get your people; I'll get mine. Let's say about six, tonight."

CHAPTER 21

THE LARGE COMMUNITY ROOM AT THE Grove was full, almost to capacity. The tables were covered with food: meatloaf, root vegetables, fresh-picked green beans, a salad from the Havensrest garden, hot rolls, and, of course, apple pie. Jim noticed that Morey and Maggie Farmington had joined the group. Pete and Melanie Wilson were there, as were Jen and Dan, with Kat asleep in her bassinet next to them; Bridgette, with Mike Cullen hovering nearby; Brett and Miranda Michaels; Arthur and Finn; Linda, with Will firmly latched to her breast; Jeremy and Harve Sanders; Ben Jenkins; and Charity. They were all eager to hear the rest of the story.

"I wish Zak could be here," said Ben, "but someone had to stay and keep an eye on the campers. I'll fill him in when I get back."

"I'm guessing that all of you, including the ones who weren't here when Charity began this tale, have been brought up to date?" asked Jim.

There were nods all around.

Finn was busy stoking a fire in the giant open fireplace, as the others gathered 'round in the couches and stuffed chairs that faced the hearth. Even though it was almost summer, the windows were left open, letting in a slightly nippy evening wind. It was refreshing after the long winter months with no fresh air. Bridgette tucked a knit shawl around Charity's shoulders after she helped the old woman settle into her favorite rocking chair. Jim placed a small tumbler of bourbon, neat, on the table next to her.

Charity looked old and frail. You could see the faces around the semi-circle slowly registering this. Not so long ago, she had seemed full of energy and life, riding Birget to town weekly, tending the orchards, and preparing her tinctures and teas. Now she seemed almost translucent, as if the light of the fire could penetrate her skin and reveal her soul from the inside. Her voice, however, was as strong and vibrant as ever.

"As I told you, back then the residents of the Grove all knew that when spring came the Lesheye would resurrect. What they should not have assumed was that they would be happy with their new home, or be willing to protect the forest that surrounded the Grove along with the small village below. In fact, Zandar was curious about his new home, but his wife Zoya was far from happy. The pair had spent all of their existence far away from humankind, and she had an inbred distrust of all things human. She recognized that the houses and some of the sidewalks were built of wood, so she was certain that wood came from the forest she was tasked with protecting. She was not wrong.

"The first years were relatively quiet. Hunters went south to find deer, to stock the winter cupboards. Those who reported local encounters with strange, threatening creatures were too many to ignore. Fishermen, on the other hand, were left alone. The Harasemchuk family, who first settled near the village, at what is now Sanders Pond, became the major suppliers of fresh vegetables. Their farms were large, productive, and provided a variety of crops. They changed their name to Harper, which was what the immigration officer had written on their papers when they first arrived in America. They were the ancestors of all the Harpers who live here today, as well as the Sanders twins, and Morey Farmington."

Charity took a sip of bourbon, followed by a long drink of water. She sat silent for a while, leaning against the solid comfort of Galen's chest and arm. Everyone sat quietly, sipping their chosen drink, enjoying the evening. Finally, Charity sat up and resumed her story.

"The year I turned twelve, several new families arrived in Harper's Landing, seeking refuge. They were pagans who had fled Ukraine, like our earlier settlers. They had sought homes in the Ozarks, only to discover that pagans were not welcome there, not even in the early 1900s. One of their number had heard of our small village, and we were happy to welcome them.

"The new arrivals needed a place to live. The village's stockpile of lumber was gone. There were only two ways to get enough to build new homes: bring it upriver from St. Louis, which was expensive, or build a sawmill and cut the lumber right here. The residents chose the latter.

"My father, as I mentioned, was a trained architect. He had been making his living selling house plans to contractors in Chicago, St. Louis, and further east. However, he longed to do some actual building again. He had loved building our family home. So, he designed the sawmill, while Stephan and Yuri rode to St. Louis to purchase saws, planers, lathes, and the other equipment necessary to run a sawmill. They also purchased a generator, to supplement the windmill that Father designed to power the sawmill. They began building in the late fall and finished before the first winter snow. Stephan made sure the Lesheye had died before they began building the sawmill, ensuring the safety of all the workers."

Charity paused, covering her face with her hands. Her shoulders shook, and it was apparent she was crying, silently. No one interrupted, while Galen simply held her close. Jen got up quietly to retrieve Kat, who had awakened and was fussing. She got the baby changed, then began nursing before the fuss could turn into full-blown squalling. While she was tending to the baby, Dan retrieved one of Mary Harper's quilts, from the many lying about the community room, and carefully tucked it around Charity's lap and legs. She looked up and smiled in thanks.

"I'm sorry," Charity said. "This is hard for me, remembering these times. It was a time of great loss, both personal and for the town."

"I know the story well," said Jen. "You have told me many times. Would you like me to tell it for you?"

"That would be good," replied Charity. "I am tiring, anyway."

Jen carefully picked up the threads of the story.

"As Charity said, the sawmill was built in record time. Charity's father wisely designed a wood-burning stove on one side of the sawmill, where the cut and planed lumber would be stacked. Not only would the stove help in curing the lumber, but it would also keep the men warm as they worked through the winter. Everyone knew it was important to get all the trees felled and the lumber cut before spring, when the Lesheye would resurrect."

Jim interrupted her. "This whole die and resurrect thing is hard to grasp. Wouldn't it be more correct to think of it as a hibernation, like bears?"

"Not really," replied Dan. "Lesheye actually die; their bodies die, that is. Traditional tales have it that they usually turn themselves into leaves, which die and turn to ash underneath piles of other leaves. No one has ever seen one resurrect, at least not according to the books I have consulted. The few Lesheye who have been willing to converse with humans refuse to describe the resurrection process. It isn't a matter of simply going to sleep, then waking up, though. You will see, as Jen tells the rest of the story, why this is so important, this inability to do away permanently with any Lesheye that might dwell near humans."

Jen nodded. The others in the room showed varying degrees of confusion and concern.

"Next you're going to tell us their souls hang around all winter, watching us, planning new ways to make our lives miserable," muttered Jim.

The others laughed. Jen resumed her story.

"When spring arrived, and the snows melted, there was more than enough lumber to build the new houses required for the recent immigrants. They had spent the winter sharing homes with other families. They were more than ready to build their own homes. One of the families had been brewers in the old country, so were eager to open a tavern and a brewery. From late March through the early weeks of May, the village rang with the sounds of hammers, handsaws, the happy voices of the families. By mutual consent, the tavern and brewery were finished first. While the houses were being constructed, the first batches of local beer were being brewed. The Sloan family used old country methods of brewing, which required copious quantities of malt and dried hops. They brought both with them from Ukraine; further, they secured a supplier in St. Louis for their future needs. Although a good dark ale is best when allowed to sit for a period of time, people were unwilling to wait. The Happy Time Tavern and Brewery quickly became the gathering spot for nearly everyone at the end of a busy, hard day. There was even a menu for children, which included home-brewed root beer."

Jen paused to switch Kat to her other breast. The baby's appetite was more robust than Will's, and she was growing quickly. Jen waited to see if Kat was really going to nurse or simply fall asleep; she chose to fall asleep. Jen handed her over to Dan so she could continue her story. The others had taken advantage of the break in the narrative to get more of what they were drinking, go to the bathroom, and raid the kitchen for rolls or cookies. There was plenty of everything.

"I'm ready to continue," said Charity. "That is, if you don't mind, Jen. You've done a wonderful job, having obviously listened to me carefully."

Jen blushed. "Of course, you can continue. We are approaching the difficult parts, though. Are you sure you want to?"

"I need to!" said Charity, emphatically. "My time is coming. I need to shed this burden before it is too late."

The others glanced at each other, wondering what she meant. No one wanted to ask.

"The men were too careless about their building," said Charity. "I think they simply assumed that either they would finish before Zoya resurrected, or that she wouldn't care about human activities in the town. At any rate, they made serious mistakes. One of them was with the sawmill, a mistake for which they would pay dearly.

"In their haste to build, the sawmill was left open and unclean. One evening, late in May, my Aunt Aleksandra went up to see if there were more handsaws and hammers, tools there never seemed to be enough of at the construction sites in the village. It was early evening, after sunset. She lit one of the kerosene lamps, then hung it on a large hook. She found some of the tools she was seeking and laid them outside to take down to the village later. She decided to get the large push broom to clean the sawdust out of the sawmill in preparation to close it down until next fall. She was completely absorbed in her work, humming an Old World folk song her aunt had taught her, and failed to notice Zoya when she appeared at the back door. Zoya was furious. She wasn't sure what building she had entered, but the sawdust and a few remaining pieces of lumber, as well as the tree stumps outside, were all the clues she needed to know that this was a place of destruction, of the murder of her children, of all that she was sworn to protect. She seized the kerosene lantern and threw it at Aleksandra. It missed the girl and shattered against a nearby table, throwing kerosene and flames in a wide circle. Aleksandra screamed in fear, swatting out the few small flames on her skirt, then fled the sawmill. In her fear and panic, she did not see the giant bat others saw flying out the back door and over the woods, sparks flying from its singed wings.

"Her screams caught the attention of Stephan, Mikhail, and my father. Father was visiting Stephan to confer with him about the materials they would need for building a woodworking studio. The three men hurried to the sawmill, grabbing buckets along the way, while Aleksandra had controlled her panic sufficiently to ring the bell installed outside the sawmill. It had been erected to summon the villagers for such an emergency. There was a similar bell in the center of the village.

"My father took a full water bucket, and entered the sawmill intending to quell the fire along the floor. However, the kerosene had splashed against the back wall. Once he was inside, the flames suddenly exploded along that wall, blocking the exit. He found himself surrounded by flames with no way out. His attempts to create a path using his bucket of water were futile. Aleksandra saw him, trapped by deadly flames, and grabbed a bucket of water herself. She ran in before Stephan could stop her, calling to Father to come her way. Instead, the flames roared up and ignited her dress. She died almost immediately, as the flames sucked the air out of her open mouth. Meanwhile, despite the desperate efforts of Stephan and Mikhail, my father also died quickly and was consumed by the flames."

Charity stopped, overcome by grief and weariness. Galen stood, picked her up, and told everyone, "Jen can finish the story. I'm putting Charity to bed. Good night."

He left swiftly, while the others sat in silence; everyone was trying to take in the horror of the story so far. Most of them realized that if this was the same Leshachikha now attacking people as the one who had destroyed the sawmill, they were in grave danger.

Jen sighed. "I suppose I should tell you the rest now, rather than later. It will explain much of what is happening in our time."

Dan returned with a cup of hot herbal tea and some chocolate. Jen smiled happily, leaned against him, and resumed the story.

"They buried Aleksandra and Gerhard, Charity's father, the next day. As you know, the church in Harper's Landing dates back to the dark time when slaves operated the textile mill and lived in the large dormitory next to it. The slave owners had allowed the building of the church, and the slaves had made room for a cemetery behind it. Someday, I really want to try to find out how they built that church. It must have taken a great deal of extremely hard labor to carry that many stones and construct such a solid structure.

"Anyway, Aleksandra and Gerhard were buried in a pagan ceremony in the little cemetery behind the church. The entire population of the area were devastated at the loss. Of course, the villagers rallied to care for Sophie and Charity, making sure they were fed and comforted during the early days of their loss. Letters were sent by ship to Ukraine to Aleksandra's and Sophie's parents. Before long, Amon and Mikehla Bareshovna, their father and mother, set sail for America, subsequently making the journey up the Mississippi to Harper's Landing. They moved in with Sophie and Charity, where they remained for the rest of their lives. That, too, is a story for another day.

"Sophie was an amazingly talented pagan, skilled at creating spells as well as putting them into action."

Jim barely suppressed a snort at this point, then gasped out loud when Linda's sharp elbow dug into his side. Mike was working hard at suppressing disbelief, too.

"I am aware that some of you are not gifted with the ability to shape magic and nature to your will as your talents lie elsewhere. Someday," she stared hard at Jim and Mike, "we will have a conversation about the various talents humankind is capable of expressing. Not today, though."

Jen sat for a moment to gather her thoughts. She continued her story.

"Sophie's mother was as powerful as her daughter; however, it was Charity who had the strongest ability to shape and shift the elemental forces that surround us. It took all of Sophie's and Mikhela's energy to keep Charity in check until she learned to control her abilities. In the weeks after Gerhard's death, the loss of her beloved aunt, and the destruction of the sawmill, Charity spent hours attempting to fling invisible poison darts into the woods around Harper's Landing. She tried setting spells to catch the monster who had killed her beloved family members. She knew, as did everyone else, that it had not been an accident. Most of the villagers had seen the giant flaming bat headed for the river immediately after the alarm bell had begun to ring.

"Charity was not the only one looking for the culprit. The villagers combed the woods and orchards daily, looking for anything or anyone out of place. Their hunts were fruitless. Finally, one day shortly before her grandparents arrived, Charity managed to slip away from the watchful eye of her mother and Stephan, making her way deep into the woods. She set up a small altar, took out the herbs, salt, and minerals she had been gathering, then began the long process of casting a finding spell. Before she had gotten even halfway through it, she heard the sound of heavy footsteps thrashing through the underbrush, headed her way. She attempted to hide behind a tree, now consumed with fear, but the tall gnarled man with antlers growing from his head found her anyway."

"Zandar?" asked Jim, interrupting her with his outburst.

"Yes," replied Jen. "It was their first meeting. He sensed her presence, hurrying to her side, hoping to prevent a confrontation with Zoya, his crazed, violent mate."

"It seems backward," commented Pete Wilson to no one in particular.

"What do you mean?" asked Arthur.

"Well, it's usually the female of a species that is protective, while the male acts as a guardian. Now don't get me wrong," he said, holding up his hand as some of the women spoke up in protest. "I know those are generalizations, but there is biology to back up those generalizations, at least in the animal world. We humans have a long history of socialization to change some of those gender norms, but these critters you're talking about don't seem to fit the mold at all."

Everyone stared at Pete as if he had suddenly grown a third eye.

"Just because I work as a programmer at the textile mill doesn't mean I don't read," he said. "I am fascinated with biological imperatives and the like. I don't mean any insult. It's that these Lesheye things appear to be violating the usual norms. The male seems more nurturing, the female more of the guardian."

"That certainly is true of this pair," said Jen. "Charity told me how Zandar introduced himself, gently reassured her that he meant her no harm, and told her that she must go with him quickly out of the forest back to the village, before Zoya found her."

"Did he take her all the way to her home?" asked Finn. "If so, that must have been a shock to the residents."

"I really don't know. I suspect he did. I do recall Charity telling me that everyone in the village, as well as all the Grove residents, was aware of the presence of the Lesheye in the forests. All of the children were strictly forbidden from going into the woods. Charity herself was forbidden to leave her home for a week after her dangerous journey into the woods."

Bridgette spoke up.

"Charity told me a few days ago, during one of our lessons, that she learned later, at the Leshachikha's trial, that Zoya had first become aware of Charity's existence that day she went into the woods to try to find her father's killer."

"Trial?" said Finn, sitting up straighter.

"We're getting ahead of ourselves," said Jen. "Bridgette, you seem eager to tell the story too. Since you are likely to be Charity's successor in caring for the orchards, I am sure she has told you the same stories she told me. Why don't you finish the tale? I'm tired and want to sit, enjoy the fire, the tea, and the company."

Bridgette glanced at Mike Cullen, who put a reassuring arm around her shoulders and gave her a slight hug. The girl blushed, took a hasty sip of tea, and continued the story.

"I'm not going to go into all the details. You would all be asleep before I got to the juicy parts."

They all laughed, including Jen who was beginning to nod off, curled in Dan's lap.

"The week after Charity made her perilous journey into the woods, Stephan and Kateryna sent word around the village that everyone who could come should gather at the church that evening. It was the only building large enough to hold everyone, and most meetings were held there. When Stephan stepped up to the podium, it was apparent every village resident had come, including all the children.

"As he was about to begin, the door opened and a huge, tree-like man entered the church, to a chorus of shrieks and gasps. The strange man stopped, raised his arms into the air, his long fingers pointing upward.

"I mean you no harm," he said. 'I am here to help Stephan and Kateryna explain what is happening."

Dan stretched, careful not to disturb the now-sleeping Jen.

"I presume this was Zandar."

"That's what Charity told me," Bridgette replied.

Zandar explained that Zoya regarded the cutting down of trees as murder of the beings she and Zandar were tasked with protecting."

"I can only imagine," interrupted Jim, "that some of the villagers weren't particularly inclined to forgive the killing, even if it was an accident."

"No, they weren't," confirmed Bridgette. "According to Charity, plus what Dan has been able to glean from Kateryna's diary, many of them wanted to get torches and rifles and go into the forest immediately."

"That would have been disastrous," said Arthur. "From what little I know about Lesheye, they would both have reacted badly to any fire in the forest."

"According to the diaries and Charity's memories, that idea was quickly quashed," replied Bridgette. "It was Zandar who proposed the most radical solution to Zoya's temper and growing madness."

She had the complete attention of everyone in the room now.

"He told them of the god of the Lesheye, a being named Porewit. He said he was sure Porewit, if he could be summoned, would put Zoya in semipermanent 'death,' a condition that would not allow her to resurrect for a long period of time. He told them that Porewit could impose further periods of stasis on her, requiring her to reflect on what she had done.

"Everyone agreed this would be a good solution, especially when they were reminded there was no way to actually kill a Lesheye. Several of the oldest and most powerful pagans among them joined Zandar the following day in the center of what would become today's orchards. There they joined together in a great summoning, hoping to reach Porewit in faraway Ukraine."

"I guess they forgot that gods don't think of distance the way we do," said Finn with a small chuckle. "I'm betting it didn't take him long to arrive."

"As Charity tells it, about ten minutes. He arrived, griping about their 'nagging.'"

Porewit, according to Bridgette's description, was a small, ancient man, wearing leather clothing and a bark hat with various herbs growing out of it. He arrived while pulling Zoya along behind him. A gold rope was wrapped around her waist, the other end grasped firmly by the ancient and powerful forest god.

The rest of the story was short but telling. Dan and Bridgette took turns filling in the details: how Porewit had determined that Zoya was aware someone was in the sawmill when she set it on fire, how she had fled instead of helping save Aleksandra and Gerhard, how she was unrepentant, and how she was defiant even in the face of the deity to whom she owed obeisance.

"So, tell us already," said Mike, impatiently. "What did Porewit decide to do with her?"

"Oh, it was a really simple solution," said Bridgette, "and everyone was naïve enough to think it would work. Porewit put a powerful spell on Zoya, one which kept her from resurrecting for one hundred years. He decreed that she would be able to resurrect again after a century had passed. Further, during those one hundred years, there would be times when she would be allowed brief periods of consciousness, would be able to observe the world around her, but could not fully resurrect. He believed she would come to regret her actions and accept her new surroundings."

"Boy, was he ever wrong," said Arthur. "Kinda makes you wonder what sort of deity he is."

Finn put a hand on Arthur's arm, giving him a slight squeeze.

"The lesser gods are not omnipotent nor omniscient, my love," he said. "It seems to me Porewit made a wise decision. He simply failed to understand the intensity of Zoya's maternal protectiveness. Or perhaps her madness was already there, waiting to be kindled, but not yet apparent."

It was late, later than anyone had intended to stay up. Jim and Linda were the first to retire, being careful not to wake Will. Jen woke up briefly, and Dan helped her home so she could go to bed. Blessedly, Kat had not awakened, and they both hoped, once again, that this might be the beginning of the baby sleeping through the night.

Arthur and Finn got in their car and headed for Havensrest, while the rest, too, went home. Eventually, only Bridgette and Mike were left. They cuddled together for a while, by the dying fire, until Mike hesitantly put a finger under her chin and turned Bridgette's face toward his. Their kiss was long and sweet, then finally turning to passion. Bridgette whispered into his ear.

"Are you sure?" he asked. "Really sure?"

"Oh, yes," she replied. "I've never been more certain of anything."

Without a further word, Mike turned off the lights in the common room, banked the fire, picked her up easily, and then carried Bridgette into her small cottage.

CHAPTER 22

THE FIRST WEEK IN JUNE WAS GRADUATION week. The elementary and high schools combined their ceremonies. The entire town turned out, filling the bleachers in the gymnasium.

The twenty high school graduates were especially antsy. Rumor had it Saul Grossman was going to make a special announcement which might involve scholarships. Most of the graduates planned to go on to college or trade school, making the rumored announcement thrilling to contemplate.

"I don't know how I'm going to afford culinary school," said Rhona Porter. "There's a good one in Hannibal, which is expensive. I also don't know anyone I can live with up there, which means rent."

"Get a job as a sous chef," said Tiffany Ryder. "You know you're good enough, and Maggie will give you good references."

"Yeah, well, my dad has been saving money for years," said Tyler, the son of Deputy Harry Randle. "But he and mom are going to…" he stopped. "Um, they have plans for my living arrangements, plus I got a state scholarship and a Winfrey Award. I guess I'm one of the lucky ones."

"You're always lucky," said Brad Melnik, Tyler's best friend. "I'll bet you've saved up money too, working for the newspaper and Harve Sanders. What will you major in?"

"Black history and pre-law."

"I preferred shop class," said Brad. "Aside from not being named after anyone famous, I doubt there are any Ukrainian mechanical engineers whose footsteps I can find."

Tyler snickered at that. *He's my best friend, but I wonder if that will last. We are so different.* He felt a wave of sadness flow over him, but it didn't feel like sadness for the end of a friendship. It felt like a premonition of something greater, and he shuddered a bit. *Oh, stop. It's graduation jitters.* He joined the others sitting on the main floor after waving to his parents.

The ceremony was simple, moving, and meaningful for graduates and parents alike. Each student received a certificate of completion. The kindergarteners, all ten of them, put on a short play they wrote, about blossoms opening and growing into fruit. They sang short songs, happily acknowledging the cheers and applause of everyone. The fifth graders, who would move on to middle school, also put on a play, a reproduction of the Salem witch trials, ending with a moving plea of a girl sentenced to hang.

"Am I not known to all of you? Do you not see me every Sunday at church, praying the same prayers, singing the hymns? Would not God, in His infinite wisdom, strike me down before Him in His sacred place, if I were what you say I am? Have you no faith in God and His plan for us, that you would pretend to dispense His judgment?"

The entire crowd was reduced to tears and silence as Sable Kolchak pled her case once she was led to the gallows.

The trial was performed exactly as described in the history books, and the place for hanging was so accurately prepared that some people later declared they could actually smell the wood. The curtain dropped as the head judge brought forth the hood. After a few moments of silence, the entire gymnasium erupted in cheers, applause, and stamping of feet.

The high school graduating class was the largest in Harper's Landing history. They wore caps and gowns and received their diplomas. Then, they did the traditional tassel switch from one side of the cap to the other. All twenty students were also in the high school choir and took center stage as the choir ended the formal part of the ceremony.

They were about to process out when the principal took the stage again and said, "All of you need to stay in place for now. We have some special announcements."

There was a stir of excitement in the air as the students looked at one another and whispered behind their hands. The hushed conversations increased as Saul Grossman took the stage.

"Congratulations to the Class of 2018! We are all so proud of you!"

More cheers erupted.

"But we aren't quite done yet."

There was a rustle of hushed whispers. Looking eager and impatient, the graduating seniors were shuffling about on the stage.

"As some of you know, I am what you might call 'filthy rich,' though I don't think my money is that dirty," Saul said with a look of self-deprecation and a small chuckle. "I cannot lay claim to having acquired it. My parents were remarkably successful, both in business and investing, and they left it all to me, their only child."

There was more murmuring throughout the hall. This was a strange speech to be making at a graduation ceremony. What was it about?

"I know you are all wondering why on earth I'm nattering on up here. So, let's get down to business. It seems that no matter how hard I try, I can't stop making money. I pay my employees more, increase their benefits, and they turn around and up production, so I sell more stuff and make more money. It's impossible to stop it."

He fake cried, while the audience roared in laughter and applause. Saul Grossman was universally loved in Harper's Landing. He raised his hand to quiet the audience.

"I've actually found a way to give away money, despite all of your efforts to the contrary. I have established the Grossman Foundation, the Harper's Landing Textile Mill Educational Foundation, and the Stephan Harper Memorial Foundation. All three are funded for as long as the money lasts, which appears to be forever at the rate we are going. Thirty percent of all profits from the textile mill will be added to the foundations yearly, ten percent to each."

The audience and the students broke out in cheers and applause. Saul once again waved them to silence.

"The Grossman Foundation will provide grants to individuals wishing to build small businesses or expand their existing businesses. Although the grants do not have to be repaid, it is our hope that you all will be so successful that you will be able to help fund the foundation for future businesses."

Saul looked down at his notes.

"The Stephan Harper Memorial Foundation exists solely to help with the final costs of anyone who dies, whether by natural causes or through tragedy, and to assist any family impacted by the loss of a loved one. No one in Harper's

Landing need ever worry again about meeting the costs of burial, nor about how to provide for their family, should tragedy strike. The Foundation will help families, not only with money but with financial advice, educational assistance, and solutions to the loss of income if that should happen."

There was a stunned silence in the gymnasium, and then the applause began slowly and built until everyone was standing, cheering, and laughing. Some were crying, for they knew that the help they needed was now available. Again, Saul lifted his hand for silence.

"And now, the real reason I chose to make this announcement on this occasion. The Harper's Landing Textile Mill Educational Foundation has been set up to fund post-graduation education for Harper's Landing students. First, every graduating senior will receive $1,000." Saul began passing out envelopes to the seniors who had been kept on the stage.

As the kids opened the envelopes, they gasped, cheered, and screamed. All of them were waving checks in the air, jumping up and down, and hugging each other.

"That's not all," yelled Saul, which made everyone quiet down again. "First, the Rory Harper Memorial Mechanics and Engineering Award. For this first year and every year thereafter, this award will fund two years of technical education at Moberly Area Community College in Hannibal. Further, it will pay for room and board, books, tuition, and a monthly stipend of $300.

"The Sanders Pond Botany and Biology Award, granted to the student who demonstrates the most skill and interest in botany, wildlife management, or related areas, is a four-year scholarship to the college or university of the student's choice. The award will cover room, board, tuition, and books, along with a monthly stipend of $200 for all four years.

"There are three more awards, which will also be given annually. The Mary Harper Excellence in Textile and Fine Arts Award is a $5,000 grant, given to the graduate who has demonstrated the most proficiency and interest in the fine arts or work in textiles. The grantee may use the funds in any manner they wish, be it training or materials or both.

"The Morey and Maggie Farmington Culinary Training Award is a $3,000 grant for the winner to use at a culinary arts school of their choice. The winner is recognized for excellence in the preparation of traditional dishes as well as creativity in presenting new and exotic foods to the community.

"And finally, the Harper's Landing Journalism Award goes to the intern at the *Gazette* who has shown the most dedication and commitment to reporting the news accurately and timely. The award is a $2,000 grant to be used for such expenses as a computer, camera, or other tools the winner might require to continue their pursuit of the news on behalf of our community. The Grossman Foundation will fund the budget for the high school paper, as well as provide guidance and assistance when necessary or appropriate.

"This year's inaugural winners will find the notice of their award in their envelope, along with details on how to obtain the funds and get assistance if needed. Please wait to share the good news with all your friends and family until the final service is over. Mayor Farmington will lead us in closing ceremonies."

Morey Farmington took the podium and signaled for silence.

"This year, we have a special ceremony as part of this graduation celebration. Please remain quiet and seated until it is complete."

A group of small children, dressed in white, appeared at the door, each holding a candle. One by one, they climbed to the stage, spoke a name, and stood holding their candles.

"Rory Harper."

"Billy Martin."

"Steven Binder."

"Mike Stoneman."

"Jimmy Barton."

"Benny Jackson."

"Betty Camby."

"Ethan Burns."

"Ashley Swanson."

"Davin Crow."

The last child, older than the rest, said, "All those from outside our town who lost their lives in Harper's Landing."

He was a tall, lanky sixth grader, who spoke quietly and seriously. "For all of these we have known, and those we never knew, who died long before we came to live here, we ask the gods, old and new, to give them rest and peace for their souls. We will not forget them. Remember their names, those we knew, and those who were never known."

The children snuffed out their candles and left the stage with the graduates following behind.

The silence in the hall was broken only by the occasional sniffle. Finally, Charity climbed the steps to the stage. She was provided a chair and a stand microphone lowered to her level.

"The time has come," she said forcefully, "for the residents of Harper's Landing to lay down their complaisance, to take up the responsibility that comes with living in a place of power."

The audience stirred. A bit of quiet whispering was heard, which ended as quickly as it had begun.

"Our ancestors came here not simply seeking refuge from persecution. They also sought a land attuned to the magic of Mother Earth. They found it here. I am not speaking of the magic of silly crystal woo-woo practitioners, or even the sincere, if misguided, neo-pagans. I speak of the Old Magic, the power which shaped the Earth and the creatures that live and walk upon her."

Arthur climbed the stairs to the stage and took the microphone Charity handed to him.

"As most of you know, Finn and I are Druids, trained in the Old Magics. We were drawn here, or, rather, I was. When I found Finn, he readily agreed to come here to live. Lucky me!"

The audience laughed quietly.

"But Finn and I have a duty to the Earth, as do you. Charity is right. It is time to acknowledge our gifts, for want of a better word. Each of you who lives here has been chosen. You are not here by accident, though some would argue you are here by accident of birth. If your family was called here, recently or in the past, you share an affinity with this place."

Charity took back the microphone, while Arthur sat on one of the chairs on the stage.

"Power attracts power," she said quietly. "Some of us have taken oaths to maintain the attunement of this area with the Earth. Some of us bake pie, because, as you know, all pie is not created equal."

There was laughter again and a few groans from those who had learned the hard way to heed Maggie's warnings.

"Some of us are Guardians. Well, one of us at a time. That has been my job. Unfortunately, I have been remiss in not training someone to take my place. For the past six months I have been training Jen Balanchuk to assume the role of Guardian of the Grove."

She waited for the quiet murmuring to die down again.

"You graduates who have been given scholarships earned them for more than your outstanding performance in school and in real world applications. You were chosen because you also have special talents that the town will need in the future. You are not the only ones with uncanny talents. For that reason, Arthur and Finn will begin classes next week. It is mandatory that all children above the age of 12 and all adults attend the classes."

There were groans from all the children, as well as many of the adults.

"Hush!" Charity said, power emanating from her voice.

Everyone hushed.

"Power does not attract only like power. We have learned the hard way these past three years that power seeks power, sometimes seeking it for evil intent or personal gain rather than for good. The fact that we lost so many children, yet almost no adults, should tell us all we need to know about power seeking the most vulnerable. These classes will help you identify your strengths, your talents. The real work will begin by teaching you how to use those talents and strengths to protect yourselves and to benefit our community."

Arthur stood and said, "The schedule of classes will be posted at Morey's and at Havensrest. I promise, you will enjoy them. And there will be no grading."

The audience laughed and applauded.

Arthur then gave the benediction.

"May your feet be steady as you walk your path.

May your heart be open as you feel your path.

May your eyes be clear as you see your path.

May your mind be humble as you study your path.

Walk your path with truth, with passion, with honesty.

And above all, honor the elders and the earth,

For they are the source of all that is good and strong about you.

Go in peace and celebrate this new beginning."

The party after graduation was epic, even by Harper's Landing standards. Instead of the usual buffet, the bleachers were pushed back against the walls, while the high schoolers quickly set up round tables in half of the gym and then covered them with white cloths. Plates, silver, and glasses were placed in settings of ten per table. The graduating class and their families were seated first, leaving enough places for the town officials. The other half of the gym was set up with long tables, providing enough room for any people who chose to remain. Most everyone in town did.

While the folks at the long tables served themselves from the buffet table, the seated guests were treated to plated dinners, followed by exquisite desserts of macarons, truffles, and, of course, apple pie.

Once the eating was done, the tables were cleared out again. Then the music and dancing began. By mutual consent, most of the parents and adults disappeared, leaving the high school kids to enjoy the night with minimal supervision. However, if anyone had looked, they would have seen Jim, Mike, Dan, and several other adult men standing guard at the doorways as well as along the paths and roads leading to the gym. They would also have noticed that there were more outside lights left on than usual. As the evening wound down, the town's two school buses pulled up to the front door. Jim and the others were not persuaded by the pleas of any of the students that they could find their own way home. Instead, all the students were ushered onto the buses and driven to their homes.

CHAPTER 23

JIM SAT, STARING AT THE LETTER LYING ON his desk. It was late morning, the June sun already burning into his small office. He got up, turned on the overhead fan, opened the front door, and returned to his contemplation of the letter. Harry Randle had dropped it off earlier that morning and left about fifteen minutes ago.

"I'm sorry to give you such short notice, Jim," Harry had said as he dropped the letter on Jim's desk. "It's just that things moved faster than I thought they would."

Jim had been Sheriff of Middlewood County for about four years. Harry had been his deputy that entire time. He realized, when Harry came into his office, that he hadn't even thought to call him when the troubles began in the woods. He further realized, with no small amount of guilt, that he hadn't noticed Harry's absence at the meetings, both in the village and with the group Jim had come to consider the "keepers of the peace."

"What's in the letter?" asked Jim.

"My resignation," the big man said. "I'm enrolled in training down in Jeff' City on Monday. I know it's not enough notice, but..."

"I'm sorry to hear that, Harry. I know we haven't been in contact much lately, which is my fault. I presume you've heard about all the happenings. Damn, I feel terrible that I didn't contact you first."

"Don't," said Harry. "I've known for a while now that it was time for me to move on. This town, heck, the whole county, doesn't need a full-time deputy. Plus, you've got a good bunch helping you out."

"True enough," said Jim. "But that still doesn't excuse me cutting you out of the recent events. It all happened so damn fast."

"Wouldn't have mattered. I was down in Jeff' City the whole time."

Snagging a cinnamon roll off Jim's desk, Harry sipped his coffee. He munched for a while, swallowed, and sat up straight.

"I'll be honest with you, Jim. I resented the hell out of you at first. I guess I always thought if anything happened to John while I was still here, I would take over as sheriff. Then there you were, fresh in town from the big city, all new and everything, and suddenly you were sheriff. No one even thought to consult me."

Jim sat silently. *He's right. They said "yes" when I blurted out my desire.*

"I know this place has always summoned the people it needs. I wasn't ready to be sheriff, and the town knew it. I sure couldn't have handled that *bolotnik* thing that was killing everyone two years ago."

Jim, open-mouthed, stared at him.

"I didn't think you knew. I thought you bought our story about the bodies being torn up in the waterwheel, the drownings all being accidental."

Harry laughed heartily.

"Jim, I've lived here for nearly fifteen years. You can't be around that long and not know that half the people here have abilities that would get them a stretch in Fulton State Hospital if they ever talked about them." Pausing for a moment, he took another bite of roll and swallow of coffee. "Plus, I didn't really know anything about police work until you came. John would send me to chase the kids out of Happy Time or help get loose cattle back where they belonged. You came along, and you taught me stuff. How to tape off a crime scene, how to take pictures and notes, how to keep people away. You made me feel like I could actually be a cop, something I always wanted to be."

Jim sat back, looking a bit sheepish. It was the longest speech he had ever heard from Harry. He had to admit to himself that he hadn't really conversed with him all that often. It was obvious that Harry was thoughtful and observant.

"I'm glad I trained you. I'm glad you are moving on to do what you dreamed about doing. So, what are you moving on to?"

"Well, I spent the last three months on and off down in Jeff' City, like I said. My boy is going to go to school down there. He got a full scholarship, but it doesn't include room and board."

"So, you're moving to stay with Tyler?"

"In part. His momma, of course, loves that we will be there, and he can live at home with us. At least until he gets more acclimated to a big city. Also, well... I passed the State Police examination first try, after only two months of training. I was going to tell you, was just trying to figure out when and how.

Then I got this letter yesterday. They want me to begin next week. I got two days and the weekend to pack and move. I'm hoping to fill the U-Haul and leave on Sunday."

"How about some of us come and help with the packing up, so we can throw you a proper goodbye party this coming Friday, up at the Grove?"

"That would be nice. The U-Haul is coming Saturday morning, so if we could get some help, we could be ready by then. We could probably stay at Havensrest Saturday night, then drive down to our new home on Sunday. Tyler is already down there, sleeping on the floor, waiting for the rest of us and our stuff to arrive."

"It's done," said Jim. "Party on Friday night at the Grove. Say 6:00 p.m.?"

"Sure. Thanks, Jim. I've come to really like and respect you. I'm going to miss this place. Even if it has changed a lot."

Jim stood up and shook Harry's hand. To his surprise, Harry grabbed him, giving him a huge bear hug. He left, headed for his home where the dreaded packing was waiting. Jim watched him go, realizing he would miss Harry, even though he hadn't been in his thoughts during this current crisis.

Jim stopped musing, slipped the letter into his desk drawer, and started calling around for people to go help with the packing. As usual, word spread quickly. Very soon, the Randles had more helpers than they had room for. Of course, Morey and Maggie made certain that all the helpers had food and drink.

Jefferson City was a little over an hour's drive from Harper's Landing. Two of Tyler's friends loaded up all his stuff in their pickup on Thursday. They added a couple of air mattresses and sleeping bags, Tyler's computer, plus a television to hook up his video game system. The plan was to drive the truck down to the Randles' new house and keep Tyler company until the rest of the family arrived. Of course, they promised there would be no drugs or drinking, just lots of watching sports, playing video games, and playing music.

The Friday evening going-away party was a roaring success. Nearly everyone in town attended. A few stayed back to help Ben Jenkins at the campgrounds. Galen Burns' people kept their "village" open to amuse everyone, while two of the high school girls kept Morey's pop-up going with loaded hot dogs and lots of apple pie and ice cream. At the Grove, everyone who knew Harry and his family brought food and housewarming gifts for their new home in Jefferson City. Harry's wife was a skilled quilter and seamstress, so the gifts were non-traditional, such as a handcrafted mirror for their bedroom, a small handmade desk for Quincy, who would be attending high school in the fall, and several framed prints of the boys and their family, documenting their history in Harper's Landing.

At one point during the evening, Jim managed to get Harry away from the rest, for a private conversation. He offered him a small shot of bourbon, neat, and poured one for himself.

"I'm going to miss you," Jim said. "I'm going to need another deputy."

"You've got your team, you know."

"Yeah, but I need someone official, someone sworn in and on the payroll of the county or the town. In case someone gets arrested by someone other than me and it goes to trial, it needs to be someone else with bona fides to hold up."

"I guess you never heard of a citizen's arrest before," teased Harry. "Yeah, I get your drift. You have the perfect candidate. He arrived at the right time, but the town always does that, doesn't it?"

"Who?" queried Jim.

"Mike Cullen, of course. Ain't no way he makes enough pruning trees for Harve. It isn't a full-time job anyway. He's got the training, the common sense, the need. Plus, he can do both jobs with no problem."

Looking out at the orchard now dimly lit by the summer moon, Jim took a sip and leaned on the deck rail.

"He might have some mental problems. You know, PTSD, something like that. Three tours in Afghanistan are a lot, especially with dark ops, wet work."

"I know," said Harry. "He's solid, though, and I think he's of the kind to ask if he needs help. Also, Bridgette needs someone who can provide for her."

Jim raised an eyebrow. "Is nothing secret in this place?"

"Probably not, you know that." Harry laughed. "Time for me to gather up the missus and the boy, go home for one last evening in the house. You know, I built that house with my own hands. My great-grandparents were slaves at the textile mill; got one of the first houses when they were freed. They stayed on, worked the textile mill, and raised two generations of Randles. The original house wasn't well-built, so when me and Martha inherited the place, we demoed it and built a new one. Quincy will really miss it, I think."

"You sell it?"

"No. I offered it to Mike. He needs his own place, not a room at Havensrest. I also think the time will come when he needs more room." He winked, glancing across the deck at Bridgette and Mike, who were sitting together, heads bent, whispering about something.

"So, you're renting it to him?"

"Nope, letting Mike be the caretaker until the boys are grown enough to decide if they want to come back here or go elsewhere. If one of them wants to come back, it will be his house. Otherwise, I might sell it to Mike if he wants, for a few bucks."

Jim looked perplexed, trying to take this in. *A house? With land? For free?*

"Jim, Harper's Landing is never going to be what you think. Accept things as they are, as you encounter them. The town gave my ancestors land and a house at no charge when they were made free. These folks have never treated us as anything but fellow residents. We never really owned the land or the house. We were using it. Now, someone else needs to use it."

"Okay," said Jim. "Now I understand why Charity refused to let us pay for the space up here."

"I'm gonna miss you, Jim. If things get bad up here, you know I'm a call away. Along with the other state guys. You have a reputation with them, you know."

He gave him a big wink then wandered over to his wife and younger son. The three of them hugged everyone, got in their car, then headed to town for one last night in their ancestral home.

CHAPTER 24

BRAD AND NICK HAD BEEN FRIENDS WITH Tyler Randle all their lives. As they left town, their pickup full of Tyler's belongings, the boys vowed they would make the hour-long drive down to Jeff' City as often as they could.

"Hey, Nick? I have an idea. It may be a stupid idea; I don't know."

"What is it?"

"Why don't we stop down near Harve's place, where those flowering shrubs grow wild on the hill above the pond. We could dig up one of them, take it with us, so Tyler has a piece of home with him."

"That's a great idea. He loves those bushes. Don't know why. Something about the flowers, I guess. I got an empty bucket back there, under the pile in the corner next to my door. Let's do it."

"I dunno, Brad. Remember, we aren't supposed to go into the woods."

"We aren't going to. We'll find something right next to the road. If we don't, well, no plants for Tyler. But I saw a bunch of them in bloom on the hill the other day."

The boys drove to the spot and found a nice specimen. It was in full bloom, so while Nick dug it out of the ground with the shovel he had in back, Brad took the bucket down to Sanders Pond and got some water. He returned to the hilltop, put some of the dirt Nick had removed into the bottom of the bucket, and the two carefully pulled the shrub out of the ground and set it in the bucket. They put the remaining dirt in and packed it down around the roots.

The bucket was now quite heavy, taking both boys to lift it to head for the pickup truck. They were so absorbed in their task they never saw the tall, gnarled figure, with eyes blazing in rage, reach out and grab them by their necks before they got to their truck.

CHAPTER 25

THE U-HAUL TRUCK ARRIVED AT THE RANDLE house early Saturday morning; it had been driven up by two of Harry's classmates from the state police academy. Their possessions were loaded quickly, the family leaving amidst much waving and goodbyes. At the last minute, Maggie Farmington came running out, waving the car down so she could give them the dozen frozen apple pies she had made.

Shortly after they left, Mike walked up to the house and just looked at it. Jim and some of the other men who had helped load the truck watched the big man as he stared at his new home. Jim suddenly realized that Mike was crying.

"It's yours for now. Do you need furniture?"

Mike hastily brushed away the tears before turning to talk with Jim.

"Yeah. Suppose I will. Haven't thought much about that, but I don't have the money yet to buy stuff."

"Let's see what we can find," replied Jim. "Maybe they left some things behind for you."

Jim and Mike went into the house. There were curtains on the windows. A small table and chair sat next to the largest window, which overlooked the side garden. In the kitchen, there was another, slightly larger table with two chairs but no dishes, pots, pans, silverware, or other kitchen tools. Upstairs, they found two bedrooms and a small bath. There were no towels or other personal care items in the bathroom, and neither bedroom had a bed or linens.

"Well, looks like more roughing it until I can save up some money," said Mike.

"Let me make a phone call or two. I know some folks that have extra stuff they'd be happy to let you borrow."

Jim went outside and called Linda, briefing her on the situation. She immediately agreed to take charge, telling him to make sure that if Mike left the house, he should put the key under the flowerpot on the porch by the front door. Jim wisely didn't ask how she knew about the pot.

As he went back inside, Jim's cell rang. It was Harry Randle.

"Jim," said Harry, without preamble. "We, or rather you, have a problem, I'm afraid."

Jim sighed. "What now?"

"Well, as you know, Bradley Melnik and Nicholas Koval were supposed to drive down here yesterday to stay with Tyler, unload his stuff, then help unload the truck today."

"Yup. I helped them load up."

"They never arrived. We stopped on the way down here to pick up some handmade bowls and things that Martha had ordered online. Then we spotted a nice-looking little restaurant in Fulton, so stopped for lunch. We figured the boys would have everything of Tyler's in the house by the time we got there."

"But they never arrived? The truck?"

"No, the boys never arrived. Tyler forgot his phone charger, or he would have called us last night. He slept in today, waking up when the guys were pulling the U-Haul in. That's when Tyler realized that Brad and Nick never arrived."

"Have you tried to call them?"

"Yeah. Both phones go to voicemail."

"Harry, see if you can get the state police to track those phones. If they are going to voicemail, they are still on. Let's see if we can get a fix on their location before they run out of battery."

"Good idea, Jim. I'll call you back soon."

While he waited for Harry's call, Jim filled Mike in. He decided there wasn't going to be a better time to offer Mike the job. He told him about the duties of a deputy in Harper's Landing, or rather Middlewood County, though to the best of his recollection Harry had never done more than drive through the county once or twice a day.

"I'd love to do it," said Mike, "but I don't have a car. Or a weapon for that matter, other than my bow. I'm damn good with any type of bow, but I suspect I should have a sidearm."

"The car and weapon won't be a problem," said Jim. "I've got a spare .357 in my office safe. Further, the garage behind the courthouse has at least two, maybe three cars parked there. I haven't looked at them for a while, but I'm betting that the high school shop class kids can get one of them running and souped-up as much as we need."

"Well, how can I say no? It feels right, like I was supposed to come here. This town..." He shook his head.

Jim's cell rang. It was Harry.

"Their cells pinged over near Sanders Pond. Not *in* the pond, thank goodness."

"Thanks, Harry. We'll let you know what we find. Mike and I are headed over there now."

Jim turned to Mike and frowned. "We need to get you armed and mobile. First, we stop at my office downtown. And let's be careful not to attract a lot of attention. I want to check this out quietly."

"You got it," replied Mike. "How about I stroll over to Morey's to get us some coffee and maybe a couple of sandwiches? Been a long time since breakfast."

"That's a great idea. See if they have any pie, too. I'm suddenly starving."

Mike placed the order and told Morey he would be waiting out on the sidewalk. He wanted to look around a bit. Morey's Diner was at the eastern edge of town where the road led into the dense deciduous forests that separated Harper's Landing from the Mississippi River. He wasn't happy about the woods being in such close proximity to the town. So far, the only attack he knew of that had not occurred in the woods was the fire at the sawmill. Havensrest was surrounded on three sides by rather dense stands of trees. Mike knew as well as most that attacks did not necessarily confine themselves to the same place, even with a previous pattern. He went back into the diner and engaged Morey in a quiet but intense conversation.

When Jim was ready to leave, Mike got into the Explorer; he was carrying a large bag filled with apple pie and sandwiches, plus a thermos of coffee. He sat all of it on the floor between his feet, put on the seatbelt, then cleared his throat.

"Jim," he said, as they headed out west toward Old River Road and Sanders Pond. "I had a talk with Morey, and he agrees with me."

"About what?"

"About the need to barricade the east end of Main Street, make people head south on First and join up with Highway 2 further down where the woods are sparser. The barricade also needs to dissuade people on bikes, people walking, and such, not only cars."

"You may be right. Those woods are pretty thick there at the edge of town. I'll get Dan and Ben, if he's available, to pull some barriers out of the courthouse garage and set them up. Put a big detour sign on them. We can route them back out to Highway 2 further on south."

"Also," Mike continued, "I think we should tell Arthur and Finn to set up some motion sensor lights on the sides of Havensrest, as well as in the gardens. I'm not comfortable with how close the forest is to the building."

"That's a damn good idea," said Jim. "You got a cell, or you want to use mine for now?"

Mike took Jim's cell and called everyone while Jim drove as fast as safely possible out to Sanders Pond. As they went through the dense forests that crowded the two-lane road, Jim realized that Mike was absolutely right. Even in the protection of the big Explorer, with his gun resting under his arm, Jim felt the slight twang of nervous anxiety he experienced in every dangerous situation. He was relieved when they finally left the forest, speeding down the open road with grassy meadows on the west side.

Dan had been reluctant to leave Jen and the others at the Grove, asking if he could send Finn instead, to take care of the barriers. Jim readily consented, especially since it meant Finn would be in town and could stop in at the hardware store near Crafters' Square to pick up motion sensor lights. Ben was done working for the day. He was more than happy to go along to help make sure the barricades and detour signs were in place. Finn promised to call when they were done.

Jim decided to eat on the way to Harve's, since Morey had made sure the sandwiches were hearty without being messy. Mike opted for dipping sauce for his, with Jim sneaking a few dips when he thought Mike wasn't looking. By the time they arrived at Harve's, the sandwiches and most of the coffee were gone. Jim was dying to dive into the large piece of pie sitting in a box, but he put it aside for later. Instead, he focused on the pickup truck sitting on the side of the road.

The truck bed was full of Tyler's belongings: television, bed, clothing, video game system, some random pieces of furniture, computer setup, and several boxes filled with books. The motor was off, and there was no sign of either boy.

While Jim took pictures of the truck, its contents, and the inside of the cab, Mike searched the ground around it; he was looking for footprints or any signs of foul play. When he crossed the road, he called for Jim.

"There's footprints over here, leading into the woods."

"Wait for me," said Jim. "I'm on my way."

"You're taking this Lesheye thing seriously, aren't you?"

"You're not? You've seen what she can do. And count your blessings you didn't see Galen Burns' grandson. I still have nightmares."

"Nightmares are something I've got enough of, thank you very much. Plus, you forget that I saw her in action too. Let's go, Jim. Those boys may be okay, but in a spot of trouble. I'm hoping they didn't go far."

"Nope," said Jim, "they didn't. Look at that bush over there. Sitting in a bucket, next to that shovel on the ground. Looks like a hole over there, several feet in. I wonder if they dug up that bush."

"I reckon," said Mike. "There's a pair of footprints, led in here, stopped, and made a right mess; at one point, one of them left and came back. I'm guessing it was to get the bucket and some water from the pond over there. At some point, we should look for footprints going to and from the pond. The footprints coming back are deeper, so he was carrying something. See here, side by side, and stop on either side of the bucket. They were carrying the bucket when something caused them to drop it. What bothers me is the footprints stop here, too."

Jim was in awe. Mike had great training; he knew that. But a master tracker? He wondered if Galen Burns was as good.

"We need to find those boys, Mike."

"I know."

Mike suddenly went still, staring at the ground, his body shaking.

"What is it?" asked Jim. "Mike? Talk to me."

The big man was trembling, his arms rigid at his sides, sweat pouring off his face. Jim knew better than to touch him, but he did get in front of Mike to speak quietly to him. Finally, Mike focused on Jim, moved a bit, and stopped shaking. He pointed to the ground, apparently still unable to speak.

Jim bent down to look closely where Mike was pointing. There on the soft forest floor was a pair of round indentations, with five small, rounded impressions on the edge of each. He had seen these before, at the scene of Ethan Burns' murder, and again, where they found Ashley and Davin. Mike had seen them, too. Jim combed through his memories of the notes taken, swearing when he realized they had failed to look for prints when Melanie Wilson was injured. He knew that Mike had seen at least some of what happened to Melanie, and now he was sure that Mike had seen these prints there.

He led Mike back to the Explorer, sat him on the running board, and rummaged around until he found his hip flask under the passenger seat.

"Here. Drink some of this. Go easy; a swallow or two."

Mike took the flask, tipped it up, and swallowed. His eyes widened. He took another sip, this time rolling it about in his mouth until he swallowed.

"You have fine taste in bourbon, Sheriff. But should we be drinking on the job?"

Jim laughed. "I won't tell if you don't. Feel better?"

"Yeah. Sorry about that. I thought the only flashbacks I would have would be, well, combat. That print brought back everything, including stuff I didn't think I saw."

"Can you wait a moment while I give Dan a call?" asked Jim. "I'm going to ask him to bring Marvel down here to help us."

"The dog?"

"Yep. Best dog I've ever worked with for finding people. Wolfhounds have a great sense of smell, and Marvel is 'special' in ways I've learned not to ask about."

"I'm gonna have some more coffee while you make that call. That bourbon is hitting my head already."

Mike drank coffee while Jim made the call. Dan said he would be there right away, about ten minutes or so. Jim shook his head, imagining Dan's well-traveled pickup banging down the road toward Sanders Pond. Dan also made a point of telling Jim that Galen and two of the men from his small tribe were at the Grove, ensuring the safety of everyone there.

"While we wait," said Jim, "I need you to tell me everything you remember. I know my people—Dan, Arthur, Finn, and most of the womenfolk—think that some tree monster who looks like Zandar is killing people. I never thought I would see anything like Zandar, but I'm not going to go 'the monster did it' route until I have proof."

"She tore that poor boy to pieces," said Mike. "She chased him down, picked him up, and smashed his head against a tree."

He paused, tears pouring freely, and took a large gulp of coffee.

"Jim, I couldn't do anything to stop her. I shot her with every arrow I had. She didn't even notice. Now that I think about it, it's probably a good thing she didn't, or I likely wouldn't be here, either. She was Zandar in female form. I don't mean actually Zandar, but she looked like him except with breasts and hips. She is every bit as tall as him, and instead of antlers, she had plants growing out of her head."

He stopped, breathed deeply, and took another swallow of coffee. He reached into the Explorer, grabbed the two cartons of pie, and passed one to Jim. Then he ate his own in three large bites. With each bite, he appeared to grow calmer, more centered.

"Ah, that's better," he finally said, with a small belch and a happy sigh. "I decided at the time that it must have been some really, really weird flashback. I ran to my cave, stayed there for two days, and finally went back to the site. There was no body, and I found all of my arrows among the trees, so I decided it was a hallucination."

"We didn't find any arrows that I remember," said Jim.

"They were in the bushes. I make my arrows, try to keep them looking like any other dead branch you might find on the forest floor. It would take someone like me to find them."

"Did you see the attack on Melanie?"

"Guess I did. I thought it was another hallucination, until I arrived at the Grove and saw that poor woman in that bed, all pale and tiny. Jim, I didn't stand by that time. I scared off that thing. I hollered, shot arrows at her head, hit her with one of them, threw rocks. When she came for me, I skedaddled out of there, swinging from trees, running low to the ground. Lost her at the river. It was uncanny how she followed me, but as soon as I ducked under the water, she lost me. Even when I stuck my face up for a quick breath, she couldn't find me."

"She's a being of the forest," said a voice from the road.

Neither Jim nor Mike had heard Dan drive up, engrossed as they were in Mike's story. In the two years since Dan moved to the Grove, he had finished his doctoral degree, published two books on mythology and its meanings for the modern world, married, and fathered a baby girl. In addition to all that, he had managed to work out regularly with Jim and at the new martial arts center that opened near Crafters' Square. He was muscular and strong, a huge change from the skinny guy who had arrived during the drownings that occupied all of Harper's Landing's attention two years ago.

"You guys better be more careful. You were sitting ducks out here, though I don't think she much likes cars, either."

"Took you long enough to get here," said Jim.

"Well, I showed a little initiative. Went down to the high school and found one of the boys' lockers. Got his gym shorts here. If he's like every other high school boy, there'll be enough scent to send Marvel into hysterics trying to find him."

All three laughed. Teenage boys rarely washed their gym clothes. Marvel's snort, when he sniffed at the shorts, confirmed Dan's earlier suspicions. The dog turned away, sniffed the air, then took off at a slow trot. The three men followed him, all on high alert. Suddenly, Marvel leaped over a bush and took off as fast as his long, muscular legs would carry him.

The dog let out a howl that pierced the ears and the heart. When Jim rounded the corner and came into the clearing, he wanted to howl too. Dan abruptly turned and left. Jim and Mike, who both thought they were inured to the horrors of violent murder, were utterly unprepared for what lay before them. Without speaking, they both removed their jackets and covered as much of the boys as they could. Marvel's howls had turned to whines and whimpers, as he nosed the boys' shoes. He lay down between the bodies, with a paw on each chest. Jim knew he couldn't touch anything until the scene had been walked and documented. Instead, he took off his shirt and covered the two heads where they lay a few feet from the bodies.

Dan returned, grateful to see that the boys' bodies and heads had been covered.

"Sorry about that. I don't have your stomachs."

"Not to worry," said Mike. "Almost lost mine, and I've seen a lot of really bad stuff. I don't even want to think about how this happened."

"Yeah," said Jim, "but we're going to have to. Or at least, Brett is going to have to. I guess I'd better call him. Plus send Arthur and Finn to the boys' parents. Dammit!"

He made the calls. Arthur and Finn agreed that they would each go to one of the boys' homes to bring all four parents to Havensrest. Brett was visiting Melanie and Pete at the Grove. She was anxious to go home; he was there to see if it was safe for her to travel. Jim told him to keep her there and to make sure the alarm systems were on before he went to the clinic to get the coroner's wagon. Jim called Harve and Jeremy Sanders.

"I want you both up at the Grove," he said without preamble when Harve answered. "Don't object. Lock up your house, get into a vehicle, and get up there. Harve? If you have a weapon, take it with you. Also, even though it's summer, get a fire going, please. I think a machete, or a chainsaw would be the best weapon. I don't think guns are going to be enough."

"On our way. I just got home; Jeremy hasn't begun dinner yet. What about the people in town?"

"I'm going to let things be there for now. I think there's safety in numbers. However, I will call Ben over at the campground and tell him to step up the activities. We need to keep people either there or in town, and not tempted to go into the woods."

"It's bad, isn't it, Jim?" asked Harve.

"About as bad as it can get. Oh shit, I forgot. When you get to the Grove, get Galen to bring all of his people who haven't yet moved into houses in town to the community room and deck. I don't want anyone out alone or unprotected."

"Consider it done. I'll call him on the way."

Brett arrived shortly after Jim finished his call to Harve. Jim merely pointed toward the two bodies and turned away. He didn't think he could stand seeing them again. Brett let out a yelp when he removed the jackets.

"Holy crap! What the hell...?"

"Yeah. That's how we felt," called Mike. "I've seen a lot of bad stuff, but that was almost too much for me."

"Jim? Would you please get a couple of body bags from the back of my van? And I'm sorry, but I'm going to need help getting them bagged."

"Yeah, we know. I'll get the bags now."

Jim headed for the van. In addition to the two bags, he grabbed Brett's evidence kit. He was sure they were going to need more than the small one he kept in the back of the Explorer.

Jim, Mike, and Brett got the two bodies into the bags. Jim recognized the heads of both boys: Bradley Melnik and Nicholas Koval. They had interned for Linda at the newspaper last year. They were good kids, reliable and friendly. He called Arthur to confirm that they had found the boys. He stopped short of providing any details, knowing that he needed to leave the formal identification to Brett. They carried the bodies to the back of the van. Then Brett started on his way back to his clinic. Cause of death was obvious in Jim's opinion, but he had seen cases that looked one way and then turned out to be something different. He would wait for Brett's report.

Once Brett was gone, Jim and Mike set about collecting evidence. Blood and tissue samples were photographed, bagged, and labeled. They took multiple pictures of the strange prints as well as what they assumed were the boys' footprints. Plaster casts were made of all the prints for comparison with the boys' shoes, as well as for comparison to the strange print casts obtained from the other murder scenes. Jim also wanted to compare them to the casts he had taken of the prints leading from the forest to the now-destroyed sawmill.

Jim carefully placed the bucket in the back of his truck. He took multiple pictures of the bush, which he was certain had been dug up by the boys. He assumed he would never know the answer to that puzzle, although he had some fairly good guesses. He didn't like any of those guesses.

I don't believe in walking trees. Yet, I've seen one! Well, I still don't believe... oh hell, I don't want *to believe in these things. It offends my sense of order.*

It took Mike and Jim about two hours to feel confident they had photographed, bagged, and tagged everything that might help solve the brutal murder of the two boys. Still, they lingered in the Explorer, both of them staring out the open windows, not wanting to return. There would be parents wanting answers, as well as the townspeople who saw the coroner's wagon. News spreads fast in a small town.

Jim had about forty or so voice messages on his cell. He ignored everything except the call from Linda, who assured him that Galen's people had gathered at the Grove and they were preparing dinner for everyone. The tribe members who were at the campground would stay for the evening. One of the women had come up with the idea of teaching everyone some tribal dances. There was also bead making and storytelling for the children. Rather than check his voicemail or respond to the calls individually, Jim sent out an email blast to the town. In the blast, he requested that everyone come to the campground tomorrow at ten, after breakfast, for a meeting. He called Ben, asking him to make sure that all of the families camping there would come to the meeting. Furthermore, he asked Ben to make sure that benches, logs, and chairs were available for everyone, arranged so that Jim and some of the other members of his team could talk to them about what was going on.

Finally, when he could stall no longer, he drove Mike to his new home, then took himself slowly up to Havensrest. Jim hated this part of his job. Always had. The family invariably wanted to know how their loved ones died, and in Jim's world such descriptions were almost always not the ones you wanted or even could provide. Brett would not be providing details on these boys, either. He wanted to give just enough information to satisfy the curious.

Jim steeled himself for the anticipated meeting as he entered the library of Havensrest. Arthur, Finn, and four adults Jim barely recognized were sitting in the comfortable chairs facing the bay windows; they were sipping bourbon and listening to soft music. Arthur pulled up another chair for Jim, poured him a small shot of bourbon, and made the introductions.

Helen and Silvan Koval were both tall, slim, and muscular. Helen remained seated, her eyes red-rimmed and puffy, while Silvan rose and shook Jim's hand. The man was obviously barely holding in his emotions, working hard at being stoic and supportive of his wife. Ivanna and Stephan Melnik sat staring out the window; they barely acknowledged Jim when he was introduced. Ivanna had long, thick red hair that reached her mid-back. Stephan's hair was black, long by Harper's Landing styles. These were hard-working people, farmers by occupation. Stephan and Silvan planted the fields that grew most of the produce sold at the small Piggly Wiggly on Main Street. Their wives were regulars at Mary Harper's quilt shop, where they purchased fabric and thread for making clothing which they sold at the Crafters' Square.

Jim sat for a while, trying to find words, praying they wouldn't ask how their boys died. His phone vibrated in his pocket. He excused himself to step out to take Brett's call.

"Well, if there is any blessing to be had in this," said Brett, without preamble, "it's that the boys were both dead before their bodies were..."

"Yeah, no details please," said Jim. "Dead, huh. That means the desecration was post-mortem. What killed them?"

"Both had broken necks. The breaks are consistent with being shaken, vigorously and with great power. Their tracheas were crushed. Whatever or whoever killed them had to be extremely strong. The fingers left bruises, and the patterns are left hand on Nick and right hand on Brad. Jim, I have absolutely no idea how someone could be strong enough to crush and shatter the necks of two nearly grown boys, each with one hand, and probably both at the same time. We must shut down the town. Now!"

"I've been thinking the same thing. This is too dangerous. We have to find this killer, quickly. I'm not sure anyone is safe, anywhere, as long as he or she is out there."

"Jim?"

"Yeah?"

"You're not going to like this."

"Oh, go ahead. Not much more can bother me at this point."

"There were wood particles in the torsos. Freshly broken off, from a limb or branch. I think, whether we like it or not, we have to consider Zandar's story seriously. I know Arthur and Finn are both convinced. Charity has the Grove locked down tight. She and Bridgette were out doing some dance around the entire area, according to Miranda. She went up to stay with Pete and Melanie, to make sure Melanie is okay."

"Once you get the bodies stored away, can you and Miranda go up there, too? I would feel better knowing that everyone is there, watching the perimeter."

"Of course. Oh, and Galen wants you to call him. I'll pick up Mike too, and bring him up there with me. See you at the Grove, Jim."

Jim stood in the garden and breathed in the early evening scents. He suddenly realized that he was hungry, very tired, and incredibly sad. He usually felt anger after a horrific crime scene, but his connection with these people and this community was being assaulted. It was easy to remain detached when the victims and their families were strangers, just a crime to be solved, justice to be served. He no longer had the luxury of that distancing. These people were his community, in a real way his extended family. He felt their grief, down to his bones, and it exhausted him.

"You need to find a practice that will give you strength," said a familiar, comforting voice from behind him.

Arthur moved to stand next to Jim, his hand on his shoulder.

"Come to me when this is over," he said. "I will teach you some practices that will help you regain your strength and composure, while not losing your newly found compassion."

"How did you know?" asked Jim.

"A lifetime of learning to read the faces and postures of people in stress. It is part of my training as a shamanic Druid. I suspect Galen has had much of the same training, though not nearly as many years of practice. He has asked me to help with his training."

"I suppose I had better go talk to those people," said Jim, jutting his chin toward the parents sitting inside, still staring out the window. "First, I want to check in with Galen."

The call was brief. Galen reassured Jim that the Grove was safe and well protected. He also stressed that everyone was staying inside. Jim thanked him and explained that he would be there as soon as he finished his duties at Havensrest.

"Arthur? How do I tell them? What can I say?"

"There isn't anything you can tell them that will change how they feel," replied Arthur. "Finn and I will comfort them. They will stay here for the night."

"What about their other kids?" asked Jim.

His face fell when he saw Arthur's expression.

"Oh, no. Only children?"

"Nick was an only child. Bradley's brother is in the Marines, stationed in Afghanistan."

"Get him home, dammit. Arthur, do whatever you have to do, but get them to send that boy home. His family cannot sustain another loss. Hell, I don't know how much more this town can bear. Get him home!"

"I will, Jim."

"Arthur, I'm sorry, but I can't do it. I can't talk to them. Tell them I am looking for the murderer. Tell them whatever they need to hear. I'll be back in the morning and fill them in then. I just can't do it now."

Arthur watched as Jim strode to his car, his shoulders hunched, his fists clenched at his sides. He spoke a few quiet words in a strange language, and Jim's fists uncurled as his shoulders relaxed. Arthur sighed in relief and turned back toward the library. Again, he whispered a few quiet words as he returned to the side of the grieving parents. It would be a long night for Finn and him. He quietly explained to the parents that everyone felt it was safest if they remain at Havensrest. He assured them there was clothing for all of them, but if they wanted, Finn could take the men to their homes to pick up personal items. The couples chose the latter, so Finn set out with them while Arthur called Morey to order dinner for all of them.

The late afternoon sun no longer heated the outside porch, the shadows of the forest providing a cool respite from the hot summer. Arthur took his tumbler of bourbon and a glass of water to one of the tables. He sat, enjoying the small breeze that flowed in across the flower beds, listening to the rustle of leaves and the chirping of the birds. Gradually, his head nodded, and he finally dozed off for a late afternoon nap.

Damned Druid! I could take him now, with him never knowing what happened. He's probably behind all this, this desecration. Cutting up my children for their comfort. I could take him now.

Zoya moved silently, careful not to step on any branches; she was coming closer and closer. As she reached for the fence around the porch, to climb up and snatch him away, a car door slammed; then, a tall thin man came running up the path.

"Arthur! Arthur! Wake up!" Finn screamed.

He began to sing, a loud, guttural, unpleasant song with a cadence not unlike the drums of war. She felt the heat building in her center as he continued his song. He switched meters, first three-quarter time, then six-eight time, and then five-eight. With each switch, she felt more fire building, while the twitching of her body became painful. Swiftly, she turned and disappeared into the forest whence she had come.

CHAPTER 25

Arthur woke slowly. He had been exhausted, emotionally and physically, from the pain of helping the grieving parents and the energy required to keep Jim in check. The two women inside had gone to their rooms, not seeing him go to the porch, nor the approach of Zoya. The men accompanying Finn had hung back at the car to unload their clothing and personal items. They heard Finn calling, heard the strange and frightening song, but by the time they arrived at the porch, Arthur was almost fully awake, and the Leshachikha had disappeared.

Finn, visibly shaken, herded them all inside and locked the doors. For good measure, he closed the curtains, despite Arthur's protestations. When Finn filled him in on what he had narrowly missed, Arthur stopped objecting. He was now fully awake, fully aware of the danger he had escaped.

"Tomorrow morning, we will join Jim and the others at the campgrounds to inform everyone of the danger. For now, we need to trust that everyone will pay heed to Jim's email warning, as well as Dan and Brett's verbal warnings, and stay inside and out of harm's way."

CHAPTER 26

THE NIGHT PASSED WITHOUT INCIDENT, AS far as anyone knew. There were no fresh reports of any missing persons. Although there had been considerable grumbling, especially among the younger campers, no one had wandered away from the campgrounds.

By ten in the morning, the entire town was gathered at the campgrounds, including all of the workers from the textile mill and all of the Osage. Maggie and Morey had enlisted the help of about a dozen high school kids, setting up early in the morning at their pop-up with cinnamon rolls, fluffy scrambled eggs, piles of maple-roasted bacon and sausages, along with lots of hot coffee for the adults and hot cocoa for the kids.

The crowd was now either sitting on the logs lined up on the campground or on camp chairs they had brought. Many were sitting on the grassy play area. Most were still eating or finishing their morning coffee. The soft buzz of conversations filled the air, as Jim and Mike took their place in front of the campground office; they sat in front of the microphone Ben Jenkins had set up for the occasion.

Jim did not want to do this. He hated this part of his job, almost as much as he hated having to tell families and friends that their loved ones had met with an untimely, and too often grisly, death. It was his job, though. As sheriff, and in the role he had somehow accepted to be the foundation of the community at the Grove (a role he still did not entirely comprehend), it was his duty to inform and warn all of these people of the deadly danger lurking in the forests. He knew now that he should have done this in the beginning, instead of a stupid and inadequate "poison ivy" warning. He sighed, sipped his coffee, then turned on the microphone.

"May I have your attention? Please?"

The murmured conversations slowly died away, until everyone was looking at Jim, either in puzzlement or anticipation.

"For those of you who don't know me, I am Jim Burch, Sheriff of Middlewood County. Harper's Landing is the county seat, so my office is here, over in the courthouse. What I am about to tell you will be disturbing. I'm asking you now, before we go into details, to save your questions until I am done. This fella beside me is Mike Cullen, my new deputy sheriff. Way over there," he pointed to Morey's pop-up kitchen, "sitting on the camp stools, are Brett and Miranda Michaels. Brett is the county coroner, in addition to being the best doctor we have in town. Not hard, considering he's the only doctor in town."

Everyone laughed at this, which relaxed the growing tension a bit.

"But jokes aside, like me, these men are here to answer your questions."

Jim paused, gathering his thoughts.

"Some of you will want to talk to Charity, Jen, and Bridgette, up at the Grove. They are quite happy to have you come. They only ask that you not travel alone, especially in the forest, and that you drive up, not walk or bike."

There was a quiet mutter of conversation among some of the townsfolk. Most of the campers looked confused, some outright worried.

"Alright," said Jim. "I've put this off long enough. Here's the deal. We have a serial killer in the area."

Hands shot up in the air, some folks yelling out questions, others looking shocked. Jim held up his hands.

"I told you, no questions until I'm done. Between us, we will try to satisfy each of you before the end. Let me continue for now."

The crowd quieted, though one family simply got up, went to their campsite, and began packing to leave.

"We didn't realize, though I admit we should have, that we had a remorseless murderer on our hands. If we had, we would not have opened the town for summer camping season. For that, I apologize.

"Now, Ben here has offered either to refund the balance of your payment or extend you a free week of camping next year. Zak, our fishing guide, has offered the additional gift of a free guided fishing day for anyone who chooses to come back next year instead of taking the refund now. In addition, Maggie and Morey and their wonderful kitchen crew spent most of last night baking apple pies for each camping family, to take with you. In any case, we are going to close down the campground, today."

One of the townsfolk held up his hand.

"What about the textile mill, Jim? Is it going to shut down, too?"

"I can answer that," said Saul Grossman, standing up to address the crowd. "The textile mill will stay open; all workers will continue to have jobs. Don't travel between work and home alone unless you are driving a sturdy vehicle. However, the museum will be closed until this killer is caught."

One of the campers jumped up, face red, shaking his fist in the air.

"We ought to sue you for carelessly endangering our families. This is unacceptable!"

"You're right," said Jim, pulling the microphone over to his chair. "We simply didn't realize the gravity of the situation. We did our best, and it worked, to keep you folks out of the forest. We also provided a lot of extra entertainment and opportunities for learning. Sue us if you like, but I don't think it's gonna get you anywhere, and it sure ain't gonna win you any friends."

"Or a future camping spot," muttered Ben, barely loud enough for the people next to him to hear and chuckle a bit.

The red-faced heckler sat back down next to his mortified wife and crying children. He then immediately stood back up, yelling at his family to get their butts to the campground so they could pack up and leave. Others followed suit, more subdued.

Morey, Maggie, and their gaggle of teenage workers wandered through the campground and handed out free ice cream bars to anyone who wanted them. Most of the parents were grateful to have their kids occupied in slurping down the treat, therefore keeping out of the way as they packed up to leave. With the help of some of the townspeople, it took only three hours to get all forty families packed up and on their way home, a pie box safely tucked away in each car. Except for the family of the man who had threatened to sue, everyone chose to take the free week and one-day fishing trip the following summer. A couple of families even asked if they could stay if they signed waivers. The answer to them was "No, but thank you for your support," as Jim and Mayor Farmington were adamant that everyone needed to leave.

A few people wandered over to ask Brett about how the victims had died or how many there were. They were disappointed when Brett refused details, only saying that there were more than two, which made it a serial killer. Jim and Mike were equally taciturn about who they thought was doing the killing. Jim found himself quite unnerved when it became apparent that at least two thirds of the townspeople were certain it was a being of magical origin. He had not realized how many of the people he was sworn to protect had their trust in quite different protections.

It was long past lunchtime when the last of the campers pulled out of the parking lot. Maggie and Morey did not fail those remaining, however. Morey and his serving crew suddenly appeared in the pop-up kitchen seating area where Jim, Brett, Mike, Arthur, Finn, and the others were taking a break. The serving crew carried trays stacked high with smoked brisket sandwiches, dripping meat juice and barbecue sauce. Jim was surprised to see Linda and Jen walking toward them; both were carrying their babies. Next came Charity, riding Birget, with Marvel trotting at her side. When the dog smelled the smoked meat, he hastily made his way over to Morey. Sure enough, the man had prepared a plate without barbeque sauce for the huge dog. Dan, Galen, and the Osage staying at the Grove were also walking up, as were Pete and Melanie Wilson at the rear of the group.

"I didn't think we should encourage people to come up to the Grove," said Charity, as she motioned to Galen to help her off the ever-patient Birget. Jim suspected it wouldn't be long before she could no longer ride her beloved pony.

"Besides, who could pass up smoked brisket and Maggie's homemade potato salad?" asked Jen.

Jim looked around for Arthur and saw him and Finn standing in line to get sandwiches. He hastened over and got his share, grabbing one of the teenage servers in the process long enough to ask that she bring a tray with sandwiches for the two nursing mothers and Charity. Soon everyone was busy eating, too busy to ask questions for the moment.

Mike Cullen sat to one side, eating his third sandwich and second helping of potato salad. The big man had been hungry for so long, now he was visibly beginning to fill out. It was easy to see that, with some diligent workouts, he was going to be a force to be reckoned with. At the moment, he was trying to take in the scene before him.

Everyone from town. Even the parents of those poor boys. All sitting together, eating, laughing, hugging. It's hard to believe they know the danger they are in. But I know they do. Of that I am certain. This place... these people... and no question that I belong. Ain't many big Black men, especially now that Randle is gone to Jeff' City with his family; but don't seem to matter.

He bowed his head, sending a prayer of thanks. It had been too long since he had a home. He lost his first home when his mother died. That time, he hid from the social services people. He was only sixteen, but he knew how to take care of himself. He knew where Mom had kept the papers. After the police and social workers left, he crawled out of the cramped hidey-hole with his birth certificate and the other papers he might need safely tucked into his shirt. There was a small bank book, a savings account book, and the debit card. Mom had given him the code, so if ever there was a need, he could get money. She also knew her boy could survive.

"If anything ever happens to me, you get those papers, that card, and that account book. You go get the money. Then you go to Breaux Bridge. There's a small 'que joint there called Quincey's. You tell Bill Quincey that you're Martha's boy. He'll take care of you, keep you away from the social workers and such."

It had taken four days to transfer the money from the savings to the checking account, then withdraw it from the ATM. There was a limit on the amount he could withdraw daily. He made several purchases, mostly clothing and travel food and a bus ticket to Breaux Bridge. Every day he approached the ATM, he blocked the camera, holding his breath for fear that the bank would have been notified of Martha Cullen's death and frozen the account. He succeeded in getting all the money out by the end of the fourth day. The following day, he burned the card and boarded the bus, never looking back at New Orleans, the city that had failed him so badly.

Bill Quincey was a huge man with a hearty laugh and a bear hug that took all the wind out of you. Mike wasn't quite sure what to make of him. Bill insisted that Mike stay with him and his wife Sarah, finish school, and never want for anything. He had his second home. For the first time in his young life, Mike had enough to eat, and he began to grow. Three years later, when he graduated from Breaux Bridge High School, he hugged Sarah and Bill, entrusted them with all his worldly goods, then climbed aboard the bus to Fort Polk for basic training. A year later, he was accepted for Ranger training, passing the training at the head of his class.

During his second tour of duty in Afghanistan, Bill and Sarah were killed in a gas explosion at the restaurant. The fire destroyed everything, including the apartment above the 'que joint. Mike found himself alone and devoid of earthly goods once again. He was near the end of his tour and instantly signed up for a third tour. The Special Forces unit had become his third family; now they were his only family.

During his third tour, Mike and his unit went on a rescue mission to liberate a small covert ops team that had been taken hostage. The location, provided by an informant, was actually an ambush. Though they recovered the ops team, two members of that five-man group, plus five of Mike's team of nine were killed. The six survivors held out until rescue came in the form of Cobra helicopters, when they and the bodies of the slain were choppered out safely.

The unit fell apart after the loss of so many of their members. The six survivors all sustained wounds, many of them psychological. Mike was ultimately discharged for medical reasons, with full benefits and the promise of lifetime care. An account was set up for him, where his VA benefits were banked monthly. Mike, however, soon disappeared into the woods and pathways that led north along the Mississippi.

Now, eighteen months and many nightmares later, he found himself, once again, among people who cared; he'd found a home. He got up, carrying his nearly empty plate, and sat down next to Jim. It was time he really joined this community. They needed him—the townspeople, the orchard, Jim—all of them needed him. He also realized he needed all of them. The apple pie with ice cream cemented the deal.

Harper's Landing was a small community. Between the residents in the downtown area, the workers at the textile mill who chose to live in the renovated workers' quarters, the few who resided on the outskirts of town like Jeremy and Harve Sanders, and the residents of the Grove, and now the Osage, the total number of souls who called it home was about 1,450, including children. And all of them were gathered together that evening, sharing sandwiches, beer, lemonade, and pie. And worry. Despite the apparent good cheer of the gathering, everyone had taken Jim's announcement and warnings quite seriously. Most of them understood that a monster lurked in the forests. Those that did not were equally fearful of a serial killer strong enough to kill with such force and viciousness, as there was no denying this killer was highly skilled at sneaking up on its victims.

"I appreciate your concern, Charity," said Morey, "but as mayor, I must point out that there simply isn't enough room at the Grove for everyone. Galen, I'd like to suggest that those folks who live alone or with only one or two other family members might want to seriously consider moving into Havensrest temporarily. I've already spoken with Arthur and Finn; they have agreed and will open not only the rooms, but also the dormitory."

Morey sat down, flushed as much with embarrassment as exertion. He might be mayor, but he hated making speeches or being the center of attention.

"We've finished the restoration of the former slave quarters," Saul Grossman interjected. "There's room for about seventy people, if you don't mind doing dormitory sleeping. There are also some single rooms. You'd need to bring bedding, but we have beds and mattresses."

"Jim," asked Brett, "do you really think folks won't be safe here in town?"

"I think they will in the main part of town. It's the folks up on the hill, and the ones like Harve and Jeremy, out on the edges, that worry me. This killer seems bent on revenge for something, attacking without warning. The fact that she, or it, was willing to take the chance of approaching both Havensrest and the Grove worries me. There is safety in numbers."

Mike Cullen slowly stood up, getting the attention of everyone in the crowd.

"Hi," he said awkwardly. "I'm Mike. Jim introduced me. You don't know me, but I'm here to stay. We will get to know each other."

He stopped a moment, cleared his throat, and stood up straighter.

"I'm a veteran, seen a lot of bad stuff. Stuff I would rather not remember. What I saw here in these woods, the day they found that Burns boy murdered? I still have trouble believing what I saw. A woman slaughtered that boy, right before my eyes. She was huge, maybe seven-foot tall, long arms and legs, with, I swear to God, moss growing out of her head. She picked up that boy like he was a rag doll. She's out there, and she is dangerous."

Mike sat back down, flushed and sweating. It was the most he had said to anyone in public since leaving his cave in the woods. He was amazed at himself that he had spoken to all those people. There was considerable muttering among the crowd. Ivanna Melnik raised her hand.

"Sheriff, do you think this same creature killed my boy?"

Jim stood up slowly, gathering his thoughts.

"As sheriff, I have to keep my mind open to the possibility of a human killer. As a member of this community, I have come to realize that I must also accept the possibility of a killer of unnatural origins. I have seen Zandar, who claims to be the mate of this female that Mike saw murdering Ethan Burns, the first victim. I cannot deny my own eyes, though I sure would like to."

A low chuckle spread through the townsfolk. Most were pagan, descendants of the original founders of Harper's Landing. Those who were not descendants had come to live here for various reasons, most of them having to do with a desire to escape the norms of living among non-pagans.

"For now," continued Jim, "I guess my answer would be yes. I think it is one and the same creature doing the killing. The fire at the sawmill was most likely her doing also."

"So, we have Lesheye in our midst," said Ivanna. "I have heard they sometimes take children, but always return them. I've never heard of them being murderous."

Several hands shot into the air. One teenager stood up, ignoring the raised hands.

"What the hell is a Lesheye, and why is she trying to kill us?"

His embarrassed parents pulled him back into his seat. Ivanna stood up slowly. The weight of her grief hung on her like an old shawl around her shoulders. But she stood up anyway and spoke loud enough to be heard by all.

"As your high school history teacher, Ashton, I must first caution you not to use swear words in public."

The teenager blushed bright red, trying to make himself small at the same time.

"I am sure," continued Ivanna, "that Charity will have all the information on how Lesheye came to be in Harper's Landing."

"If anyone really wants to know the story of how they got here," interrupted Dan, "Charity and I will be happy to tell the story again if enough people want to hear it at the same time. It is a long story. Neither of us are in the mood to retell it more than once. We, first and foremost, have a community to protect."

Jim stood, taking charge of the meeting with his bearing. The fact that he was wearing his uniform and carrying a sidearm in full view didn't hurt. Many of the townsfolk had never seen him in his official dress. The crowd, again, grew silent.

"For now, you are probably safe as long as you don't go wandering in the woods and stay in groups of at least four people. She may be large, but I don't think she'll take on a group of people who are likely to defend themselves. My deputies and I will be attempting to hunt her down, to trap her if possible. While we are doing that, Charity and her group of students will be searching the history books for a possible solution to the problem of her immortality."

Arthur and Finn stood.

"Before you go," said Arthur, "we have another matter to attend to. We have two more of our children, our teenagers, who have been taken from their families in a brutal murder. We propose holding their funeral as soon as Brett releases their bodies. The families have consented to a closed casket burial, so we will gather at the church and the cemetery behind. Brett? Do you know when the parents can have their children?"

"They can have them tomorrow. There is nothing more to be done. Cause of death has been established; all trace evidence has been gathered."

The quiet sobs of the two pairs of parents could be heard in the back of the crowd. Several couples rose and gently led the Koval and Melnik families out and up the road toward Havensrest.

"Tomorrow," said Arthur, "I will gather with you, Finn will sing of their memories, then we, as a community, as a family, will bury the children, afterward feeding the bodies and souls of the living. At noon, please."

The meeting broke up. Families huddled together, making plans as to how they would deal with this threat. The general consensus, which Jim and Mike heartily agreed with, was that staying within the confines of the town, venturing out only to go to Havensrest or up to the Grove, was the safest course of action. Maggie and Morey assured everyone that the diner would stay open. The manager of the small Piggly

Wiggly said the same; Happy Time Tavern owner Parker Malone also planned not to close, though for the foreseeable future, he would be locking his doors at nine rather than eleven.

Maggie headed for the diner to do the prep work for the following day.

Maris Jacobson, a new resident and retired chef, went into the diner with Maggie. Maris found a towel, filled a bucket with warm soapy water, and began cleaning. Morey and Maggie headed for the kitchen, where they began preparations both for the regular dinner crowd, as well as for the mountain of food that would be available after the funeral.

The three looked up when the door to the diner opened. It was Mike Cullen.

"I didn't think you should be alone here," he said. "Do you mind if I stay and keep watch?"

"Not at all," said Maggie. "I'm happy you're here. Would you like a soda? A piece of pie?"

"Both?" asked Mike, hopefully.

They all laughed. Maggie disappeared into the back of the kitchen, coming back with a large piece of pie, vanilla ice cream on top, and a glass of Pepsi with a small amount of ice.

"You remembered. I left you a note once, a long time ago now, asking if maybe I could have a Pepsi with a bit of ice."

"Of course, I remembered. You were always so polite, always paying or leaving fresh fish, sometimes both. That is why I keep some bottles of Pepsi in stock just for you. You're a good man, Mike Cullen; you know the value of food, goods, and service."

"I grew up in a restaurant," he said. "Food is special."

"It is," replied Maggie, sitting at the table with him for a moment. "Food, lovingly prepared, nourishes more than the body. A lone meal, cooked with care while favorite music plays in the background, served on a plate full of memories, eaten with silverware brought down through generations, is a solitary celebration of the senses and the soul."

Maris Jacobson had been listening as she replaced the tablecloths in the main dining area and took orders from the regulars. She snagged a cup of hot tea, then sat down with Maggie and Mike. After a few sips of her tea, she looked up and spoke.

"You are so right, Maggie. Additionally, a dinner made by a couple, perhaps as a date night or a sudden desire for intimacy, served with wine, candles, perhaps a winter log burning in the fireplace, unites their love and commitment. However, when a community comes together to eat, whether in celebration for a wedding or, as it will be tomorrow, a communal mourning for the loss of one or more of their own, that is healing. It is the gathering that cements a sense of belonging, of partnership, of compassionate care for one another. Small towns like Harper's Landing haven't forgotten this. That is why we do this, Mike. We cook to feed the body, the heart, the soul."

"I reckon I knew that once," he replied. "It isn't so different on the battlefield. We don't think about it that way. We hunker down, grab water and food when we can, doing it together."

He began to shake with the memory. Maris put an arm around his shoulders, while Maggie grabbed another piece of pie, muttering something before handing it to Mike. He took a bite, sighed, took another, and looked up at Maggie in wonder.

"This pie is magical. How do you do it? It has to be more than love when you make it. What did you say, right before you handed it to me?"

"Think of it as a prayer, Mike. Someday, I will teach you some prayers for the orchard, when you go out to prune and care for it. For now, though, how about some KP duty?"

"Now that's something I haven't missed. I guess I could, as long as I can do it right here, in this window, keeping watch over you all. Further, please, don't be going out the back door tonight. Okay?"

"Okay," said all three together.

Maggie handed Mike a large basket full of potatoes. He groaned.

"I hate peeling potatoes."

"Then you will love this. They've been partially boiled. Slip the skins off, like this."

She picked up a warm potato and gave it a small squeeze, deftly removing the peel. Mike tried it, crushing the first one he picked up. He tried again, gentler this time. Soon he was in a rhythm, removing peels swiftly.

"If you ever tell the army about this," he said, "they will lock you up. Potato peeling, according to the drill sergeants, builds character. This is subversive; I'll happily take it."

They all laughed.

The door opened again. It was Helen Slovak. She was crying, nearly collapsing as she sat on one of the benches at the tables in the front window.

"I couldn't go home. I just couldn't. Silvan wanted to go out and hunt for that... that thing that killed our boy. Stephan wanted to go with him, as did Ivanna. She's a good strong hunter. The other men stopped them, took them home."

"Where's Silvan now?" asked Mike.

"Arthur took him to Havensrest. They were all so worked up they forgot about me, so I walked over here. I guess we can have them pick me up."

"We'll get you back, if you want to stay for the company," said Morey.

Helen smiled weakly, nodding her head.

Mike motioned to Maggie and Maris to go finish their preparations. He moved over next to Helen in the window seat, where they sat staring out into the growing dusk, watching.

Finally, it was time to load everything into the diner's van and Mike's car to take it to Havensrest. Tomorrow, while the others attended the funeral, Maggie, Maris, Morey, and the high school kids who were helping at the pop-up kitchen would assemble to cook all the food. Mike, with Jim's help, had found one of the cars in the courthouse garage to be in good working condition. He invited Helen to come with him; she climbed into the front seat. Pan after pan of prepped food, ready to be cooked, was loaded into the two vehicles. At this point, all the regulars had eaten and left. Morey turned off the lights and locked the doors; then, they slowly made their way up the hill.

Once everything was unloaded and tucked into the huge commercial fridge in Havensrest's kitchen, Mike put an arm around Helen's shoulders.

"I think you and Silvan should stay here tonight," he said. "They have an extra room for you. I checked with Arthur. Silvan is in the library, getting thoroughly smashed. I don't think you should be alone, especially not in your house tonight. Would that be okay with you?"

Arthur walked into the room and smiled at Helen, nodding his agreement with Mike.

"If it's okay with Silvan, I would like that."

She slumped into a nearby chair, nearly asleep, so Maggie and Maris helped her to the room Arthur and Finn had set up for them. There was a lovely, fresh nightgown laid out on the bed. It was a huge four-poster with down pillows and soft cotton sheets. A beautiful quilt (obviously one of Mary Harper's) covered the bed, with flights of cranes outlined by a full harvest moon. Helen smiled wearily at the sight, readily allowing herself to be helped out of her clothing and into the nightgown. Before Mike and Arthur could even peek in to let her know they were going to bring Silvan, she was sound asleep.

CHAPTER 27

JIM BURCH SAT AT HIS DESK, RAKING HIS hands through his hair in frustration. It had been two weeks since Bradley Melnik and Nicholas Koval had been buried. Jim, Mike, Dan, and Brett had reviewed all the evidence multiple times. They were no closer to finding an alternative explanation as to who had killed those two boys, plus Ethan Burns, Davin and Ashley. Sooner or later, Jim would have to call the state guys up to help, and no way was he going to convince them that a mythical monster was killing these kids. They would undoubtedly see Zandar as someone hiding in a costume and attempt to arrest him on sight.

Even so, there was absolutely nothing pointing toward a human killer. Brett had found trace evidence of wood particles in the wounds of all the victims. They were all from the same source, but Brett hadn't been able to match the wood to any local species. A sample he'd sent to the state lab in Jefferson City came back as a species of hornbeam, found in eastern Ukraine. It also contained unknown organic cells combined with the wood. The lab report labeled them as "apparently hominid, of unknown origin."

Jim got up abruptly, stomping over to Morey's Diner. He was hungry, pissed, and confused. It was late morning. The scent of bacon and eggs still hung in the air, along with the ever-present smell of strong, dark coffee. Jim had the place to himself. He chose a table in the back room and requested coffee, scrambled eggs, hash browns, and a cinnamon roll. Linda would be annoyed that he hadn't come home after his run to have breakfast with her and help with Will, but he'd make it up to her later. For now, he wanted to be alone.

Morey himself delivered Jim's order, along with a cup of coffee.

"Eating alone today?"

Jim grunted in assent. Morey, recognizing a bad mood when he saw one, slipped quietly away. Jim had begun eating the eggs when he realized someone had sat down at the table with him. He looked up, irritated, and his fork hung in mid-air, while he stared at the strange little man sitting opposite him.

The stranger was barely more than five feet tall. He looked incredibly old, with wrinkles everywhere, but especially around his eyes and mouth, speaking of a lifetime of laughter and smiling. He smelled faintly of dark tobacco and old leather. He pointed at the cinnamon roll.

"Mind if I try a small piece?" he asked in a thick, almost indecipherable accent.

"Go ahead. Here, let me cut you a chunk."

Jim took his knife, cut off about a quarter of the roll, and put it on a napkin.

"You can get another when we are done," said his unexpected companion. "My, my, Maggie hasn't lost her touch, has she?"

"Done? Done with what? Who are you? Can't you see I want to be alone?"

The ancient stranger sighed, smiled, then laughed gently.

"He Who Does Not See sees quite well. I am happy that you can see me."

Carrying a coffee pot, Morey came into the room. He refreshed Jim's cup and frowned at the piece of cinnamon roll sitting on a paper napkin.

"Something wrong with the roll, Jim?"

"No. Simply sharing. Why don't you bring my friend a cup of coffee and his own roll?"

"Your friend? Oh, you're expecting someone to join you. Sure, I'll heat up a second roll. Let's wait on the coffee, though, until your friend arrives."

He left the room. Jim sat still, trying desperately to keep control of his emotions.

"He couldn't see you?"

"Nope. Maggie could, if she came in. But she's busy making pie."

"He Who Does Not See," muttered Jim. "I see fine. Apparently, I also see more than I ought to. Unless you and Morey have decided to cook up some practical joke on me?"

"Nope," replied the man. "These cinnamon rolls are amazing." He popped the whole piece into his mouth, rolling it around, beaming at the taste. "Maggie can see me; Morey can't. He doesn't have the..." He paused, thinking. "There's really no word in English for me to describe it properly. But you, Jim Burch? You see fine."

"Who are you?" blurted Jim.

"My name is Porewit. I have come to help you with your Lesheye problem."

My Lesheye problem. More like "our" Lesheye problem. Please, God, let me be seeing things.

"As I live and breathe, it's Porewit!"

Maggie came bustling into the back room and plopped down on the bench next to the little man, giving him a smooch on his wrinkled cheek.

"You can see him, too?"

"Well, of course, I can. It's Porewit! You've been gone so long. Are you here to teach me more recipes?"

Her face suddenly grew sober, the smile fading from her lips.

"You're here about her, aren't you?"

"Yes, I'm afraid so. An insane Leshachikha is a problem requiring more than human intervention."

Jim had had enough.

"Who are you? Not your name, who or what are you? You look pretty damn human to me, so what else can I expect to walk in here, invisible to everyone but me and Maggie? Gods above, I think I'm losing my mind."

"Gods above would be a good phrase," replied Porewit, "though I don't do much aboving anymore. Who am I?"

"Are you the Porewit that Zandar, Charity, and some of the others have been talking about? Why would—what's her name, Zoya?—listen to you now? She apparently didn't the last time you were here."

Porewit stood and began to grow, up and out, his wrinkled flesh smoothing out. As he grew, an autumnal glow grew about him. The brown, orange, and yellow glow surrounded his body, increasing in intensity until Jim was nearly blinded.

"I am Porewit, god of the Lesheye and all the creatures that dwell in the forest! The Lesheye may not fear you, but they fear me! I am here to help you deal with them, specifically with Zoya!"

Jim looked about frantically. Surely most of the town had heard that booming voice! However, all he heard and saw were the customers in the original area of the diner; they were chatting and eating, now that the lunchtime crowd was settling in.

He looked back at Porewit, who began to shrink until he was, once again, the tiny, ancient, wrinkled being who had first sat down to eat with Jim. Maggie was beaming, gazing lovingly at Porewit, while Jim sat, dazed and bewildered.

Now I'm seeing gods? I need a shot of bourbon and a long talk with Arthur.

Bourbon and conversation would have to wait, though. Jim's phone buzzed. He answered, still dazed from the impossible events he had just witnessed. Before his caller could speak, Porewit disappeared. Jim let out a yelp.

"Hold on," said Jim into the phone, turning his gaze to Maggie. "You have a lot to explain."

"I know, Jim, I know. Don't worry yourself. You'll get all the details from me, just not at lunchtime. I'm visiting Charity later today. Why don't you meet me up there for dinner?"

She hurried off to the kitchen; she had left Jim holding his phone, his mouth open, cut off mid-retort. He turned his attention to the phone, only now realizing that Ben was yelling at him.

"Hold on, Ben. Start again. Weirdness here."

"We got worse than weirdness, Jim. Oh, by the gods, dammit. Get down here to Big Bass Pool as fast you can, please. Bring Brett. Hell, bring anybody you can!"

"Bring Brett? Why? Surely not another body."

"Get down here, Jim! I can't talk. Not right now. Dammit, bring Arthur, too, 'cause I'm gonna need help staying away from the bottle on this one!"

He hung up abruptly. Jim ran out of the diner, jumped into his Explorer, and roared off toward Big Bass Pool. He activated his Bluetooth and called Arthur.

"Something's happened at Big Bass Pool. Call Brett, hell, call everyone—Mike, Dan— and tell them to get down there and meet me."

"What's going on, Jim?"

"I don't know, Arthur. Ben called and sounded awful. Bring Finn with you and tell Brett to bring a full trauma kit as well as his coroner and CSI stuff. I've got a bad feeling about this."

CHAPTER 28

IT WAS A PERFECT DAY FOR FISHING. ZAK loaded the gear into the back of the van while his five customers finished their coffee, set the basket of rolls provided by Maggie into the middle compartment, and made last-minute trips to the john. They would be going downriver from below the textile mill to Big Bass Pool for a day of camaraderie, food, beer, and bass. This was his third group of the season. Zak was happy, because fishing had been great, and the word was out that the Martins Way was overflowing with potential trophy bass.

The men had agreed that a drift boat provided the best opportunity for successful fishing, but they made Zak promise they would have some time at Big Bass Pool. These men were professionals who sat at desks all week long. They wanted to walk, stretch, sit on logs, and tell raunchy jokes.

They were taking a lunch break, before casting into Big Bass Pool. Everyone exclaimed in surprise and pleasure over the rich, gravy-laden meatloaf open-faced sandwiches, redolent with sharp horseradish and earthy rosemary, as well as the indescribable lusciousness of warm homemade whole wheat bread. There was a selection of beer, coke, and coffee. Everyone but Zak chose beer. Of course, there was apple pie in abundance.

Screaming with rage at the sight of the fire and the rabbit that had been snared, she came crashing through the brush as they finished the last of the pie. She was clearly pissed off at all of them. It was difficult to know what was wrong since she was hurtling her invectives at them in a language none of them knew. What they did know was that she was huge, terrifying, human-yet-not-human, and apparently hellbent on murder and mayhem.

Most of them did not escape.

Zak's van was visible as soon as Jim rounded the corner and entered the parking lot for Big Bass Pool. Ben's car was parked there also, his door still open. Jim pulled up behind, shut both doors, then headed down toward the river. A bench had been placed about midway down, at a spot where the river and the land beyond could be seen clearly. It was a favorite spot for bird watchers, but the sole occupant was Ben Jenkins. He was pale and shaking.

"Tell me," said Jim, sitting down beside him.

"You need to get down there, Jim," said Ben. "I think one or two of them are still alive. I know I shoulda stayed with them, but I couldn't. It's..." Sobbing and shaking, unable to continue, he buried his face in his hands.

Jim ran back to the Explorer, pulled out a first aid kit from the back, and hurried down to Big Bass Pool. As he approached the clearing, someone came stumbling out of the bushes. Jim nearly drew his pistol until he realized that it was a man in a fishing vest, blood running down the side of his face.

"I'm a doctor," he said. "I hid from her, but I'm coming with you to help. Keep that weapon handy, Sheriff."

"Her?" queried Jim. "Big, woody looking, long scary arms?"

"Yeah. She's the reason you have all these rules, isn't she?"

"Yes, but we told you all, before you came, that it wasn't entirely safe. It's why you were all required to sign waivers. I really didn't think she would take on a group. How bad?"

"Very bad. All six of us. What the hell is that thing?"

"Let's get down there and attend to any possible survivors," answered Jim. "We'll talk about what she is later. Okay?"

The man nodded grimly, wiping away some blood trickling near his eye. He opened the first aid kit and grabbed a bit of gauze, holding it to his head as he and Jim proceeded cautiously to the pool.

The smell of blood combined with the scent of urine, damp soil, fire, and fish hit Jim before he saw the bodies. They were torn apart, ripped open, or flattened as if some giant foot had stomped them repeatedly. He glanced at the doctor, who was staring in horror at the remains of his fishing party.

"We were sitting there," he gasped, "having beers and telling jokes, getting ready for an afternoon of more fishing and bonding. She came out of nowhere. I'd be down there, too, except I was taking a leak over there," he pointed to the far side of the clearing. "Turned in time to see her burst in on us."

"Are you okay to come see if anyone is still alive?" asked Jim, gently putting a hand on the man's elbow.

"Yeah. Let's go. Now, before I lose my nerve."

Being careful to avoid stepping on any blood or body parts, they made their way into the clearing. Jim realized, watching his companion, that he had been at a crime scene before. He knew not to touch anything other than what was necessary to determine if someone was dead or alive. He stopped at one of the bodies and called to Jim to hurry. The man was unconscious but alive. His legs and most of his groin area were shattered. There was a huge, muddy round spot right in the middle of his pelvis, a print Jim recognized immediately.

"Do you have anything like morphine in that kit?" asked the man.

"No. Only bandages, antibiotic ointment, normal first aid stuff."

"Okay. We need to get some morphine, in case he comes to."

"We have a doctor here in town," said Jim. He hit the speed dial for Brett, who told Jim he had just left the clinic.

"I am bringing the full trauma kit, as you asked," Brett assured Jim. "You all be careful. You sound badly shaken, Jim. Arthur called me to say he and Finn are on their way. So is Dan. Finn will stay with Ben. Mike should already be there. Watch yourselves."

Jim made his way swiftly up the hill to his car, where he got some blankets. He whirled about, pulling his gun when he heard a twig crack. He gasped in relief and holstered the weapon when Mike appeared. The big man was shaking, nostrils flaring as he took in the familiar scents of death and destruction.

"I don't think I can go down there, Jim," he said. "I'm sorry, but I don't think I can. How about I wait with Ben up here? We can take care of each other, and I'll send the rest to you as they arrive. I'll also keep my eyes and ears open in case she comes back."

"Okay, I understand. Once we get things covered or bagged up, though, I need you to help with tracking and such."

"That I can do. Right now, my nose is telling me there's a powerful lot of horribleness down there. Thanks for ... you know."

The doctor yelled at Jim, telling him to hurry with the blankets. Jim continued down as Mike turned, going back to sit beside Ben. Soon the two were deep in conversation, sharing the common memories of trauma victims.

The stench at the banks of Big Bass Pool was overwhelming. Jim tried in vain to keep a keen ear on the sounds of the forest while being overwhelmed by the stink of death and the horror of the scene before him. He had to trust that Mike and Ben would warn them. He knew that Mike would be especially hyperalert.

"What is your name?" asked Jim, as he sat the blankets on the ground next to the doctor.

"Howard," replied the man."

Jim watched in silence as Howard attempted to stem the flow of blood using the blankets. Suddenly, Jim snapped out of the daze that threatened to overwhelm him. "Cop mode" took over, and he went to the other side of the gravely injured man.

"How can I help?"

"Hold these in place, applying pressure, so I can search him for more injuries."

Jim put pressure on the blankets on top of the man's pelvis with one hand, while Howard removed the man's shirt, cutting it away with his knife. The unconscious man had been stabbed in the chest twice on the right side. There were abrasions on his abdomen but, luckily, no additional bleeding other than the two chest wounds. Howard took the man's shirt, wadded it up, and had Jim press it down on the chest wounds.

"Do you know his name?"

"Yeah," grunted Howard. "He's my partner in our practice. Tom, Tom Howell. Great surgeon, my best friend."

Howard then began applying a tourniquet to Tom's left leg. The right leg was apparently shattered but not bleeding, meaning that, although the leg was severely damaged, the femoral artery had obviously been missed. Tom's left leg was a different story. It was hanging on by a few shreds of skin, necessitating the tourniquet.

"I hope that morphine gets here soon," Howard muttered.

"Howard?" called a voice from behind them. "Howard Adams, is that you?"

"Brett? So, this is where you went. Get down here. I need that morphine now. I hope you brought a full kit, too."

Brett and Dan arrived, each carrying a large travel bag, one of which was full of various medical equipment. Brett got to work setting up a morphine drip with a bag of saline. They could see the unconscious man's muscles relax. Brett monitored his vitals while Howard prepared to cut away the remaining tissue holding the mangled leg.

Jim was relieved to turn away from the grisly scene and help Dan get the forensic equipment out of the other bag. Jim and Howard had already checked the rest of the remaining bodies, all of which were obviously dead, but Dan checked them again anyway. They were both careful to avoid trampling the scene.

Jim was preparing to "walk the grid," as his favorite fictional detective Lincoln Rhyme called it, when Dan suddenly gasped.

"Jim? Where's Zak? He was the guide for this group. Where is he?"

"Oh no, no, no," said Jim. "Not Zak. He must have gotten away."

"Shall we have Mike look for him? Arthur and Finn are up there too; they can stay with Ben while we search."

"I need to talk to Ben first," answered Jim. "I want to know how he knew about this since he wasn't on the trip. Maybe he knows where Zak is. Maybe Zak... Too many maybes. Let's go talk to him."

They found all four men sitting on the bench above. Ben was still shaken, though visibly calmer thanks to Arthur's presence. Mike appeared completely in control of his emotions and even offered to go down and help. Jim asked him to wait for a minute while they talked with Ben.

"Ben, how did you know what happened here?" asked Jim. "Did Zak call you?"

"No. I was down here planning to do some fishing. Just arrived and was getting my gear ready when the guys arrived. They took their lunch down to the pond."

"What happened? Do you remember?" asked Jim.

"Remember?" Ben looked sick. "The problem ain't going to be remembering; it's going to be forgetting. Zak was screaming in panic, telling me to get down there, yelling 'Call Jim!' The other fellas were screaming, over and over. Then they stopped. I'm sorry, Jim, but I was too scared to go look. I hid up here in Zak's van and called you."

"Could you hear anything else?" queried Arthur, putting a calming hand on Ben's arm. "Any voices or noises?"

"Some woman was screaming, words I didn't understand," said Ben, his voice shaking badly. "There was also crashing noises, like tree branches falling or something. Finally, that godawful scream from the men. I'll like as never forget that."

He began to cry. Arthur quietly spoke with him, while motioning the others away. Jim turned to Mike.

"I hate asking you to go down there, but we need to find Zak. He's not with the others, and I don't think he would have abandoned them willingly. He's not that sort of guy."

"You and Dan do your evidence thing," said Mike. "I'll track down Zak. If I find anything on the way, I'll put one of those little markers by it. Give me a handful of them, those yellow flags you have. If he's down there, I'll find Zak."

Mike took approximately twenty yellow flag markers, averted his eyes as best he could while he followed the trail to the pond, and set off carefully along the narrow bank. He was looking for Zak, but he was also looking for the distinctive round prints that Zoya left wherever she went, plus anything else of interest. Jim and Dan left the care of Tom to Howard and Brett, while they began a meticulous examination of the crime scene.

The previous winter, at Dan's request, Jim had taught him the basics of a forensic examination of a crime scene. Much to Dan's confusion, Jim presented him with the entire Lincoln Rhyme series by Jeffrey Deaver.

"It's good reading. Plus, in my opinion, it is also one of the best presentations of how to handle evidence. Most of the textbooks are dry as dust. At least with these, you get a great story along with a good education."

Jim noted that Dan walked slowly and carefully, having put cloth booties over his shoes, with a rubber band over each of the booties. He had obviously read the books. In the end, there was little to notice other than the mutilated body parts, the victims, and the strange round prints they had noted at the other crime scenes. Jim was even more pissed than before. He didn't want mythological tree creatures. If he had to deal with murder, he wanted a perp he understood. He could handle a crazed killer, a sadist, or a psycho. Immortal tree gods were too much for him to grasp. He wanted boot prints, footprints, a bloody axe, anything familiar. Instead, he watched as Dan carefully bagged what appeared to be small branches, took multiple photos of the round prints in the ground, and searched for any remaining evidence.

Jim left the collection of body parts, blood, and the like to Brett and Howard. Brett was a trained forensic pathologist; he could guide Howard on the protection and preservation of evidence. After marking the scene and collecting what evidence they could, Dan and he set out in search of Mike, keeping an eye out for any disturbances of the bushes along the riverbank. They could see Mike's boot prints along the narrow shore and followed them carefully.

Jim was looking out toward the river also, remembering the quacking he had heard two years ago, which Charity and Arthur insisted had not come from a duck. They refused to elaborate, but Jim knew they attributed the noise, along with the drownings around the same time, to a mythical being. He couldn't deny that he had felt that buzzing in his head when they took him to Sanders Pond where they said the being lived. Still, despite that previous experience, he didn't like things he couldn't explain rationally, with mythical beings at the top of that list.

What the hell was I thinking, staying in this place? Although, if I hadn't, I wouldn't have Linda and Will, but damn! Mythical murderers? Can't claim things are boring.

Something in the river caught his eye. He waded into the water, while watching for the drop-off Zak had once warned him about. As he drew closer, he saw it was a body. No, not a body, a person trying desperately to make it to shore. Jim yelled for Dan to find a long branch or break one off. His yells caught the attention of Mike, who was not far downstream. Mike was examining a disturbance in the bushes he would tell Jim about later. He marked the spot and ran back upstream toward Jim and Dan.

When Mike arrived and saw what Jim was pointing at, he quickly shed his jacket, boots, and jeans and dove into the river to swim toward the floundering body. Whoever it was, he was obviously losing his battle with the current. Mike arrived just in time. He grabbed him under the arms in rescue position, then began a strong kick toward the shore. Dan arrived with a long branch which Jim extended out toward Mike. The big man quickly grabbed hold with one hand, his other arm still firmly wrapped around the man he had saved from drowning. It was Zak Millbank.

When Mike and Jim finally got Zak to shore, it was obvious he was grievously injured. His left arm was nearly torn off, with a bit of tissue holding it on, the shoulder blade and humerus fully exposed. The cold river water had apparently stanched the bleeding, which threatened to begin again now that he was warming up. Additionally, there were long wounds on his torso. The wounds extended from shoulder to hipbone on the same side as the mutilated arm. Jim hoped Zak was right-handed.

Mike picked up his shirt, wrapping it tightly around Zak's shoulder wound. He swung Zak's body over his shoulder and set off at a lope toward Big Bass Pool, where Howard and Brett were still attending to Tom. Jim assumed that Brett had called Miranda and requested an ambulance. These two men—Tom and Zak—would need to be taken to the hospital in Harwood. Brett's clinic was good, but they were not equipped nor staffed to deal with such severe injuries.

Zak was swiftly attended to by Brett since he and Howard had done all they could to stabilize Tom. As they worked, Jim heard the welcome wail of the ambulance siren. In short order, both patients were loaded into the ambulance, with Howard riding along with the EMTs to help attend to both men. Brett stayed behind to help Jim protect the chain of evidence.

"Take them to Harwood," said Brett. "They have a small hospital there, equipped to deal with traumas."

"I want both of them on a life flight to Jefferson City Hospital," replied Howard. "These wounds are serious, and I want them in ICU beds ASAP."

Brett thought a moment, then agreed. "I'll call and make arrangements for a life flight to meet you in Harwood. They have a helipad. They can be monitored there until the chopper arrives."

The ambulance took off, leaving Brett and the others behind to deal with the bodies. Brett called Miranda again, this time asking her to drive the coroner's van to the site and to bring three body bags.

"Dammit. Jim, we are going to have to involve the state boys now," said Brett.

"Why? We know what we are doing."

"Yeah, we do. But Tom Howell and Howard Adams are well-known physicians. Also, that dead guy over there?"

"Yeah. What about him?"

"He's a state senator, Jim. This guy over here is a deputy district attorney in Jeff' City. That one is a judge."

"Oh, crap. So now we get the state guys swarming all over, along with CNN, Jeff' City news, and probably some others, too."

"You're probably right. We cannot keep this quiet. Frankly? I want help. Not only with the autopsies and inquest, but with the search, and you should, too. Because despite what we've seen and heard, if this ends up being a serial killer and not some mythical forest being, there are two of them, or even more. I don't see all this mayhem being done by one person."

"You're right, Brett. But where are the footprints? Two people, no matter how careful, couldn't do this much damage in this damp soil and not leave prints. All we've got are these," Jim said, pointing at the strange round prints. "How are we going to explain to the state guys and the media what Mike saw? He won't talk to the media, but somehow, they always find out."

"Oh, geez," exclaimed Brett. "Every damn conspiracy theorist around will be up here, tramping around endangering themselves and everyone in town. What the hell do we do, Jim?"

"We need an explanation for all of this mayhem. Am I understanding that correctly?" asked Mike.

"Yeah. Something believable, or at least marginally so. No rubber duckies this time," said Brett.

"Rubber duckies?" Mike looked profoundly confused.

"It's a long story," said Jim. "We had several drownings, with some mutilation, a couple of years ago. I wanted an explanation that was believable and provable. We used rubber ducks with GPS trackers to convince people about the cause. I'll tell you the whole story someday."

"I can hardly wait."

Mike stood in silence for a while, then cleared his throat.

"Why not tell them a version of the truth? We don't know what happened yet. We are investigating thoroughly, hope to have a report soon. For now, it could be an accident, it could be a rabid animal, or it could be that we have a serial killer team on the loose. Why make it complicated?"

"That's probably what we'll say," said Jim. "But I want all of you up at the Grove anyway. Brett, Mike, Ben, Arthur, Finn, and I want Howard, too. Brett, you go get him. I'm sure his partner will be in good hands. I don't want my prime witness flying off to Jefferson City before I have a chance to interview him."

Jim and the others walked up the path to the bench, where Ben still sat. He looked relieved to see them.

"I was about to head back to town," he said. "The campgrounds need attention. I also need to secure those guys' belongings. Who's gonna make the call to their families?"

"That's my job," said Jim. "You and I can sort out their stuff and lock it up. I'll make the phone calls. I want all of you up at the Grove as soon as you have secured the evidence. Brett, store the evidence in your safe. Preserve what's perishable in the refrigerated storage in back, along with the bodies. Neither the evidence nor the bodies are going anywhere. In the meantime, we need to figure out what we are going to tell the state people and the families when they arrive. We also have to prepare for the media. I don't know what we are going to say, but it certainly isn't going to be anything about walking tree people."

"One thing I know for sure," replied Brett. "It can't be made up, can't be a lie. We are going to have to be creative, but careful, on this one."

Jim and Mike got rolls of yellow warning tape out of Jim's car to enclose the crime scene. Jim then called four of the recent high school graduates who had helped watch over Sanders Pond two years ago. He asked them if they would come down to do guard duty again, until the state police investigations team arrived. The boys promised to be there in no more than fifteen minutes.

Brett called the clinic in Harwood. Fortunately, the life flight chopper had not yet arrived. Howard Adams was not happy about coming back to Harper's Landing instead of going with his partner, but he understood the need. He also knew his friend would be in good hands. He told Brett that

Laura Millbank had arrived, insisting on going with Zak to Jefferson City. Jim saw no reason why she shouldn't, so Brett okayed her flying down there. Howard told him that she had arranged for the care of the children and that Zak's parents would be driving in from Hannibal to be with her at Jefferson City Hospital.

Jim pulled Brett aside for a moment.

"I'm dead serious about handling this properly with the state guys. We cannot lie. I can't emphasize that enough. We are definitely going to have to be creative, though."

"You let me help. You leave the problem of Zoya to me," said a deep voice behind them.

Both men whirled around, staring at the small wizened figure standing before them. It was the same man Jim had encountered in the diner.

"Porewit?" asked Jim. "What do you mean, 'leave the problem of Zoya to me?' How is one tiny little man like you going to handle an insane, raging tree-woman? If there is such a being?"

Brett sat down hard on the ground and stared at the strange little man. Jim sat on a nearby log, while Porewit paced back and forth in front of them. Finally, he stopped, sitting on a nearby trunk.

"The two of you are men of science. I respect that. Despite that, you were called to this town, which means that somewhere inside you is the ability, if not the willingness, to accept the uncanny, the different, the magical if you will. I am a magical being. There are many in your world, even in this town, who will never be able to see me. However, both of you can, and you need to trust that, to believe what I am about to tell you."

"Are you a god?" burst out Brett. "Are you the god Charity spoke of?"

"Yes, though not in the sense of the God that you were raised with, the religion of the White Christ. In my reality, of which you are privileged to get a brief glimpse, there are many gods. We each have our own duties and obligations. Mine are to train and manage the Lesheye, among other things. I fear I have neglected you badly, failed in that duty. I know that Charity told you that we sent Zoya into forced hibernation one hundred years ago. Alas, I lost track of that hundred years. I should have been here when she resurrected again. I was dealing with war in Ukraine, helping to relocate our people there. Nevertheless, I am here now."

About time, thought Jim.

"What can you do?" he asked. "Surely not another hundred-year hibernation. That will just put another future generation in danger. By then, these woods may not even exist. We humans tend to grow rather quickly, while cutting down whatever is in our way."

"This is true," said Porewit. "I have a more permanent solution in mind this time, at least where you are involved. I have every faith in your abilities, but we must find Zoya and disable her before she does any more damage. That will not be possible for you to do without my help."

"I will also help," said a deep voice. Zandar walked into the clearing, pain and anger showing in his face, in his clenched fists. "She has gone too far. She must be stopped at all costs."

He came to a stop when he saw Porewit and bowed, kneeling on one knee.

"My Lord, I did not know you were here. Forgive my disrespect."

"Oh, get up, Zandar. We've known each other too long, old friend, to dabble in trivialities. Now let's you and I help these folks by going and getting Zoya. I will subdue her. Let me think a moment..."

Porewit stood in silence; the others watched him closely. Suddenly, he looked up.

"You, all of you, meet me at the Mother Tree in the orchard, when I call you. Zandar and I will have her there. Please do not come earlier. If you hear any ruckus during the night, you must resist the urge to come out and look. I cannot stress this enough. I am counting on you to tell the others at the Grove. Wait for my call, and then come immediately."

Porewit grabbed Zandar's hand and led him into the forest. Suddenly, he turned and came back to Jim and Brett, who were still sitting in stunned disbelief.

"One more thing. There will be a price to pay. There always is with us gods, but you already knew that. Jim Burch, you must bring your wife with you to the Mother Tree when I call you all to gather."

"Linda? Why do you want Linda? I will not let you take her!"

"Oh, do be silent and don't be silly. I'm not going to hurt her. She is just a part of the cost for my services. She has a job to do, and it is way past time she accepts it."

Porewit turned and melted into the forest.

Brett finally broke the silence.

"Well, that was interesting, to say the least. I'll take Mike to help with securing the bodies and evidence. Then I'm going to drive to Harwood to get Howard."

He left abruptly, waving at Mike to join him when he got to the top of the path. Jim and Ben waited until the young men arrived to take up guard duty; then, the two of them went to the campgrounds. Once they had located and locked away the belongings of the dead and injured men, Jim drove to the Grove.

The phone calls Jim made to the families were as horrible as he knew they would be. He was grateful for the calming presence of Arthur and Finn, as well as the tea Charity provided, along with the chance to cuddle his family.

It had been an exhausting day, physically and mentally. Jim sank into one of the overstuffed chairs in the common room in front of the fireplace; he was grateful for the roaring fire and the shot of bourbon Linda had poured for him as soon as they arrived. Soon, everyone who had been at Big Bass Pool was sitting in front of the fire, sipping bourbon, and trying to relax.

"How about some dinner?"

Jen and Linda appeared, Bridgette trailing behind, carrying between them plates burdened with food, silverware, and a large basket of rolls. Apparently, both babies were asleep, leaving the women free to provide comfort and sustenance.

Not for the first time, Jim pondered the importance this community placed on food. Homemade food. There were no fast-food joints, with the possible exception of some of the bar food served at the Happy Time. Every occasion, be it a wedding, a birthday, a funeral, or a gathering like this one, was accompanied by warm, comforting, healthy food. He remembered when Beth died, it seemed like everyone had brought food. He had been forced to give away a lot of it. He decided it wasn't something to be examined. As long as there was food and good bourbon in the world, everything would work out.

CHAPTER 29

THE GATHERING AT THE GROVE WAS LARGER than Jim had expected. Looking around, he realized that every person in the room had, at one time or another, actually seen one of the Lesheye. Dr. Howard Adams was the only outsider; however, he had not only seen Zoya, but also seen her in action. He looked the worse for wear, having endured his own injuries on top of tending to his critically wounded partner. It was obviously weighing heavy on him to know that Tom would probably die, or, if he survived, would never be able to practice again. Howard had also assisted in the care of the grievously injured Zak, as well as witnessed the murder of three friends. Jim made sure that the bourbon bottle was nearby for him.

Brett cleared his throat to speak before Jim.

"As coroner, it is my sad duty to tell you that three men lost their lives today at the hands of Zoya, the Leshachikha. Additionally, Dr. Tom Howell was seriously injured. In my professional opinion, he likely will not survive his wounds.

Zak Millbank was also gravely injured, but he is young, healthy, and, so far, is doing quite well."

"The families of the dead are on their way here," interjected Arthur. "Finn and I have prepared rooms for them in case they want to stay overnight. They might arrive this evening, though we urged them to wait until tomorrow to drive up."

Jim waited until the expected soft conversations died down.

"We have a problem. One that requires careful thought and input from all of you. We know what killed these men, plus the members of our own community that we have lost recently. While we are familiar with—unusual—happenings, I'm sure you can imagine the reaction if we try to tell the media or the state police that a walking tree-woman caused all this mayhem."

Everyone began talking at once. Some of them were talking to each other, while others were yelling, trying to be heard over the noise. Jim let them vent for a couple of minutes, then bellowed, "Quiet! All of you!"

Everyone stopped talking, mouths dropping. Jim wasn't known for losing his cool. Right now, he was obviously peeved. As if to emphasize his point, both babies began to cry. Linda and Jen hurried to their bassinets. Soon after, both infants were happily nursing.

Jim continued.

"We cannot lie. Aside from the fact that it's a felony to knowingly provide false information in a murder investigation, it would be difficult to concoct a believable story to explain the condition of the deceased or wounded. However, we should be able to omit information. I want Mark Whitaker's opinion on that. He's the only one who hasn't seen what the rest of us have. Further, I want his opinion before we tell him what we saw. In fact, he may tell us he doesn't want to know what we saw."

Mark Whitaker, the county's district attorney, walked into the community center at that moment. He looked around, spotted Jim, and headed his way.

"Okay, Jim. Got your call and came as soon as I could. How can I help?"

"We have a situation. I'm going to give you the skeleton version. You tell me if you need or should know more or not, before rendering an opinion."

"Okay. I'll do my best."

"A lot of people have recently been killed or injured in the forests, as I am sure you know."

Mark nodded. "Hard not to know in a county this small, and this talkative."

"The problem is, everyone in this room except you knows what caused those deaths and injuries, as well as the fire that destroyed the sawmill. But it will bring a world of trouble down on us if we tell the media and state police what we saw. I would prefer to simply say that the cause of the deaths and injuries is still under investigation. While not the whole truth, it would be true. What is your opinion?"

"Here I thought I had a simple life," mused Mark.

Everyone laughed.

"I think you're treading on fairly thin ice. Let me ask this: if you were to tell the full truth, if everyone here was to tell the state guys what they saw, would you be believed?"

"Probably not," said Arthur, emphatically. "It would require a great stretch of the imagination, a suspension of disbelief most people are not capable of."

"Well, in that case, I think you would be safe in saying that the investigation is ongoing. I do think that, unless the families demand it, you would be better off trying to limit the involvement of the state as much as possible. Is it true what I heard, that one of the victims is a state senator? Another a judge?"

"You heard right," said Brett. "I would say fat chance keeping the state boys' noses out of our business, with those two plus a deputy district attorney all dead. I will try to convince them that we are capable of doing a full investigation. I still have some clout with them, or at least I think I do. A couple of years ago they were impressed with the thoroughness of your investigation, Jim."

Mark, obviously deep in thought, had gotten up to pace back and forth in front of the fireplace while the others spoke.

"I think we need to make every effort we can to keep the investigation under our control," he finally said. "If we lose that, which I think is quite possible given the state senator and all, we need to hold firm to the 'investigation is ongoing' response for as long as we can."

"Do you need to know what we know?" asked Arthur. "I don't know if it will make your life easier or worse, to be honest."

"I've been thinking about that," replied Mark. "It's a choice between full disclosure and plausible deniability. However, since I am the district attorney for the county, I think you'd better tell me. I'd rather not try to convince them I didn't know if whatever it is you are keeping from me were to become public knowledge. I'm assuming we don't have a poison ivy outbreak."

Mark and Arthur retired to a far corner of the room, with bourbon and plates of food, where Arthur filled him in on the history of the accidental transport of the Lesheye to America and Harper's Landing. Jim glanced over once in a while, amused by the looks of stunned incredulity on Mark's face as Arthur told him the whole story.

"I suppose we are going to have to show him all the evidence," Jim said to Brett. "We are also going to have to be careful about everything we say to anyone, including townsfolk who don't know about Zoya and Zandar."

"I'm not quite ready to accept that Zoya is responsible for everything," said Brett. "I know she's done some of it. We have eyewitnesses, including poor Howard over there who is really enjoying your bourbon. May have to carry him back to Havensrest."

Howard looked up at the mention of his name.

"Did I really see what I think I saw?" he asked Brett. "Because either there were mushrooms of a certain type in that meatloaf gravy, or I drank too much beer, or I'm going to have to change my religion."

He let out a loud belch, turned beet red, and bolted for the bathroom.

"Well, that's a waste of good bourbon," mused Jim. "Unless he had to pee really bad."

"The latter," said Howard, as he returned to his place in front of the fire. "I'm known for being able to hold my liquor. Now give. What the bloody hell did I see out there? What was that thing that killed George, Franklin, and Harold? And probably Tom? I don't expect him to make it, even with the good care he'll get in Jeff' City."

Suddenly, he put his face in his hands, shaking with sobs. It all hit him at once: the loss of three good friends with the probability of losing his partner of many years.

"He's all I've got. Peggy and I never had children. When I lost her last year, it was Tom who kept me going. The other three, too. What the hell was that thing, Brett? Because it took away everyone left to me that was precious. By God, I want it dead!"

Charity whispered to Galen. He got up, went to her house, and returned a few minutes later with a steaming mug of something. Charity took it to Howard and persuaded him to take a few sips. After he tasted it, he drank the whole mug. He looked much better, soon gathering his composure.

Howard, Arthur, Charity, and Mark went into the dining area, where they sat, ate pie, drank coffee, and listened to Charity tell more stories about the Lesheye. Meanwhile, Jim and the others debated what they would tell the state authorities if required.

"Are we all in agreement regarding the 'investigation is ongoing' comment to the state police?" asked Jim. "That is unless Mark disagrees after what he is trying to digest over there."

They all nodded.

"The media is a whole different kettle of fish," said Brett. "There's no doubt they will arrive *en masse*, especially after the media circus two years ago. A noted doctor stomped to pieces, along with a dead senator, judge, and prosecutor? Not including all the locals that have died or been injured? Well, that's raw meat for the news folks."

It was quickly getting dark outside. Jim wanted anyone who didn't live at the Grove, including all the people staying at Havensrest, to get back safely inside before dark.

"Let's meet here again tomorrow morning. We need to be here anyway, for Porewit's meeting, if he calls it that soon. Before you go, however, there is one thing that has been bothering me."

Jim walked back into the dining area, the others following him.

"Mike?" he asked, "Didn't you say that, when you dove into the river, Zoya ignored you?"

"Yep," Mike replied. "She was chasing me, but when I hit the water, she just turned and left."

"I believe that you, Arthur, said it was because she is a creature of the forest?"

"I don't recall who said it," replied Arthur. "But it is true. She would ignore anything that wasn't a direct threat to her 'children' and the other creatures of the forest."

"So why did she just kill a fishing party? Plus, nearly kill poor Zak?"

"I can answer that," said Howard. "We got the bright idea of cooking our fish and a snared rabbit over an open flame when we got back to the campground. One of the guys, I think it was Senator Hailey, pulled out a small hatchet from his gear and started to hack down a couple of small trees. We were going to use the limbs as skewers. That's when she came bellowing out of the woods. I don't think I'm ever going to forget that, and I wasn't in her way."

"Well, that explains why you guys were targeted," said Finn.

"Let's continue this tomorrow, before Porewit's meeting, after breakfast," said Jim. "By the way, Charity, what is the Mother Tree?"

"It's the original tree planted in the orchard. The big one at the center. It was already here when Maria, Yuri, and the other immigrant relatives of Stephan and his siblings arrived. Stephan convinced them to use this meadow as the apple orchard. The Mother Tree is over 150 years old. Many of the other trees were grown from seeds retrieved from her fruit."

The visitors quickly herded themselves out to their cars. Galen helped Charity back to her cottage, where the two of them disappeared inside. The lights soon went out. To Jim's surprise, Bridgette joined Mike in his car, the two of them headed off for downtown and Mike's new house.

"You approve?" he asked Jen.

"Yes, I do. Not that it would be necessary. She is eighteen and quite capable of making her own decisions. But there is something special about Mike. He needs her. Once he is rid of his demons, I think we are going to find Mike an indispensable member of this community. The town has called him; of that, I am sure. The reason will become apparent someday."

"You really do believe the town calls people," said Jim.

"No. I know the town calls people, like it called you, Dan, and Arthur. Now Mike. Galen, too, I think. Or perhaps Galen's grandson was the one who was called. We will find out soon enough when Galen begins serious training of his new replacement."

"Let's hope that is far in the future, the replacing I mean," said Dan. "I like Galen a lot. Charity has needed a caregiver for a long time."

"Yes," replied Jen, "though that won't last much longer."

"What do you mean?" asked Linda. "Is he going to leave?"

"No, Galen won't be leaving."

She left it at that, swiftly entering her house, carefully putting Kat in her bed. Linda shrugged, picked up Will, and took him to his crib. Dan and Jim followed their wives. Soon everything at the Grove was quiet.

CHAPTER 30

JIM WOKE AT TWO IN THE MORNING. HE had heard something, a noise loud enough to penetrate his usual deep sleep. He got up, careful not to wake Linda, and pulled on his bathrobe. After a quick bathroom trip, he stepped out onto the porch. The night air was brisk. The scents of damp soil, night-blooming jasmine, and the steer mulch he had put on the vegetable beds competed for attention. The last full moon of July streamed through the branches of the orchard, casting shifting shadows, as the gentle night breeze made the leaves flutter.

He was certain he saw movement on the ground but couldn't make out any recognizable shapes.

Probably the moonlight through the trees, he thought.

A hoot from the owl that lived in a tree above the community house startled him. He looked up and saw the owl take off suddenly, flying low over the meadow. It swooped down after some unsuspecting night forager but suddenly rose high in the air and hooted loudly, a panicky sound. Jim heard the crackling sound made when someone steps on a dry, dead branch. Looking for anything or anyone out and about in the orchard, he peered into the night.

Gonna take my own advice, he thought, and headed back into his house. It was not a night for wandering about in the dark to look for what was likely a large animal. He climbed into bed, careful not to disturb Linda with his icy, cold feet.

At the southernmost end of the orchard, Zandar and his companion—the tiny, ancient demigod perched on his shoulder—were following the footprints they had found at the Martins Way River. The footprints headed toward the Grove. The moon was their only light, as they diligently hunted for the insane, dangerous Zoya. The silence of the night was ominous. There were no rustles in the bushes of tiny night hunters, no voles searching for bugs, and no echolocation of bats seeking night-borne bug swarms. Even the scent of the night-blooming jasmine seemed muted.

"Stop for a moment by that tree," whispered Porewit. "I would like an apple. Perhaps if we sit for a while, she will think we have gone and try again."

"I don't like this," replied Zandar, also whispering. "If she thinks we have gone and goes for the Grove again, we may not be fast enough to stop her. For all we know, she could be down by Havensrest, or even in town. She holds a grudge against Maggie too, for taking 'her' apples."

"You spend the night at the Grove. I will send some of the animals to help watch."

Zandar's eyes widened.

"You can do that? I never knew. I mean, I guess I am horribly selfish. It never occurred to me that you took care of everything in the forests, not only us Lesheye."

"You become more 'human' every year. We will have to discuss my plan for Zoya, since it might involve you. But not now. First, we must find her, or, rather, I must find her. You must guard the Grove. Go, and do not sleep, old friend."

Porewit disappeared into the forest, while Zandar made his way slowly back to the Grove to sit on the deck in silence. He barely acknowledged the four bucks who prowled back and forth on each side of the area. Zoya would have a hard time getting to the residents here if she were so inclined.

Zandar's sadness was palpable. He loved Zoya. They had been together for hundreds of years. He had long since stopped counting. The hundred-year hibernation had been almost unbearable for him. He had visited her every day. His long wait was over, and now he felt it had all been for nothing.

Havensrest was also dark, though the motion lights outside had been left on. The residents slept soundly, unaware of the circle of animals standing watch around the entire periphery.

Downtown in Harper's Landing, Mike couldn't sleep. Once he was certain Bridgette was sound asleep, he went down to sit on the porch. He sat in silence and listened to the sounds of the night. An owl glided silently over the buildings, its shadow catching Mike's attention. Somewhere a coyote yipped; another returned its call. The bullfrogs from Sanders Pond could be heard all the way up to town, their deep-throated croaks echoing through the still night air. The hum of most insects was barely discernible, but the crickets were out in full voice. All in all, it was a normal Missouri July night. It was about half past two when Mike headed upstairs and slipped into bed; he was careful not to wake Bridgette.

I'm going to have to decide. I can't continue with this girl unless I commit. It isn't fair to her, or to me for that matter. Can she handle my demons? What about the nights when they won't rest? Can I ask someone to share that with me?

He fell asleep, determined to talk with Arthur and perhaps Charity, too, in the near future. In fact, he knew that a conversation with Charity could not be avoided, and Jen would probably be a part of that conversation. His sleep that night was uninterrupted by the dreams that usually haunted him.

CHAPTER 31

AUGUST ARRIVED, AND WITH IT CAME THE stifling heat and humidity so common to the Midwest. It had the fortunate effect of keeping daily tourists down to a minimum. The campgrounds had already been closed to outsiders for the rest of the summer. Saul Grossman made sure that Ben was adequately compensated for the loss of income by having his workers agree to take their vacations in town, which made use of the camping areas and the new castle playground.

Things were relatively quiet, considering the spotlight that had been put on Harper's Landing by the media. Word of the gruesome deaths of a state senator, a judge, and a prosecutor had gotten out almost immediately after the bodies arrived in Jefferson City. Shortly after they finished interviewing the state police and tormenting the families of the victims, the media swarmed like locusts all over the town. Brett was their primary target since he had performed the initial autopsies before sending the bodies on to the state lab.

A few of the reporters had come to Harper's Landing two years ago, when all those children and the federal judge from St. Louis had drowned under mysterious circumstances. They were eager to explore the possibility of something new and uncanny happening in Harper's Landing. Even those who had not been present back then knew about the drownings. Despite all the efforts by Jim, Arthur, and the other residents in the know, gossip started to flourish. Several reporters were pressing anyone they could corner about whispers of strange beings in the forest.

Jim's primary concern was that some blockhead looking for a Pulitzer would wander into the woods alone and end up ripped to pieces. *Wouldn't that make dandy headlines?*

Shortly after the breakfast crowd cleared out of Morey's, Jim headed there, hoping to retreat from the constant questions of the press. He had not slept well and was nursing a headache which threatened to blossom into a full-bore migraine. He ordered a cup of coffee and a plate of scrambled eggs with lots of bacon and shredded cheese mixed in. He would exercise it off later. For now, he wanted sustenance and caffeine.

The smell of cinnamon drifting out of the kitchen reminded him of his last visitor. He wondered if he would see the man again. Even though he knew Porewit was real, he could not quite bring himself to acknowledge that he was a god.

Gods don't exist. At least, not as little old men or people who look like trees.

"You would think so, wouldn't you? I mean, we should be thunderous of voice, towering in physique, not a little old man with long gray hair, or a tall, spindly tree-thing with antlers growing out its head."

Jim nearly jumped out of his seat.

"Will you please stop sneaking up on me? If you have to visit, at least be civil about it. Now that you know I can see and hear you, the games can stop."

Porewit leaned back in his chair; he stared at Jim while chewing on a piece of a cinnamon roll. He swallowed, took a sip of coffee from the cup he had apparently brought with him, and cleared his throat.

"We can't let her kill anyone else, Jim Burch. We can't let her get her hands on a newsperson, a visitor, or a local resident. The more she kills, the more she will kill. She must be stopped."

"Well, you're the god here. Surely you must have some way of stopping her."

"When's the last time that God of yours interfered in the mayhem of your lives?"

"You've got a point. You aren't like Him, though. We, at least some of us, can see and hear you. You promised me that you and Zandar were going to stop her. You said something about restraining her and bringing her to the Mother Tree. What happened to that grand plan?"

"We can't find her," replied Porewit. "She knows I am here, so she has disappeared. Probably shape-shifted. She can do that, you know. So can Zandar."

"There was a bat. Flying away from the sawmill."

"Yes. That would have been her. We have no way of knowing what form she has taken now. We must provide her with bait."

"Bait! You mean... oh hell no. I'm not putting one of my people in danger."

"I'm afraid it's not your choice to make. In any event, the volunteer was the one who suggested it. She's beyond her time to have left anyway, as she has already told you. I have promised her a reward, not as a bribe, but as a recognition of what she is doing. The risk she is taking."

"Why must it be Charity? It is Charity, isn't it?" demanded Jim. "Why is she being so damned foolish?"

"That is not for me to reveal, especially to you. I know you. You will try to talk her out of it, try to prevent her, do everything in your power to stand between her and her destiny. I can assure you that she will not be harmed by Zoya, hard as that ancient Leshachikha might try. It will be her final act, an act of sacrifice for her beloved Harper's Landing, even if Zoya is not the architect of her departure."

"If it is Linda, I swear, god or not, I will tear you limb from limb."

"Oh, don't be silly. Of course, it isn't Linda. Hers is a different destiny. Enough posturing. We must prepare. If we wait too long, Zoya will find another victim, which absolutely must not be allowed. You need to find Mike Cullen, Dan Balanchuk, and the two Druids. Galen Burns will need to come, too. We will assemble at the Mother Tree, the source of all power for the Grove and for the town, at noon tomorrow. Don't be late."

Porewit faded from view before Jim could say more.

At least I have a day to prepare, maybe to find out who this is and stop her from doing something rash and permanent. Jim sat up straight, suddenly. He remembered Charity's words from earlier. *"I know who it is. She will not be stopped."*

Jim sat for a while, nursing his coffee, picking at his breakfast, and alternating between wanting to cry and wanting to throw something. Finally, he picked up his phone to call the five men Porewit had named.

"Meet me at Morey's" was his entire message to each of them.

He waved over the new waitress, one of the high school seniors, and asked her to tell Morey there would be five of them, wanting pie, coffee, and cheddar cheese. She refilled his coffee cup, then hurried off with his order. Jim sat back, nursing his coffee, waiting for the others.

We will find another way. We have to. How can we survive if we lose her? Why should she sacrifice herself because some tree-woman has gone mad? I need to get my hands on Zandar and perhaps even Zoya. I need to know how to deal with them.

He paused, holding his head in his hands, shocked to realize he was holding back tears.

If I continue down this path, is it the way to madness, to despair, to the long dark night of the soul? Why is my life so filled with loss?

"You must learn to embrace what you have, to balance loss with gain."

What the hell? Now I'm hearing voices?

Dreading the onset of another migraine, Jim scrubbed his face with his hands.

"Once you stop fighting with yourself, the headaches will go away."

"GET THE FUCK OUT OF MY HEAD!" roared Jim.

Morey, Maggie, and several of the customers came barreling into the back room where Jim had moved to hold his meeting. Mike Cullen showed up behind them, worry creasing his face.

Maggie moved ahead of them all to sit down next to Jim. She put an arm around his waist and pulled him close. He gradually relaxed, letting his head rest on her shoulder. She whispered quietly into his ear, her arm firmly wrapped around his left side, holding him close. As the others watched, Jim finally nodded his head in assent, apparently to a whispered question. Maggie got up, making shooing motions toward the gathering crowd.

"Go on over there, Mike. Sit. Let him talk if he wants."

Mike nodded, heading over to the window table. He took a chair opposite the bench where Jim was sitting, still looking slightly shell-shocked. Mike recognized the look, the ongoing internal battle between what was real and what was not. He sighed softly, knowing he was pretty much useless in Jim's search for a solution.

Finn and Arthur arrived about five minutes later, with Dan right behind. Jim's cell rang. It was Galen.

"Jim? I'm not going to leave Charity. I won't bring her down there, either. You have to do without me, or you guys have to come up here. I'm going to stay with her. Try to talk her out of it."

That was confirmation of what Jim had suspected. No, not suspected. Known.

"You stay with her. We'll work on a plan here and see you tonight. I think we are all going to be together tonight. I suspect things are going to get a bit hairy."

"Where's Brett?" asked Dan. "Shouldn't he be here, too?"

"I dunno," responded Jim. "Porewit didn't include him on the list."

"Porewit?"

"Yeah, it's a long story. Let me call Brett."

Brett was having problems of his own. Jim put him on speakerphone.

"Miranda and I are on a helicopter, with Pete and Melanie Wilson, headed for Jefferson City."

"What's up?" asked Arthur.

"Melanie's got all the signs of preeclampsia, which we aren't equipped to deal with. We will stay in Jeff' City until she has the baby. Probably be a week or so before we can come back. Don't worry. Dr. Monroe from Harwood is coming over to tend the clinic while we are gone. Frankly, we—me and Miranda—need a vacation. I will call when we are ready to come home, and one of you can come get us."

"You're going to miss all the excitement," said Finn.

"Frankly? I won't miss it at all!"

They all laughed, except Jim, who was still nursing his coffee and fighting off a headache. He sat, just listening while Brett and Mike worked out the details for picking them up for the trip home when mom and baby were ready, then disconnected the call when they were done.

"At least we don't have to contend with the state cops for now," said Jim. "They are all down at Big Bass Pool poring over the crime scene. They made casts of Zoya's footprints, or what we assume are her footprints, then sent pictures of them down to Jefferson City for identification. They're taking water and soil samples. I suppose, at some point, we are all going to have to answer a lot of questions, mostly with 'darned if I know,' which is pretty much the truth anyway."

"Brett won't be here to help," said Arthur. "That's inconvenient."

"Damn. I understand why he's gone, but I sure would like to have him here," said Jim. "I hate having to explain to someone else what is going on. They wouldn't let Harry Randle come with them. Said he was too new to the force."

"I don't think that us understanding what is going on is going to be a problem," replied Arthur. "Porewit has filled me in."

Jim shook his head. "He fills you in yet tells me absolutely nothing."

"I suspect he is waiting for you to accept what you do know," said Arthur. "You really do know more than you are letting on, to yourself and to us."

"We've had this conversation before, Arthur. It goes against everything I've practiced, believed in, and acted on all my life. As a cop, I must rely on facts."

"What? You're going to take a mad tree-woman to court?"

"You have a point. That's not why I've asked you all to come here, though. We have a situation that needs to be stopped, which it can with your help."

"If it's what I think it is," said Finn, "we won't be able to stop it. Further, we shouldn't even try."

Jim's cell rang.

"Jim! It's Galen! You gotta help me, man. You gotta come now! Oh God, she's gone, Jim. I tried to stop her, but she blasted me with something. I came to, and she's gone. Please, please, please! Come now!"

Galen began to sob, as Jim told him they would come immediately.

"You stay there, you hear? Do NOT go after her until we get there."

Jim hung up, then immediately dialed Linda.

"Linda? Find Jen and get to Charity's house. Do not let Galen go after her."

"What do you mean, 'go after her,' Jim? What is going on?"

"Galen will explain. Get over there now, and do not let him leave until we arrive."

Jim knew there was panic in his voice. He tried his best to find the "Jim the Cop" inside of him as he ended the call. There would be hell to pay at the Grove, so he needed to be calm, professional. He realized the others were staring at him.

"Come on. We got to get to the Grove as quick as possible. If you didn't drive here, hop in my car."

Mike got into the passenger seat, and Arthur and Finn piled into the back. Dan drove his truck, following Jim as he barreled up the road to the Grove.

CHAPTER 32

"WILL YOU STAY WITH ME?" Charity's voice wavered.

"Did you ever doubt it? We have known each other for over a hundred years. We have forgotten the promises we made, which must be fulfilled. It is the reason we have this trouble now."

Porewit put an arm around her. Charity spoke quietly.

"I did my job. But you are right. I didn't train anyone. That has been fixed. Jen is ready, as is Bridgette. Maggie is training two girls for pie duty. Jen has found a girl capable of keeping the town attuned. Until she is trained, Jen will do that job."

"I will stay with you. Zandar will, too."

"I am afraid."

"Of dying?"

"No. Of her. She is mad, insane. I want to heal her, but she is unreachable."

"She will heal, just not by your hand, Oathbound. It is not your destiny."

"I do not wish to leave. This body is done, but I am not. Will you, at least, grant me that? A way to stay?"

"It was always my intent. Your journey is far from done."

"I feel her coming. Stay with me. Please do not let her hurt me."

"I will be with you. Her rage and strength may be beyond my ability to restrain, but I promise to try. I am calling Zandar. I feel her, too. Do not be afraid, little mortal. This is your destiny. You have a long journey ahead."

CHAPTER 33

JIM DROVE INTO THE GROVE PARKING AREA and slid to a stop that barely missed the bottom steps. He was out of the car and up the stairs before the others had their seat belts off, Dan right behind. Jen stood at the top of the stairs, where she tried in vain to stop them from reaching the deck and heading toward Charity's cottage. She had no better luck with Finn and Arthur, though Mike read her posture and gaze, so he stopped mid-stairs.

"Well, you're all stuck here now," she said in exasperation. "Except Mike."

"What do you mean, 'stuck,'" snarled Jim. "You can't keep me from going to find her."

"Jim Burch, don't you speak to me like that!"

Jim stopped in his tracks, suddenly realizing how out of control his emotions were. He walked over, stood in front of Jen, and took off his hat.

"Jen, I am sorry," he said in a quieter voice. "Truly, I am. But I need to get Galen, and we need to go find her."

"I'm afraid that won't be possible."

Galen came out of the community rooms; he was walking slowly as if he were extremely tired or in a lot of pain.

"Go ahead, Jim. Give it a try."

He watched, a mixture of amusement and dismay on his face, as Jim walked to the top of the stairs, tried to descend, and found himself thrown back about four feet where he landed on his butt. Finn reached out a finger and got pushed back, as well, though not as hard.

"I'm going to take you guys' experience for it," said Arthur.

Dan took Jen to pick up a squalling Kat and an equally unhappy Will. Jim ignored them and concentrated on Galen and his story.

"She knocked me out for an hour," said Galen. "When I woke up, I hurt all over; then, I did myself more damage by trying to run down those stairs."

"Mike?" queried Jim.

"Yup, I'm on it. I'll find them. Although I suspect it may be a matter of lending help, rather than stopping her." He held up his hand, palm out, stopping Jim from responding. "Don't worry, Jim. I'll do everything in my power to keep her from getting hurt."

Mike turned his attention to Galen.

"Was there anyone with her? Or did you get that far?"

"An old man came to the community room door," replied Galen. "He said, 'It is time,' and she got up and went with him. I tried to follow, to stop them; and that's when she turned and pointed at me. Knocked me out on the couch."

Mike nodded, leaving the stairs, his eyes looking for footprints on the ground. He must have found something, for he suddenly took off at a ground-eating lope and entered the forest about midway down the orchard.

They went into the community room, where they found Jen with Kat and Linda with Will, both happily nursing. Someone—probably Galen—had laid and lit a fire. The room was comfortably warm. Once they were inside, Finn and Arthur retreated to the back of the room, where they sat, facing each other on the floor, their palms together, their eyes closed. Jen shook her head when Jim started to head over to them.

"They are speaking with either Zandar or Porewit, perhaps both. Maybe even Charity. The best thing you can do is get some food ready. They will be starving after so much exertion," said Jen.

"Exertion?" exclaimed Jim. "They're sitting there!"

"Oh, Jim, you have so much to learn," said Galen. "I am training my replacement, but at some point, you and I are going to do a sweat. There is much to be learned in a sweat."

"Right now, I'm more concerned with not being able to get out there. Mike, Porewit, Zandar, and Charity? Against her? They don't stand a chance."

"There are others," said Galen.

"Who?"

"That is not for me to tell. At least not at this time. Just know they have help. Charity will not be harmed, even though Zoya will come for her."

"As I recall, less than an hour ago you were utterly panic-stricken," said Jim. "Why are you so calm now?"

"I had a visitor."

Galen refused to say more, instead turning his attention to preparing food for everyone. Jim shrugged, then joined him. They decided to grill venison steaks and fresh vegetables. While Jim prepped the grill, he realized that the simple act of preparing food was doing wonders to calm his tangled emotions.

While the meal was cooking, Jim and Galen watched the full moon, with a few clouds scudding across it from time to time. The night air was chilly, and sounds were carrying on the cold air. They heard the hoot of the owl who lived in the orchard, the chirp of crickets, even the bullfrogs all the way from Sanders Pond.

Jim nudged Galen, pointing toward movement in the shadows at the center of the orchard. Whatever was there could easily have been assumed to be shadows created by waving leaves or the passing clouds, except that both men could see there was purpose in the movements. Jim felt deep frustration at being unable to go confront whatever was there.

"I know you can't relax, but listen," said Galen. "I have decided to tell you about them."

"Well?" queried Jim.

"I'm trying to decide where to begin, and how to explain this to you."

Galen stayed quiet for a while longer, lost in thought. Finally, he cleared his throat.

"Long ago, before the White man came to America, even before the People of the Great Nations walked on these lands, the Mialuka watched over Mother Earth and her children. They are tiny, very tiny; some call them fairies. Today there are books that call them Osage fairies. They are not fairies, and they are not known only to the Osage. The Mialuka are our Guardians, as the Lesheye are the Guardians of the forests of Ukraine."

"I take it you have met these Mialuka? Or some of them?"

Jim sounded dubious, not quite doubting Galen but reluctant to accept the reality of fairies.

"I talk to them," said Galen.

Sighing, he did not seem inclined to continue; then, he abruptly resumed his narrative.

"As the forests dwindled, torn down by civilization, as the great plains lost the giant herds of buffalo, and as the western lands sprouted great cities and large logging operations, the Mialuka dwindled in number. They died as the land died. There are few of them left, in the ever-decreasing wild areas. They tell me that most of them are concentrated here along the Mississippi, as well as in Oregon and Washington where there are still great swaths of dense forestland.

"They came to me today, shortly after I called you, to tell me they would be helping Porewit and Zandar, plus now Mike, in protecting Charity as well as trapping Zoya."

"How can fairies do anything against a mad, seven-foot-tall tree-woman?" asked Jim. "She will squash them with ease."

"Nothing 'squashes' Mialuka. Do not mistake size for strength. I would think knowing Charity would have taught you that."

They both chuckled.

"Yeah, you're right. I hate sitting here, though, doing nothing."

"You'd better stop 'doing nothing' and get that food out."

Jim leaped up, dashing to the kitchen to get serving plates. He found Jen and Linda warming bread and making other preparations for dinner.

Jen shooed him out of the kitchen once he had what he had come for. He and Galen piled steaks and vegetables on the platters and carried them inside. Jim, Galen, and Linda then went to the couch, where Dan was already curled up, a pot full of hot spiced cider, along with mugs, on the table.

"Let me know when Arthur and Finn are done."

"We are here," a melodic voice spoke behind her. "Arthur is making a 'visit' and will be here shortly. As you might have guessed, we are both starving."

Finn sat down and took one of the mugs; he poured himself some hot cider. They had just begun to eat when Mike Cullen appeared at the door; he was banging on it with his foot. He carried Charity in his arms, Birget right behind him making small whickering noises and pounding her hoofs on the deck floor.

Jim ran to the door, while Jen and Linda grabbed nearby quilts, then leaned back the spacious, well-padded recliner that was Charity's favorite. Mike laid her down gently, the women covering her cold body with two heavy, warm quilts.

"Is she hurt?" asked Galen, anxiety cracking his voice.

"No," replied Mike. "She is cold and very frightened, though. It was a close thing. Zandar, Porewit, and a large group of what I can only call fairies are guarding Zoya. The Mialuka—that's what the fairies call themselves—dug a hole next to the big tree in the center of the orchard; then, they all forced Zoya into the hole, buried up to her knees. Additionally, Zandar wrapped vines around her, tying her to the tree."

He began shivering so hard his teeth clacked. Dan pulled him to the couch, literally forcing him onto the cushions. Linda put a quilt around his shoulders, while Arthur and Finn sat on either side of him.

Arthur began whispering quietly into Mike's ear, while Finn hummed a quiet, soothing melody. Gradually, Mike's shivering calmed. He gratefully accepted the proffered cup of spiced cider from Jen.

"What happened out there?" demanded Jim. "Did they put Charity in harm's way?"

"Yes, they did. She demanded they do it, Jim. She was watched all of the time. Those fairies are hell on wheels. I sure wouldn't want to take them on."

Galen snickered in the far corner. Everyone turned to stare at him.

"What?" he said. "Mike's right. The Mialuka are more powerful than any being I know of. Like I said earlier, don't mistake size for weakness."

"They were the ones who kept Charity safe," said Mike. "Zoya suddenly appeared out of nowhere. I thought I saw a large bird, figured it was an owl. Then, boom! She was there. She went right for Charity, but those Mialuka guys tripped her. She fell flat on her face, and I ran in, grabbing Charity before she could get up again. Birget was there, waiting in the trees; she came trotting out, and the two of us rode her home as fast as she could go."

He suddenly looked out the door.

"Someone should be taking care of her."

"I already did," said Dan. "While you guys were getting settled, I took her to her stable out back, rubbed her down, put on a blanket, and gave her oats and water. She's a good pony, strong and loyal."

"We can leave now?" asked Jim. "Then I'm going to the orchard. It's my job."

Charity slowly sat up, gesturing for someone to raise the recliner. Her skin was almost translucent. Galen sat beside her, holding her hand, tears flowing freely down his sun-browned cheeks. He held the mug as she sipped some hot cider. She spoke, her voice soft and shaky.

"Jim Burch, you will do no such thing. I need you here. Your wife needs you. Zoya is being guarded by beings much stronger than you could ever dream of being. Tomorrow, at noon, we will gather at the Mother Tree. Everything will be finished. Zoya will be dealt with, no longer a problem or threat to you or Harper's Landing. Oaths will be sworn. Promises will be fulfilled. You will be there, as will many others. I need to sleep. Galen, make sure all your people are there, please."

She closed her eyes and put her arms around Galen's neck, letting him carry her to bed in her small cottage. Galen returned shortly after.

"Make a good breakfast tomorrow. Please. It will be the... I cannot say it. Make a good breakfast. I must rest now. I will leave early, after eating, to gather my people. She asks that you make sure the people from the town who need to be there have transportation. Apparently, they know who they are. They will be waiting at the diner unless they have their own cars."

He withdrew to Charity's cottage and shut the door firmly behind him. The rest, after finishing dinner and cleaning up, also retired. Arthur and Finn decided to drive back home. They noticed that the night was still, a preternatural quiet, absent of insects, birds, or wind. It was as if the world was holding its breath, at least in Harper's Landing.

CHAPTER 34

MORNING CAME EARLY AT THE GROVE. Babies get hungry and are not shy in making their demands. Will and Kat seemed determined to compete for who could squall the loudest. Jim brought Will to Linda, who was settled up in bed with a mound of pillows behind her. She loved these early morning feedings, where she sat, warm and drowsy in her comfy bed, with her feet crossed, while Jim made tea for her and coffee for himself.

Next door, at the Balanchuk home, Jen got up, then picked up Kat from her bassinet. She preferred to go sit in the rocking chair in their warm, cozy kitchen. Dan woke up more slowly, wandering in, ready to make coffee for the two of them. Jen was certain Kat would end up hyper, but she refused to give up her morning coffee, not even for tea.

Dan gave Jim a call in order to plot breakfast, which they would prepare in the communal kitchen for everyone. When they arrived, Arthur and Finn were already there with a big box of cinnamon rolls sitting in the middle of the large dining table. Eggs were being whipped in the mixer, while Finn was grating cheese. Jim set about washing and chopping green onions, while Dan fried copious quantities of homemade belly bacon.

By the time Dan announced breakfast was ready, everyone was up and setting the table. Mike Cullen showed up with Bridgette in tow. The table was laid, the food set out to be served family style. Everyone sat and dug in, feeding their huge appetites.

Charity and Galen were somewhat slower in arriving. Galen was as hungry as the rest, but Charity simply drank tea and nibbled at a bit of cinnamon roll. Galen was finally able to persuade her to eat some eggs, although she did so with little enthusiasm.

Once breakfast was done, Mike stood up, blushing, awkwardly shuffling his feet.

"I need to ask you something. Bridgette here says I need to ask you all."

Everyone was staring at him, waiting for him to speak.

"Um... I... Oh heck! I want your permission to marry Bridgette. She and I have talked. I proposed, but she says I need your permission. So, can we please?"

Laughter and cheers erupted in the room.

"Of course," said Jen. "As her mother, I choose to speak for the entire group. You have my permission. However, if you ever hurt her in any way, well, I pity you the revenge of this company."

"It will have to wait, though," said Arthur. "I would love to perform the ceremony if you will have me, but there are other things that must be attended to now."

"We were thinking in the spring," said Bridgette. "I have some training to do or, rather, to complete. Also, Mike has yet to discover why he was called here, other than to trim the trees and make love to me."

Everyone laughed again, while Mike blushed. His dark skin turned deeper, almost purple, when he blushed. The sweat on his face was obvious. He still laughed with the others, though.

"I think I know what my gifts or, rather, talents, are. I can talk to the dead. If they want to talk to me, that is."

The room fell silent.

"Comes in handy in war," he said. "First time it happened, though, it scared the crap out of me. I had lost my buddy. I was telling him goodbye. He up and spoke in my mind. Told me he wasn't ready to leave yet, because me and my platoon—what was left of them—were walking into a trap, according to him. I decided to listen. Sent a couple of scouts ahead, up on the hills above the road we were told to use to get back to our HQ. Sure enough, they spotted a group of Isis setting IEDs on the roadside. Saved our lives."

"Seems like you were ready to listen," said Arthur.

"When you're raised in a community like mine, in NOLA, you learn to accept such things."

"You've seen several of the people who died at Zoya's hands. Why haven't you told us what they said?" queried Jen.

"Because none of them stuck around to talk. Like I said, if they want to talk to me, they stick around to do so. Otherwise, they just move on."

"You can see them?" asked Finn.

"No, it's more like I can feel them. I know they are there. I'm not certain how useful it is going to be here. Unless a murder victim tells me who done it."

"Perhaps you have other, additional talents," mused Dan. "The orchard is far healthier since you arrived, and that, for me, is talent enough. If the dead choose to speak to you at some point in time, I am certain it will be because we need to know something."

"Enough chitchat," interrupted Charity. "Time to talk about more serious things, especially since noon will be here soon."

Settling in to listen, everyone pulled up a chair, couch, or cushion.

"Today I am one hundred and twelve years old," began Charity. "No, you didn't need to know. At my age, presents are nonsense. It is enough that you are here with me. Don't stop me with idle questions. I have little energy left. Today will also be my last day with you. It is time for me to leave, or at least leave this body. I am tired. My body is worn out. You have all you need, and the people you need, to continue the Grove. Whether you realize it or not, you are making an impact on the world.

"Every craft you sell, every piece of furniture that leaves here, every bolt of fabric, every quilt, all go into the world with intention. There is a reason your creations are sought after, and it isn't simply the quality of your workmanship, though that is indisputable. You are making a difference. Don't stop!

"Galen and the Osage have brought new life to Harper's Landing. Heed them well. They have a connection with the land and skills to share. They wish to integrate into the community. I expect you to accept them wholeheartedly. Use what they bring to you and share your traditions generously."

Breathing slowly and deeply, she paused for a moment, eyes closed. She opened her eyes, took a long sip of tea, and continued.

"Zoya has been contained. Her fate is not yet sealed, however. Porewit has a plan, but it is one which you must approve, because it is you who have suffered the most at her hands. I hope you will approve. It is kind, it is compassionate, and it guarantees no further damage from the Leshachikha. Oaths will be made and shared on this day. Some will be freed of old oaths while some will be newly bound to those same oaths. When we go to the Mother Tree, which must be soon, you must listen seriously to everything that is asked of you. Do not make promises you cannot or will not keep. It will be bad for you and for the town if you do. Now, bring Birget for me to ride so as to meet with the others at the Mother Tree."

The apple trees were heavy with fruit, the meadow grasses and wildflowers beginning to die away. The leaves were turning yellow on the cottonwoods, and small flocks of ducks and geese could be heard heading south. The summer buzz of insects had died away, and the happy chirps of birds no longer filled the orchard. Labor Day was on the horizon with fall around the corner. Soon enough, the nights would turn icy, the morning dew frozen.

The crowd slowly gathered at the tree. Linda stood with Jim; she was carrying Will in a baby sling. Jen wore a similar sling with Kat cuddled up to her, Dan standing at her side. The two women decided to sit in the grass, where their husbands joined them. Arthur and Finn stood next to the great tree, Zandar behind them, with Porewit beside Finn. Zoya was firmly tethered to the tree and buried in the ground up to her knees. She was obviously furious but silent.

The crowd included a group of recent high school graduates, their eyes wide. They, too, were sitting in the grass, several looking like they couldn't have stood if they wanted to. They were awestruck, perhaps a little fearful. Maggie and Morey were there, along with Galen and the Osage men, women, and children. Mike and Bridgette stood next to Birget, holding on to Charity, while Galen stood at the front holding Birget's halter.

Mike was aware of a substantial number of small beings surrounding the area, mostly perched on the tree branches, with a few on the ground near Porewit. He looked at Galen with a raised eyebrow, and Galen mouthed back, "*Mialuka*." Mike nodded.

Once everyone was settled, Porewit stepped forward and began to grow. His body straightened, the wrinkles on his face and hands disappearing. As he grew, his clothing fell away, revealing a body built of wood and moss; his arms were branches, and his feet were entwined roots. He spoke, his voice deep and powerful. Everyone there could see and hear him.

"You have gathered here today, many of you seeking revenge. That will not happen!"

There was angry murmuring among the crowd, and some of them started to rise.

"Stay seated!"

The crowd quieted, riveted by his voice and appearance.

"Zoya has done you great harm. Unfortunately, it is not the first time. We thought that with time to contemplate her actions, as well as to observe you and your ways, she would come to accept you in the way that her mate, Zandar, did from the beginning of their journey in this strange land. That did not happen."

Charity was sobbing, tears pouring down her face. Galen came around to Birget's side and lifted her to the ground. Bridgette spread a blanket where Charity and Galen sat together, her head on his shoulder.

"Charity has lost more to Zoya than you can possibly know," continued Porewit. "And yet, when I told her of my proposal, she agreed. It is her right. She is the Guardian, Oathbound to this place, this sacred ground. It is needful for the health and vitality of your community that you all agree with my justice.

"I am Porewit, Guardian of the forests of Ukraine and the surrounding countries. These," he pointed to Zandar and Zoya, "are but two of the many beings who owe me fealty. Fealty is a two-way bargain. They promise to defend and obey me; I promise to defend and protect them. I failed here. These two were brought here by an unfortunate accident, to a land strange to them, among people, which is not where Lesheye wish to be.

"I have no power over you. I do, however, have power over them. If you demand it, and it is your right to do so, I will have no choice but to destroy them. Keep in mind, though, if they are destroyed, it will not be without harm to you. I propose, instead, to permanently remove them from your lands. If you will allow it, as Charity wishes and as these two Druids," he pointed at Arthur and Finn, "desire, I will have them taken back to their homeland, and beyond, to the steppes of Eastern Russia where the only humans are small groups led by shamans who understand and revere such beings."

Porewit sat down. Arthur stepped forward.

"I have led you through joy and sorrow. I have helped you bury your dead, welcome your babies, pledge your love. Though I have not been here many years, I am Harper's Landing; I am the Grove, as only an earthbound Druid can be. Finn now shares that binding with me. If you choose to destroy these two, know that it will do potentially irreparable harm to your souls and minds. It is not an act you will forget. You will not forget forgiveness, either, but forgiveness will be a blessing to your minds and hearts.

"I ask you to forgive for two reasons. First, because Zoya believed that you were killing her children. Every tree that was cut, every trunk that was dug out, every plank and board that was sawn and sanded, was a stab to her heart. Further, it was not only the trees. Zoya and Zandar also protect the creatures of the forest. Every deer hunted and killed, every rabbit or squirrel or bird, was one of her children. That is why she turned on your children. Second, because the continued desecration of the forests which she discovered had continued apace when she awoke from her hundred-year hibernation. This drove her to madness. We do not destroy humans who have gone mad; we help them. We should show the same compassion to all sentient beings."

A tall, muscular woman emerged from the trees to stand next to Porewit. Her face was browned by the sun, and her clothing was leather and fur. She was also accompanied by the biggest bird any of them had ever seen. The bird wore a saddle, which caused a great deal of comment among the gathered residents. Once they had calmed down, Porewit spoke again.

"This is Aruvqan. She is my messenger; she flies on the wings of her companion. If you allow it, I will command Zoya and Zandar to shift into leaves, which we will place in a secure container. Soon those leaves will turn to ash, as the Lesheye do every fall. Aruvqan will carry them safely to their new home, far away in the high steppes as I have told you. There, in the spring, they will resurrect to find themselves home again. I will return to my duties also and do what I can and must to heal Zoya. These beings are immortal. Unless I destroy them, they will live forever, repeating the cycle of death and rebirth as they care for the great forests where they belong. Now you must vote."

Morey Farmington stood and looked at the people around him.

"You made me your mayor many years ago. I do not possess any uncanny talents like the rest of you, yet you have trusted me again and again to lead you in mundane matters. I vote aye. Return them to their home. None of this was really their fault."

Jim felt the need to speak also.

"You accepted me as your sheriff. As far as I know, I do not possess any weird talents either, although there are things I have seen and heard that others have not. Nevertheless, it is my job to keep you safe. I agree with Morey. None of this was their fault, though if there were no way to remove them, I would demand that they be tried and punished. I vote aye."

Steven Binder's mother stood.

"She killed my son. Now that I understand why, though I cannot forgive, I do understand. I vote aye."

The parents of the other children who died at Zoya's hand also stood one by one, expressing similar feelings. They all voted "aye."

Morey stood again.

"I ask that we agree to a unanimous aye vote, that Zoya and Zandar be taken from our midst, returned to their homeland to heal, so that we can get on with our own healing."

There was no objection. They all watched as Zoya and Zandar turned into leaves, unable to resist the command of Porewit. Aruvqan brought out a satchel, big enough to hold the two leaves. It had a flap and a lock which Finn secured. He handed the key to Aruvqan. She mounted the great bird, and they took to the sky, streaking away as soon as they were far enough above the crowd to avoid harming anyone.

"Now," said Porewit, "I have one last duty. It will be the last time I perform this duty, the first time being nearly two hundred years ago when your first ancestors came to this land. They called me, not knowing of the existence of my counterparts. I ask now that my friends come and join me in an Oath binding."

The Mialuka who had been flitting about the trees came to stand next to Porewit. The townsfolk whispered quietly amongst themselves. They had never seen Mialuka, though several of them admitted to having heard of them. Gradually, they quieted.

Galen lifted Charity, blanket and all, carrying her to the base of the Mother Tree, where she sat with her back against the trunk. She appeared ancient, far more wrinkled and tired than anyone there had ever seen.

"I told you there would be a price, Oathbound. It is time for me to collect," said Porewit.

"I am ready to transfer my duties to Jen," replied Charity. "She is ready."

"It is not Jen. She is not destined to be the Guardian."

"What?" cried Charity, as Jen gasped. "What do you mean, Porewit? I have trained her."

"You have trained her to heal, to maintain the connection between the town and the earth. You have trained her in the ways of herbs, potions, and growing things. She is a fine teacher as well. You have done a good job, as will she. But the Oath of the Guardian does not require training. You know that. Once the oath is taken, the Oathbound knows all that she will need to know."

"Then who is it?" asked Charity.

"It is Linda Burch."

Jim audibly gasped. Linda nearly dropped Will.

"No! I am not powerful, I am not worthy, and I am not going to embrace any talent I might have. It nearly cost me my life once. That will not happen again."

"Linda, dear mortal lady, you cannot deny your power. If you continue, some day it will destroy you. It was not your abilities that nearly cost your life. It was the anger and jealousy of the one you chose who could not accept what Mother Earth gave you."

"But why me?"

"Have you not wondered why you can see the future? Have you not longed to understand why you feel the stirring of life underfoot in the spring and the increasing quiet of winter? Have you not been fearful of your inability to comprehend the danger you felt but could not see?"

"All of that and more," replied Linda.

"You are the Guardian, meant to be united with the town, the Grove, the earth, and the waters of this place. It is time for Charity to let go. You must take up the mantle. It will not be hard; it will not hurt."

Linda turned to Jim, kissing him.

"Don't worry," she whispered. "For some reason I know this is right. It will not change me or us."

Reluctantly, he let go of her hand and watched as she sat next to Charity. Galen moved away, letting Charity lean into the support of Linda's arms.

Porewit shrank, once again the tiny wizened old man they had first seen. Miraculously, his clothes appeared back on his body, complete with his comical hat. He stood before the two women and whispered words none of the rest could hear.

As he spoke, light rose from the earth, up the trunk of the Mother Tree, along all of her limbs. The light spread, enveloping Charity, Linda, and Porewit. Suddenly, it blazed briefly around Linda, then slowly faded. Charity slumped, Galen leaping to hold her. He laid his head briefly on her chest and looked up, tears flowing down his cheeks.

"She is gone."

CHAPTER 35

A GRAVE WAS DUG AT THE BASE OF THE Mother Tree, where Charity was laid to rest as the entire community looked on. Galen refused to leave, even after everyone else had either gone home or to the Grove to eat, remember, and reflect. Finn stayed with him, relieved first by Arthur, later by Jim. As night fell, Dan came, bringing hot tea and blankets, both of which Galen accepted. However, he would not leave. Dan slept beside him until Mike relieved him in the wee hours of the morning.

Linda ate and drank copious quantities of food and water, while her mind and body adjusted to the instantaneous pairing she'd experienced with the Grove. She later told Jim it was as if she felt and heard everything all at once. She was overwhelmed at first, but Arthur led her through some gentle meditations that helped her begin to sort things out. She knew it would take weeks, perhaps months, but she would be able to separate the various voices and sensations, learn which were simple murmurings and which were calls for help. Jen provided tea and other herbs to help keep Linda's mind and body calm as she adjusted to her new sensations. Jen was still trying to understand why she had not been chosen as the Oathbound, but gradually, she realized that her power lay in her ability to create potions, healing teas, and spells. She would soon become Linda's strong right hand, her partner in maintaining the Grove, the town, and the people under their care and protection.

Galen refused to leave Charity's gravesite. After four days, Linda began to worry about him; she sent Jen down with some healing tea. Linda's phone rang. It was Brett.

"Hi! We rented a car and are on our way home from Jefferson City. Should be there in about an hour."

"That's good news, Brett. You might be needed here. Galen is having problems."

"What happened? Oh, Charity. Yeah, Arthur called us and told us. Well, it's a good thing I had reason to call you. I have Pete and Melanie Wilson here with me, along with Bethany Anne."

"Oh! That's a lovely name."

"She's a lovely baby. Anyway, it was an exhausting delivery, and they are both worn to the bone. I was wondering if we could tuck them in at Bridgette's former cottage now that she's living with Mike. I don't want them alone just yet."

"Of course. I'll make sure that it's warm, clean, and ready for them. You should get here in time for early supper. Venison stew is on the menu."

"I'll probably want to go check on Galen first. Pete's driving right now, and when he heard venison stew, he sped up a bit. Seriously, I think we are about forty-five minutes away. We also have news regarding Howard, Tom, and Zak."

Linda hung up and told the others. Bridgette and Mike hurried over to her former cottage, where they dusted and vacuumed. They made sure there were clean sheets on the bed, with lots of quilts, as well as clean towels in the small half-bath. There was a little kitchenette that Bridgette used when she was learning to make potions. A pan was procured from the community kitchen in case Melanie wasn't nursing and needed to warm bottles. If she was nursing, she would probably pump and store bottles anyway. They made sure the small fridge was plugged in to cool.

It was nearing five when Brett, Miranda, Pete, Melanie, and Bethany Anne arrived at the Grove. The sun had set, the night air was brisk, and a waning full moon was rising over the tree line. The small group had been smelling the stew all the way from their car, so they hurriedly unpacked and climbed the stairs. Bethany Anne was sleeping so soundly in a sling that she had not awoken when moved from her car seat. Pete took their belongings to the small cottage and was pleased to find that Linda had placed Will's bassinet in the bedroom. Will was now sleeping in a crib in his own room, much to his parents' relief.

Brett looked down toward the Mother Tree, where he saw Galen, now accompanied by one of his tribe members, still sitting at Charity's grave.

"I need to go to him," he said. "Perhaps I can persuade him to come up and get some food. At least I can try."

As Brett walked out to meet Galen, Miranda updated everyone on Howard, Tom, and Zak. "After Howard knew Tom and Zak were being taken care of, he had himself checked out to make sure there were no hidden injuries. Luckily, there weren't; he will make a full, physical recovery. His friend and partner, Tom, was not as lucky, and succumbed to his injuries. Zak, however, is expected to make a full recovery. He will have extensive physical and occupational therapy to learn to deal with having an amputated arm, but otherwise will be physically fine and returning to Harper's Landing as soon as the doctors will let him."

As she finished, Bethany Anne woke suddenly and let out a squall that shook the timbers. Everyone jumped. Such a loud noise from such a tiny baby! Melanie offered a breast, but Bethany was having none of that. She was dry, so it was not at all clear what she was yelling about. The strange thing was it didn't really sound like a cry. Her voice had a different quality than is usual for a newborn.

Brett saw Galen and Mike headed toward the Grove. Galen bounded up the stairs and came inside.

"You're back!" he exclaimed. "And with a baby!"

"Here," said Melanie. "Have a look."

She held the baby out to him. Galen took her in his arms gingerly. It had been a long time since he had held a tiny baby. Her eyes were squeezed shut; she was still bellowing that strange noise. As abruptly as she had begun howling, she stopped once Galen had her firmly in his arms. She opened her eyes and stared long into his. Galen stared back. He then said,

"Oh! There you are."

THE END

BOOK CLUB QUESTIONS

1. Zandar, the Leshy, has developed a fondness for human beings. His mate, Zoya the Leshachikha, hates them and wants to destroy them. Do you agree with Charity's explanation for why this is?
2. Porewit, as well as Charity and Arthur and Finn, believe Zoya can find redemption. Do you think she deserves it?
3. Food plays an important role in all of the Harper's Landing books. The main characters believe in the healing power of food and the importance of eating together. Discuss the role you think food plays in building community. Does our society's fascination with fast food and "eating on the go" cause harm to us socially and emotionally?

4. Saul Grossman has invested a lot in Harper's Landing—a lot of money and a lot of time. Are his contributions about helping, or are they about ego?
5. Does Arthur and Finn's relationship, being a gay couple, detract from the book? Does it add any dimension to the community and its acceptance of people?
6. The town relies on tourists for a significant portion of its income. Does the book adequately address the problem of income when the tourist trade is discouraged?
7. What role do you see Galen playing in the future in the town? Mike Cullen?
8. What is your feeling about the townspeople's acceptance of a solution for dealing with Zoya?

AUTHOR BIO

SHOSHANA EDWARDS IS A RETIRED PROfessor who lives with her husband in the Pacific Northwest. When she isn't writing, she enjoys quilting and gardening, boasting a front yard with twenty-two rose bushes, forty varieties of iris, and certification as a pollinator garden.

More books from 4 Horsemen Publications

Crime, Detective, and Noir

A.K. Ramirez
Secrets & Photographs
Memories & Scars

D.A. Spruzen
The Turkish Connection
The Witch of Tut

Joe Davison
Journey to Hell

Mark Atley
Too Late to Say Goodbye
Trouble Weighs a Ton
A New Day Starts Here

Horror, Thriller, & Suspense

Alan Berkshire
Jungle
Hell's Road

Erika Lance
Jimmy
Illusions of Happiness
No Place for Happiness
I Hunt You

Maria DeVivo
Witch of the Black Circle
Witch of the Red Thorn
Witch of the Silver Locust
Witch of the White Serpernt

Mark Tarrant
The Mighty Hook

October Kane
Nothing Will Be Left
Everything Will Burn

Steve Altier
The Camping Trip
Jimmy's Curse
The Ghost Hunter

Discover more at 4HorsemenPublications.com

Printed in the USA
CPSIA information can be obtained
at www.ICGtesting.com
LVHW091731220124
769281LV00006B/456